CW00798957

# HEAT TO OBSESSION

## NOLON KING

STERLING & STONE

# HEAT TO OBSESSION

# ONE

## Amanda

*Happy anniversary. Maybe now we won't get divorced.*

An ugly thought, but I couldn't keep it out of my mind. Same for the many unpleasant memories that kept slapping at my head to remind me of why I was here and what I needed to do. Of my responsibilities to Mike and my family. Of penance owed, and atonement still on its way.

Because yes, it had been a very long year, but I'd never stopped thinking about what I did, why I did it, and how it nearly destroyed everything.

Our wedding anniversary is on August 23. But Mike insisted on a new day to celebrate the strength of our marriage. Or maybe its rebirth.

For weeks he had been telling me we'd earned it, that the date was important to acknowledge all we'd done to turn our lives around after flirting with marital disaster. The children were with his mother, leaving us alone in the house. Mike had poured his heart into making dinner for the two of us. I was pretending the meal wouldn't be a disaster and everything between us was truffles and saffron.

I reminded myself to stay present, to appreciate all my husband was doing.

Otherwise, there wasn't any point. Cooking taught me how to learn from mistakes. Many of my best recipes came from my worst disasters, or from times I went left when I should have gone right.

This entire last year had been a second chance for our marriage, another shot at tweaking the recipe of my life closer to perfection, or at the very least further from misfortune.

Mike still had no idea what had turned me around, only that I came running home a month after our big blowup, begging for forgiveness and a chance to prove myself, pretty please with crystalized sugar on top. All I needed was another chance, and I'd never make the same mistake again.

He took me back without making me feel miserable over what happened between us, and our marriage had steadily improved ever since, even if my professional life was slowly rotting.

I went to therapy and got my priorities straight. I stopped criticizing Mike and our children about every little thing. Started coming home from Arrivé as soon as I could, instead of when I wanted to. And on those rare occasions when I had to stay at the restaurant later than any of us would have liked, I called home to let my husband know, so he didn't keep the children up waiting for me.

Yet, no matter how hard I tried to see it some other way, my life still felt like a little like a lie.

Maybe that's because of the big one I was keeping all to myself.

"We're almost ready!" Mike called out from the kitchen.

He sounded excited. Pleased with himself. I was sitting at the dining room table, trying not to think any critical thoughts, working to keep myself away from commenting on his setting's many clichés. Reminding myself that the best meals, the ones that nested deepest into our memories, didn't necessarily have anything to do with the food itself.

Probably the last thing a chef like me ever wants to hear. Still, undoubtedly true.

"I can't wait!"

But I turned my attention to the wall, studying the lovely prints and framed family photos instead of Mike's tablescape. A stem vase with a single red rose and a cloud of filler, the pair of tea lights in crackle-glass holders, the goblets already filled with wine, and the linen napkins slipped through tacky golden rings.

No. Not tacky. *Thoughtful.*

Who cared if the napkin rings looked like they came from the dollar store? What did it matter that I hate baby's breath and think the last place it belongs is kissing the neck of an otherwise beautiful rose? These were little things I couldn't expect Mike to know, and it wasn't fair to judge him for them.

My friend Thom is a special effects advisor in Hollywood. I always thought he had the most thrilling job. He used to tell me stories about the different directors he worked with, and all the celebrities. But unfortunately, Thom paid a heavy tax for his dream gig. Movies, the medium he loved more than anything before getting into the business, were in many ways ruined forever. Because now, whenever he went to a show, Thom could only see the seams.

That same thing had happened to me.

It was hard to enjoy anything when I was always measuring it against what I might do myself.

Mike beamed as he entered the dining room

with a pair of plates. Until a second ago, I could only guess at what he was cooking, but I hadn't been far off. It looked like a rosemary garlic roast with pan-roasted mixed veggies.

I deeply inhaled and matched my husband's smile. "That smells delicious!"

How was Mike supposed to know his choice was more like a rich Thanksgiving meal than an intimate dish for the two of us to share? No reason to make him feel bad about it.

He sat and shoved a forkful of meat and vegetables into his mouth, studying my face and starving for a compliment.

The roast was supposed to be juicy, fragrant, and mouthwatering. Garlic should've been exploding in my mouth. The mushrooms should have been sautéed in butter and smothered in the sauce. Instead, the roast was dry, the veggies over-charred and under-salted.

I chewed his food while biting my tongue. A year ago, I would have explained everything he'd done wrong, down to suggesting a much better wine pairing — a pinot noir with notes of plums and dried cherries, perfect for tender, slow roasted beef and the caramelized rosemary and garlic.

Instead of constructive criticism, I licked my lips. "This is better than delicious."

"Wait until dessert."

*A thousand dollars says it's lava cake.*

"I made lava cake!"

"Can't wait." I leaned across the table to give him a kiss.

Still smiling, Mike raised his glass. "To us. For getting our marriage back on track."

I picked up my glass and agreed. Then I took a sip, wanting to swallow it all.

"It feels like such an accomplishment, you know?"

"The last year?"

"Right. A year ago …" He shook his head. "I honestly wasn't sure we were going to make it."

"We've covered that." I managed a brittle smile. "Tonight is supposed to be about looking forward, right?"

"I'm sorry. I just didn't know how we were going to do it."

"It's a simple recipe. Hard work, therapy, communication. We're not the first couple to go through this."

Mike laughed. "I know. I'm sorry. I don't want to beat a dead horse, especially tonight—"

*Then don't.*

"I'm proud of us, Amanda. Proud of you. It's more than the therapy. Your follow-through has been terrific. You've established boundaries at work, made more time for us. That's made all the difference."

I had a choice to make. Ignore my half of the conversation and agree with Mike's assessment or get in a fight during our anniversary 2.0 dinner. Same as I had so many times in the last year, I smiled and said something that I only sort of meant. "We pay Dr. Walling $240 an hour. It wouldn't make sense to ignore his advice."

"Cheers to that!" Mike raised his glass again.

*Clink!*

I took another sip that should have been a swallow, still forcing myself to smile.

Because yes, our family was doing much better than it was a year ago, but the restaurant was doing much worse. What used to feed me now ate at my insides. Arrivé had been struggling for the last year, and it seemed to be getting worse rather than better. Spending less time in the kitchen led directly to a greater degree of incompetence from my staff. And Harris hadn't been much of a help. My partner made excuses for everyone and was constantly telling me I was too harsh and my standards were too high. Said if I didn't relax in the kitchen, no one would want to work for me.

He would say that. Harris could never stand the heat, which was why he dropped out of culinary school. We'd had the same teachers, but very different experiences. Some people crack under pressure, others turn their strife into diamonds.

I would have fired Gillian five times already, but Harris kept defending her. The girl couldn't seem to read a simple recipe. She always put too much or too little of something into the dish. Her instincts were awful, enough to make her unteachable. At least, that was what I kept arguing. Still, despite the restaurant bleeding money, Harris insisted on supporting Gillian's subpar work and limited potential.

I looked up and into Mike's eyes. He was staring at me. Expectant, but I wasn't sure what for.

"Did you want to say anything?"

I pulled myself out of the reverie — where I was just about to fire Gillian — and gave him my warmest smile and the words he wanted, or maybe *needed,* to hear.

"You were absolutely right, and this last year has been worth all the sweat. It's not always easy juggling it all, but I've enjoyed spending more time with you and the kids."

Mike lit up like I'd plugged him into the wall. His teeth almost seemed whiter.

It was weird, feeling good and bad in a volley. Part of me was resentful of having to go through the motions, but the rest of me — the better part — delighted at the sudden glow on his handsome face and was delighted to taste the fruit of my effort.

I really did love him.

Most of the time, Mike was more than I deserved, but I also couldn't ignore the compromises that hit my career as a consequence. Yes, everything would get better, especially once Bake It Away became something more than a dream. Until then, it would feel like I was constantly borrowing from Peter to pay Paul, at least when it came to time, money, and the majority of what mattered.

"I love seeing you be a mom," Mike said.

He'd said the same thing a little more than a year ago, and a spiteful smirk had turned his face into something grotesque and misshapen. This time, his expression was much less offensive. Still, I flinched.

But I recovered immediately. "I love being a

mom. And I love you. I'm sorry for everything. For all the—"

"Let's not do that." He put his hand over mine. "I have much better plans for tonight."

"Oh?" I raised my eyebrows.

He grinned, almost boyish, and produced an envelope like a magic trick. Then he slid it across the table.

A smile found my face without effort. Mike was making it easy, pleased with himself and finally with me. It was the balm we needed after a long and difficult year of trying and growing.

I opened the envelope and laughed, even though I wasn't remotely surprised to see what was inside. Six cards penned by him in his neat block print, each promising an irresistible present.

*Redeemable for one artisan massage.*

"Artisan massage, huh?"

Mike showed me his palms. "I am a craftsman."

Even when things were at their worst between us, the two of us never suffered in the bedroom. My husband's hands were magic, and so was everything else in that regard.

I was immediately warmer. Wet and wanting. The lava cake was even staring to sound good.

We finished eating, our conversation light and

playful. When there were two bites of cake on the plate, I fed my forkful to him, and he fed his to me.

"Let me clean up the kitchen," he said, "then I'll meet you in the bedroom."

I put my hand on his. "Let me. I'll be fast. You go set up the table."

With a grin that intensified my craving for him, he said, "It's already set up, but I'll be waiting."

I hurried to the kitchen, glad dinner had gone so well. Maybe I'd been fretting over nothing, still suffering from PTSD over what I'd almost done to our family and the year spent making it up. Everything was better at home. I'd proven myself.

It was time to fix things at the restaurant.

As I started tidying, I found Mike had plated another two servings for tomorrow's lunch. My heart melted. Even though he knew I'd need to move them into Tupperware, he still took the time to make them look pretty.

I did the dishes, put everything away, then went hunting for a lid that I couldn't seem to find. After looking in every cupboard and cabinet while trying not to lose my shit, I finally returned to the original drawer, certain that I'd overlooked it.

I thrust my hand all the way to the back. No lid, but my fingers brushed something familiar. I should have left it there, knowing what it was that had bunched in my hand. But I pulled it out anyway and let the memory come.

The apron was cheap. Probably less than ten bucks, though it was tied with a thin silk ribbon that made it look like the indulgence it wasn't.

A flare of guilt coursed through me, both for what happened a year ago and for thinking of him now. I was so glad Mike never discovered the truth. I felt guilty for my relief, too.

"Need help in there?"

His voice was faint, coming all the way from the bedroom. Still loud enough to know he was ready.

*Me, too.*

I shoved the apron back where I'd found it, slammed the drawer shut, threw some foil over the Tupperware, then hurried to our bedroom.

# TWO

## Noah

Every professional chef in the world would agree on this one immutable truth — *you need passion in this business to make it.*

But my passion had spent the last twelve months in atrophy, rotting on the vine of my withered ambitions. In the last long year, I had learned to stop caring, trying, and believing. I was a shell of my former self, and every day it felt like I was one bad dish away from burning out.

A year before, it thrilled me to be working in the Hotel Milano. It was easy when life was on the upswing. I still had faith in myself and in this place. I couldn't see all the cracks in the facade. The Milano presented itself as a charming boutique hotel, an alternative to the city's stuffier hotels, but with a level of service you could never get at an Airbnb.

But it was decaying from the inside.

Construction on the building started in 2006. Unfortunately, by the time it first opened for business in 2008, America was in the dumps and practically boycotting vacations. So the Hotel Milano was on its fourth owner, Emil Maldonado, a throbbing cock of a man who believed that smart business meant running it into the ground.

A year ago, I wanted more of everything, including responsibility. But right now, governing the three people under me felt like a pillow pressed hard to my face. Working alongside them wasn't the problem. Collaboration was part of the gig. Restaurant life meant being part of a family, usually at least slightly dysfunctional, because nothing was ever done solo. But everything about this particular kitchen in this particular restaurant had me feeling like I was cooking with one hand bound behind my back.

It was my first job out of culinary school and infinitely less glamorous than I expected it to be at every stage — when I filled out the application, when I got called in, and when I started my first shift. The fundamentals still mattered. I'm a master with my knife and can poach an egg or pan-fry a fillet to perfection. But the philosophies expelled by my best instructors had no value in my current job.

Jonas Lowry, my favorite teacher, told us if an architect makes a mistake, he can use the landscaping to cover his error, but if a chef slips up, he must cover the dish with sauce and insist his recipe is new.

That advice could only take me so far. I couldn't do that at the Hotel Milano.

I couldn't do *anything* there.

There was no glamour in this position. My job was to cut corners. Despite the menu, where prices ran from absurd to ridiculous, the budget for ingredients was embarrassing. I was supposed to spend as little as possible and have almost no spoilage. The servers were all instructed to tell the diners that everything was fresh, never frozen. We promised the guests that our food was all farm to table, out of the garden and onto their plate. But Chef Mike — the bank of oversized microwaves in the corner of the Milano's slowly decomposing kitchen — was the hardest working among us.

Lowry had also said there were no great chefs without great teams behind them.

Emil put it another way. "Being the head chef

doesn't mean shit, Noah, except that you have to tell the other assholes what to do."

"Noah!"

I looked behind me. My sous chef, Leah, was trying to get my attention. How long had I been zoning on this omelet? They were all about technique, and thus one of my favorite things to cook: heating the pan before adding the butter, letting the eggs sit undisturbed for ten seconds to form the outer crust, the jiggle to make sure the whole thing slides before you try to flip it.

"Sorry," I said. "Just give me a minute."

I gave the omelet my full concentration, hiding my annoyance at the tiny tear that formed as I folded it around bacon, onions, and mushrooms. I got it on the plate, Then turned my attention to Leah. "What's up?"

Her face scrunched. I'd seen this plenty of times. Leah needed to bitch about something without sounding like she was complaining. That was a regular thing around here. Everything was worth bitching about, but Emil didn't tolerate complaints. So, no one was willing to speak up, even when there was a legitimate problem.

"It's the freezer."

"What about it?" But I was pretty sure I already

knew.

The freezer had been behaving erratically for a while. I'd raised the issue three times but had managed to get nowhere with Emil. Food was thawing and refreezing. There were ice crystals inside our packaging, freezer burn because the water molecules inside the food were working their way out and into the colder areas of the freezer. Sure, the food was still safe to eat, which is what Emil usually argued, but a loss of moisture diluted the taste. And our proteins were changing color. A fillet should never be gray, especially not when it cost as much as we charged. Same for the dull-looking veggies that made me grateful for the restaurant's dim lighting.

"It's out of control."

Leah didn't get to say anything more because the double doors to the kitchen swung wide as Emil sauntered inside.

And of course, he'd heard every word. "What's out of control?"

Leah looked at our boss, her eyes wide and frightened. The man looked made of pudding, despite his panna cotta appetites. She didn't want to say and would never have brought the complaint directly to him. That's what I was for. But he'd know if she was being evasive and would press into her like garlic against a cutting board until she spilled it all.

"The freezer," she said, holding his gaze. "It's being erratic."

"How so?"

It took Leah a moment to select the most pressing of the freezer's many problems. "It isn't keeping things frozen, and—"

"So turn the temperature down. The high end of the fluctuation range will keep things frozen," Emil said, like we hadn't tried to solve the problem ourselves. Like we hadn't attempted a hundred little things already.

Like telling him wasn't the last thing any of us wanted to do.

Leah said, "But—"

"But nothing!" Emil was already yelling. "I don't want to hear about how the freezer's not working, or how we need more storage, or anything else. My job is to run this hotel, and your job is to cook. Without complaining."

Then he turned to me. "Your job is to run the kitchen and make it so that idiot concerns like this don't bother me. Keep our quality up and our costs down."

It was an idiot thing to say even if Emil cared about quality, which clearly he didn't. And I would have been happy to keep this situation away from his highness. But he was the one who'd asked Leah what was out of control when he came into the kitchen.

He didn't even give me the chance to respond before he turned back to my sous chef and began to berate her like the belligerent asshole he was.

"Are you stupid?"

She blinked, unsure of how to respond. With Emil, you had to get things just right. Did Leah agree that yes, she was stupid, jeopardizing her job since the big man had made it very clear on multiple occasions that he didn't suffer fools in his employ? Or did she disagree with him by defending her intelligence, thereby risking her position?

"No." Leah shook her head.

"Then why are you behaving like you're stupid? If the freezer isn't working, then make it work. This isn't hard to figure out. If it's too warm, turn the temperature down. If it's too cool, then we should probably crank it up."

Emil yelled without any regard to the spittle from his fat lips spraying on his subordinate's brow. He leaned closer and lowered his voice, reveling in her wilting posture. "Should I say it slower so it's easier to understand?"

"No," Leah said, clearly trying not to cry.

"Great." Emil turned to the rest of us. "Anyone else want to give me crap for shit they should be figuring out for themselves, thereby making them eligible for immediate termination?"

The kitchen was silent, but I couldn't be.

"Emil." I said his name without a molecule of confrontation.

He turned to me. "Noah?"

"Leah *was* trying to solve the problem herself. She was coming to me. You just happened to walk in as she was explaining it, and she didn't want to be disrespectful by not answering your very direct question."

Emil looked like he wanted to cut in, so I started talking faster.

"I would have been happy to handle it myself, but I don't think that adjusting the temperature is going to work. We've been doing that for a while now, but the freezer is having a lot of problems, and—"

"It's barely ten years old," Emil argued.

"It's a health violation, and as the head chef, I'm supposed to report it, especially now that it's gotten this bad. I won't, but this is something we'll want to fix before we're ordered to."

Now he was listening.

I kept going. "You could get it fixed cheap, under the counter. And it will save money by reducing our spoilage. Probably by a lot."

Emil nodded. To him, spoilage was a four-letter word, and now I was speaking his language.

"How do we get it fixed cheap?"

"I have a friend in trade school for repairing industrial appliances. Good guy."

"What do you think he'll charge?"

I shrugged. "I'm not sure. Depends on whether the job is more parts or labor. It's probably a few thousand dollars retail, but I bet we can get it down to a grand or so."

"Keep it three figures and I'll write the guy a reference letter when he graduates and is looking for a real job."

Then Emil turned and huffed out of my kitchen.

"Thank you." Leah only managed the two whispered words before scuttling back to her cutting board. Anything more and she might have started crying.

I went back to work, even more frustrated than

I had been before.

My life was a disaster. The only woman I'd ever loved had dumped me, trapping me in a cycle of depression ever since. I was producing lackluster meals at a marginal hotel, a job that had felt like a dream gig less than a year ago. I kept telling myself that it was no different than anything else I'd accomplished in my life. Every one of my previous victories had come thanks to my patience, intelligence, and ruthless pursuit of success.

I was a Cinderella with a fairy godmother who didn't give a shit.

But I'd been circling the drain for a year. My cooking was now questionable and getting worse as I cared even less. I spent most of the time I wasn't working either drinking or smoking, trying to silence the voice of my dead father, the asshole who haunted me with his joyful gloating, reminding me that I'm a loser, just like him.

Amanda promised me everything I ever wanted, right before she took it all away.

Why couldn't I just hate her and move on?

Sarah, my favorite of the servers, came into the kitchen with yet another customer complaint.

I apologized for overcooking the omelet, numb as I was when I did it, and tried to remind myself that life had mattered before Amanda, and that it would matter again eventually.

But now that my old man was back in my head, the fucker was refusing to leave, constantly assaulting me, his ancient arrows of insult sinking into the flesh of my psyche, telling me I would never land a job in a five-star hotel, would never save enough to start my own restaurant, and would be stuck working in places like this dump forever.

I try not to think about what my life would have been like if I could have convinced Amanda to stay, because those are the thoughts that hit me hardest, hurt me the most, making me wonder if death might be better.

If everything had worked out like Amanda had promised, I'd be an apprentice chef in her restaurant and we'd be on the way to opening our bakery. Instead, I was trapped at the Milano making chicken pot pie and Salisbury steak for folks who'd probably be just as happy eating Stouffer's at home.

I wanted to close my eyes, but I had to finish the eggs.

Then I could allow myself to imagine Amanda entering Arrivé, inhaling the scents and basking in the sights of her restaurant. And maybe even thinking of me.

# THREE

# Amanda

Bella by the Sea looked nothing like my restaurant. My attitude had always been to charge for the food, not the ambiance, so I'd kept our decor elegant but simple. It was one of the few things Harris and I still passionately agreed on. We hung pictures of the regional farms on our walls alongside their stories, which we had printed in clean, crisp Helvetica. Nooks and crannies were peppered with mason jars packed with pickled vegetables, dressings, sauces, and, according to CritEat, 'the best jam in Southern California, if not the world.'

This restaurant, however, was obnoxious, like the loudest girl at the party, squeezed into the tightest dress, after having too much to drink. Sure, she looked fantastic and half of the place had probably thought about fucking her, but everything from her platform pumps to the sway of her hips was designed to distract people from how little she had going on upstairs. All flash, no substance.

Bella by the Sea felt the same way.

At least, that's what I thought based on its façade. Then I stepped inside.

I'd expected pretentious decor designed to distract diners from the fact that the chicken dish that cost more their sitter could have been prepared by a first year at Pierpont Community College.

But the restaurant was stunning while still managing the impossible task of appearing under-stated. It even made being inside the Palms Couture Shopping Center somehow part of its charm. From a balcony overlooking the Pacific with a sweeping view to Catalina on a clear day, the place still felt private, almost like it was nestled into the side of a cave.

Only after stepping inside did I immediately realize where I was and remember where I'd heard of this restaurant before. Their business model was unlike anything else. The place was cozy enough that they could serve only three parties at a time. A micro-restaurant with never more than a dozen diners inside, all of them eating five-star food and paying a premium for the privacy as much as for their entrees.

I was impressed, though I still had no idea why I was there. Only that Harris said — practically demanded — that despite the ridiculous drive, I make time for this meeting before my shift at Arrivé

A handsome man named Matthew greeted me. He looked enough like Superman to get me blushing at the sound of my name. After taking my arm, he led me on a short walk into a shockingly intimate room.

Harris was already there, sitting to the right of two people I had never seen, didn't know, and certainly hadn't expected. A man and a woman, professionally beautiful. They looked like a couple.

"Good afternoon." The woman had her hand out, already standing.

We shook. Nice and firm.

"I'm Amanda," I said, trying to capture as much as I could without staring.

"Melinda." Her smile lit her face, and there was something so genuine inside her eyes that it managed to touch me.

She was beautiful. Probably about ten years older than me, but very well-preserved. And confi-

26

dent, with piercing eyes and hair as tailored as the rest of her.

The man beside her radiated power as he stood a few seconds behind her. I had no intention of doing so, but a bow felt almost appropriate.

"Dominic." He offered his hand.

Harris stayed seated, probably just happy I showed up. And I couldn't help but think that maybe I shouldn't have. Him not telling me why would have been reason enough. I hate surprises, and evidence suggested this would be the kind I loathe most.

Harris is a few years older than me and would be a prodigy in the kitchen if he could man up enough to survive it. Being a chef is hard enough, but being the best and living up to your ultimate potential? Few are cut out for that.

I am, he isn't. And that's why Harris needs me.

In many ways, Harris was the perfect partner. He had a knack for marketing and was great with the wait staff, along with most of the other stuff I wasn't especially good at or didn't really want to do. He was also the calm both before and after my storm. But lately, we'd been fighting. And I was certain that was the reason we were there.

"It's good to meet you." I sat feeling deeply uncertain.

A second into Dominic's pitch, I understood why Harris was being so secretive.

*Goddammit.*

"But we're happy with the restaurant." I stole a glance at Harris as he withered into his seat. Because apparently we were sitting with media moguls Dominic and Melinda Shelly, for a meeting I would never have agreed to if I'd been given the details ahead of time.

"Of course you are," Melinda said, taking the ball from her husband. "And it will be the core of everything else."

"I'm sorry. This is all just happening so fast. Can we start over?"

Harris looked hopeful after I said that, so I stared at him hard to take it away.

Dominic said, "This deal will skyrocket your careers."

Melinda added, "A cooking show together that will stream on our new media platform."

I just didn't see the appeal. "What makes your platform special? There are already too many."

"And they're all making money," Dominic said. Then, with a confidence that made it seem like he could see the future, he added, "We'll make more."

"But *how?*"

Melinda smiled. "We're happy to answer any questions you have, but that's a big topic. We're building a stable of stars for tomorrow. We'll get you on network TV now, then move you over to our platform when it's ready. In short, we're building a connective tissue that no one in Hollywood has."

"No one in the world," Dominic cut in.

"Right," Melinda agreed. "No one in the world. Juke isn't just a platform. We're also creating content."

"But so are Netflix and Hu—"

"We're everything they are and all they cannot be," Dominic cut me off with a note of finality. "Let's talk about your deal, then if you like what you hear, we can talk about Juke."

I didn't feel defeated so much as redirected, but I couldn't argue the fairness. "Okay. So if I understand your proposal, you want to create the show to drive interest in the restaurant, which you'll franchise, after it's been given a facelift to make it more marketable."

"Yes," Melinda said. "But that's only the start. We're also giving you a contract for three cook-

NOLON KING

books. The first one is timed to launch at the end of the first season, and we can guarantee it will hit the New York Times bestseller list."

"No one can guarantee that," I said.

"Melinda won't let me promise you Number One, but I don't see why she's playing coy." Dominic winked.

There was a lot to love about what I was hearing, but I hated the ambush and that I wasn't being given time to process the details. Could I take bits and pieces? Was this an all-or-nothing deal? Because if it was *all*, then unfortunately I'd have to go with Door #2 and the *nothing* behind it.

Maybe the deal could be leveraged toward my new bakery instead?

I tried to navigate the conversation, but it was like nabbing the wheel from Andretti. Harris barely said anything, but Dominic and Melinda were never out of control. We talked through one remarkable course after the other — the food at Bella by the Sea might be the best I'd ever tasted, despite having savored some of the world's finest cuisine — without getting anywhere. My questions were answered without depth, concerns pacified without getting solved, and hesitations all waved away.

By the time we were sharing a plate of

nectarine pavlovas — thin slices of the fruit on a meringue shell filled with a pastry cream that tasted like the sweetest of sins — Dominic was still talking about the new life I could have.

I was breaking out in a sweat.

Before the last of the meringue had melted on my tongue, I looked at Harris, hoping to see agreement in his eyes. All these promises were more than a little over the top. But he was still nodding along and looking more than a little hopeful.

I couldn't take it. "I need time to process. It's a lot."

"Take all the time you need," Melinda said.

Then everyone sat there.

"Do you think Harris and I could have a moment alone?"

"Absolutely!" Dominic stood before I could protest.

I wanted to take Harris outside, maybe go for a stroll through the Palms Couture. Instead, the moguls left us in the room, though they remained in eavesdropping distance on the other side of the door.

"I can't believe you set me up like this!" I whisper shouted.

"I didn't tell you ahead of time because I

knew you would shoot me down. This is a great opportunity, Amanda. And you know it. You can't say no just to say no. Not anymore. It isn't fair to me."

"I'm not trying to be unfair to you. You're the one who set me up. You *know* I don't want to be on TV. I've said that every time this comes up."

"There's no reason! You're great on camera, and—"

"YouTube and LiveLyfe are different."

"It doesn't have to be. Those little videos have done a lot for us, but this will do *everything*. This isn't the same offer as before, not even close. We've never had a chance like this. A show with investors already attached? Producers lined up? Not a pilot, but a guaranteed network run before we move to the Shelly's big new platform that—"

"Could totally flop?"

"Do you realize who they are? What they do?"

"Remind me, how is Jay-Z's thing going?"

Harris shook his head. "That's not the point. What about the cookbooks? You've always wanted a cookbook."

"I want to do a book about pastries, and they seemed completely uninterested."

"They weren't uninterested, Amanda. Said the

idea had to wait its turn. I'm sure you've heard that before."

*Fuck you, Harris.*

Instead, I said, "That's not fair."

"Isn't it, though? This bakery thing has become an obsession with you, and *that's* unfair. We should be hiring new staff, working harder to push the restaurant back to the top from …"

He didn't finish.

*From where* we *lost it.*

Meaning *me.*

"I'm fine with working hard to finish what we started, but this isn't even remotely close to what we agreed on."

"Neither are a lot of things." Harris was usually mild-mannered, but the conversation was turning his face redder and redder, thinning the patience in his voice from a bass note to a soprano. "This is our break, Amanda. It can set us both up for the rest of our lives. What are you waiting for?" He took a moment to breathe.

I gave it to him, then wished I hadn't.

"I want to sell the restaurant," he said.

"Why would you want to sell the—"

"I've told you! When are you going to start listening? I want to be the idea person in a cooking empire, rather than managing a restaurant and serving as a buffer between you and the kitchen staff."

"What do you mean *serving as a buffer?* I—"

"You know exactly what I mean, Amanda. You're difficult to work for, and everyone is afraid of you."

"That's not—"

"And it's not just in the kitchen or among the waitstaff. We're losing clientele because of you."

"I don't think—"

"If you—"

"You're cutting me off a lot today, Harris."

"Maybe I don't cut you off enough!"

It felt like a slap from someone who rarely ever threw them.

Harris drew a breath, then followed it with a long sigh and a relaxing of his shoulders. In a more even voice, he said, "If you don't do this, I'm going to sue you and force you into selling the restaurant."

"You don't want to do that." It was almost a whisper.

"You're right. I don't. It's the last thing I want to do. But I never see Emily, and that isn't fair to her. I want to get married, not lose the most important thing in my life.. I've spent more than a decade working my ass off for a restaurant that — if things go swimmingly and we manage to get back on top — will never make more than it did a year ago. Don't you want more than that?"

I didn't know what I wanted, other than to go somewhere else where I could finally process the last couple of hours. This was an ambush — how was I supposed to come up with anything cogent? I needed time to think before I respond, especially about something as important as this. And Harris knew it. He's always talking about being fair, but this afternoon was obviously, *comically*, unjust.

I was in shock. Harris had given me plenty of stern talking-tos, and half the time, I thought he enjoyed doing so. But we'd always get back to business as usual soon enough. Didn't seem that would be the case this time. The corners of his mouth were pulled down in a frown, and his usually bright blue eyes were lifeless as a pair of ancient dimes.

I took it for granted that Harris would always be there behind me, handling the stuff I didn't want to do. Honestly, he handled the stuff I couldn't do even if I wanted to.

"Give me the weekend to think about?"

It was all I could say without crying.

But Harris shook his head. "There's a signing bonus if we say yes today."

"That's ridiculous!" But after a moment, I said, "What kind of signing bonus?"

He opened his mouth but never got a chance to answer.

"You know what? Never mind! I'm taking the weekend. This could have gone differently, Harris. It's bullshit that you felt you had to do it this way."

"You're right, Amanda. It is bullshit that I had to feel this way. I hope you do spend the weekend thinking about this. It'll be good for you, thinking about someone else for a change."

# FOUR

# Noah

I was perseverance personified by the time my shift was behind me.

Emil either never visited the kitchen or he barged in three or four times a day. Today was the latter.

The man was never constructive. It was like he had a parasite inside him that feasted on the misery of others. The worse Emil made someone feel, the wider he seemed to smile. Not while he was doing it, that would be rude. But it boosted his mood every time. I wouldn't have been surprised if the fucker had sported wood after his third encounter with Leah, the one where he finally got her to cry after suggesting she consider getting a job at the Inside Scoop across the street because digging ice cream out of the carton was more straightforward while still technically being part of the food industry.

We also ran out of supplies, tossed twenty pounds of freezer-burned meat, and dealt with Jeff coming into take a look at the freezer, which was in worse shape than I thought, thanks to some Band-aid solutions from a few years ago that I didn't even know about. I had to solve the problem without Jeff ever meeting Emil because after one exchange, my buddy would be telling my boss to fuck off.

I was more fatigued than I should have been, in part because I'd gotten lazy about doing my prep-work. Efficiencies are found in all the stuff we do in the kitchen before we start cooking. It's called *mise en place*, meaning "everything in its place." A chef's ritual and religion.

But lately, I'd been an atheist.

And in truth, I'd probably been feeding on disorder. If things were muddled or messy, maybe even a ticking bomb of chaos, I could keep stumbling through the snags and complications. I could be the problem solver — a shark moving through water, knowing stillness meant death.

"Noah?"

I recognized Sarah's voice before I turned around. "Yeah?"

"Someone wants to talk to you."

*Great.*

"Who?"

"A couple of customers?" Jenna jerked a thumb behind her, out toward the restaurant.

"What did they say?"

"That they wanted to speak to the chef."

"Did they use my name?"

"Um … no, I guess not."

"So, they want to complain."

"Maybe." She shrugged. "But they don't look like complainers."

"What do you mean?"

Another shrug. "They look nice. Like they have money. And they definitely have manners."

"Maybe they would like to tell me politely that this kitchen is serving dog shit to its customers."

Jenna laughed. "What do you want me to say?"

I sighed. "Tell them I'll be right out."

I was bone tired and wanted to go home. The last thing I wanted was to field a complaint.

This had happened before, and I could already picture the couple. The man would be wearing a crisp white button down under a loose-fitting blazer, and the woman's fingers would be crusted in rings like barnacles on a boat. They would both try to save me from myself by starting with an insult thinly veiled as a compliment, telling me the meal reminded them of some other place where the food was so much better, then offering a few friendly suggestions to improve the dish.

And then I would have to thank them.

I sighed again as I walked to the dining room.

But the couple was nothing like I expected. The man was handsome. The woman too, though in a more arresting way. They looked up together, smiled in tandem, then stood as one.

"We're the Shellys," the gentleman said, as if I'd been expecting them.

"Melinda," said the woman, then she tipped her head toward the gentleman beside her. "That's Dominic."

And then it hit me.

Dominic and Melinda Shelly.

Anyone living in Los Angeles knew who they were, or at least had heard their names.

What could they possibly want with me?

Dominic gestured at the table. "Do you have a minute?"

Emil would be thrilled if he walked by and saw

me standing and shooting the shit with some of his guests, but sitting, not so much.

Still, I was curious.

I glanced back toward the kitchen. "I need to get back to the kitchen. But is there something I can help you with before I go?"

"There is." Melinda glanced at the table. "Join us and we'll tell you all about it."

Dominic was talking before my ass hit the seat.

"We've seen your LiveLyfe feed. Impressive, both the food and your followers. Can you tell us where all of those recipes come from?"

I shrugged. "It's stuff I make up. At home and off the clock."

"Obviously," Melinda said, her voice like a private joke among the three of us.

Dominic smiled. "We think you would be a perfect host for a cooking show we're planning to produce."

A million possibilities sprang to life inside me.

This wasn't just talk. This was a power couple that could make anything happen. But what would I have to do in exchange? Getting into business with a couple like the Shellys surely meant making a deal with the devil. Not that I objected.

"A cooking show? But I've never been on TV."

"You've been on LiveLyfe and YouTube. We've seen plenty."

I shook my head, having a hard time believing any of it, sure that the Shellys must be making a mistake. "Is it possible you have the wrong guy?"

Melinda pulled out her phone, then showed me the screen. "Are you @ChefHappens?"

Yep, that was my LiveLyfe feed. I could barely swallow. "That's me."

"Then we definitely don't have the wrong guy," she said. "And that's a great name."

"You want to give me my own cooking show?"

Dominic laughed while shaking his head. "Oh, no. Sorry if we gave you that impression. It isn't your show, though we might steal that name. You'll have a co-host. Two, actually. You'll be serving as an apprentice to a pair of mentor chefs."

"Am I allowed to ask who?"

Dominic laughed harder. "Of course. Have you ever heard Amanda Byrd?"

Time froze, making me acutely aware of the Earth in her orbit.

I was a little light-headed, but a little too heavy everywhere else.

But I didn't want them to know any of that,

couldn't let them see the truth on my face. So I said, "Who doesn't? I follow her on LiveLyfe."

That pleased them enough to widen their smiles.

I felt an itch for the kitchen, suddenly worried Emil would see me at the Shelly's table, wonder what was happening, then come over and make a scene right there in the restaurant, ruining my chances with the Shellys forever.

"What's next?" I asked.

"For all three of us, what's next is us making this happen. But for me, right this second" — Dominic held up his phone — "I need to make a call. You two have fun. I'll be right back, then we can finish this up."

Then he left me sitting with his beautiful wife while my kitchen staff awaited my return. I was in full line of sight, if Emil happened to be passing the restaurant.

And I had to pretend like none of that mattered. "So, when does all of this start?"

"Immediately." Melinda smiled, then said something that scared me. "But there is one more thing."

Of course there was.

What if it was something I couldn't do?

What if my chance was about to slip through my fingers, like it did a year ago?

"What is it?" I asked, already afraid of her answer.

"Oh, it's nothing to fret about!" Melinda waved her hand as if swatting my worry away, probably responding to the expression I was wearing but could not see. "It's a simple thing, really. A TV thing, specifically."

I said nothing, waiting for her to explain.

"These shows always do best with a through-line," Melinda continued. "An element that carries us from one episode to the other. Just like how, in a well-planned meal, the courses complement each other from the appetizers all the way through dessert. For the first season, we were hoping that you would be willing to have an on-camera flirtation with Amanda."

"Why would I want to do that?" I asked, my heart like a soufflé about to collapse.

"Because it makes for great TV. We would never make the relationship part of your job, of course. But Dominic and I wondered if you'd be open to letting viewers believe there might be some sort of romance brewing under the surface."

There was nothing I wanted more.

But I said, "I'm not sure. Doesn't Amanda Byrd have a family? Sure seems like it, looking at her LiveLyfe."

"She's happily married, which is why it's only for the cameras. We don't want you to have an affair or break up a marriage." She gave another laugh, followed by yet another wave of her hand. "But Shellter Productions doesn't do anything half-assed. If we're getting into the TV game, then we are going to play by the rules — until we rewrite the rule book. Do you understand?"

I might have nodded. Or I might've stared at her in disbelief.

"Are you in a relationship now?"

I'm shook my head, still in a daze.

"Good," she said. "Not that I don't want you to be happy or anything, but we don't want any open doors. One picture on LiveLyfe could ruin every-thing. Do you feel confident that you can either abstain from starting any new relationship or keep anything that does develop a secret until after the first season has finished airing?"

"I'm single, I'll stay single, and flirting with Amanda isn't a problem at all."

"What did I miss?" Dominic asked, reappearing to reclaim his seat at the table. "Have we signed?"

Melinda took her husband's hand. "He's kidding, Noah. There's nothing to sign yet. But there will be."

"Buckle up," Dominic added. "You're in for a ride."

"What do I do until then?" I meant after kicking Emil in the dick and storming out.

"Quit this place immediately," Dominic said. "You work for us now."

Melinda made a face at her plate. "And please hurry. You're not doing anything for the industry here."

Dominic continued. "We have an apartment for you downtown, near the studio. Plus a Lexus you can use for the length of your contract."

Melinda drummed her nails on the table. "Tell him about the personal shopper."

"Oh, right. You'll need some suitable clothes. To look the part."

"I can't—"

"We're giving you a five thousand dollar advance. You can buy whatever you need to get yourself ready for television."

I swallowed while I searched for the right words. "When do we start filming?"

Dominic said, "If all goes well, we'll be rolling a week from Monday."

"Wow. That's fast."

"Yes," Melinda started.

But Dominic finished. "That's how we like to do things."

They both stood, shook my hand again, and promised to stay in touch.

Sarah stopped me on my way into the kitchen. "Why do you look like that?"

"I don't know." I started to laugh. "What do I look like?"

"Like Applebee's has just been shut down by the federal government."

I laughed harder. "It's better than that."

"What is it?"

"I'll tell you next week!" I bellowed over my shoulder, practically skipping by the time I was pushing my way through the double doors to the kitchen.

I couldn't believe this.

Yes, it was the chance of a lifetime, getting to cook on TV.

But that wasn't even what I was excited about.

A year ago, everything was taken from me. My

ambition started to circle the drain, and hope seemed like something I'd never feel again.

I thought I had lost my shot with Amanda forever, and yet for some reason I couldn't yet understand, the universe had seen fit to give me something it had never given me before.

*A second chance.*

"Anyone know where Emil is?" I shouted out to everyone.

Of course not. Because if anyone was thinking about him, it was only in hoping he wouldn't be coming back into the kitchen any time soon. I wanted someone to ask me what I wanted.

"I don't know," Leah answered first. "Why?"

"Because I need to tell him that I'm out of here."

FIVE

## Amanda

*Well, you need to fucking figure it out.*

I think I said that a dozen times before leaving Arrivé today. Way to be a leader.

Yes, I needed to do better, and no, speaking that way to my staff was no longer acceptable. Never really was. I'd heard all the requests and accusations. But if Harris wanted me to be kinder in the kitchen, then maybe he shouldn't send me in after an ambush. You can't squirt Sriracha in your oatmeal and complain that it didn't taste sweet.

I'd been a lot better this last year. Still, I admit the pressure sometimes got to me. Jacques always said, "Control only what you can." Maybe that worked for life in general, but in the kitchen, I felt like I needed to control everything.

Defined lines of responsibility helped us maintain our flow and quality. Harris didn't understand that I was setting the bar and making it clear what everyone else should expect, from our staff to our customers. Someone had to set that standard, and even if it wasn't a fun job, I'd always been willing to be that person.

I only yelled when someone screwed up or refused to follow those principles because that was when everything we'd built became jeopardized. Protecting what we had was part of my job. The plating stopped with me. I couldn't keep the staff motivated through my actions alone. Everything and everyone around me mattered. If I was the hardest working person in the kitchen at any given time, then I had the right to deliver my missives with cursing and shouting.

But Harris throwing a bomb into the mix with his little trap sent me off the rails. Even if a bit of swearing and yelling could be reasoned away, my new mantra couldn't be.

*Well, you need to fucking figure it out.*

It rolled pretty easily off the tongue, but wasn't constructive at all.

David and Chelsea were on the living room floor when I walked in, both of them reading.

That was all thanks to Mike, another example of why I loved him and why he was so great for all of us. Sure, we both agreed the children should have their digital time limited, but Mike had the character to see it through and demand — without making it seem like an order — they get in their daily reading with the kind of books you have to hold in your hand and manually turn the pages.

"Hi, Mommy!" David looked up from his book and saw me first.

Chelsea glanced up a second later. "Mommy!"

I sat with them on the sofa and looked at their books. Chelsea was still working her way through *An Atlas of Imaginary Places*, but David had started on *Charlie and the Chocolate Factory*, his first Roald Dahl story.

"How do you like it so far?" I nodded at the book.

"I'm glad we're not poor," David answered immediately. Then he told me all about the four grandpas living in one bed, and I pretended not to remember the details.

When it was Chelsea's turn, she showed me the gorgeous illustrations of bubble gum volcanoes and upside-down mountains, magical archipelagos and impossible lighthouses that could never really exist and that I had to use more than a little imagination to see.

Mike entered the living room. He raised his eyebrows. "You're home?"

I pressed my lips to each of the children's foreheads before walking over to him, giving him a hug, then following that with a kiss on his cheek. "Hell of a day."

"How did it go?"

I made some sort of grumbling noise, then launched into a mini-tirade about my shift at Arrivé. Had to get that out of my system before I could effectively bitch about my being shanghaied at Bella by the Sea by my partner.

But Mike cut me off. "No, I mean the meeting with the Shellys and Harris. How did it go?"

I couldn't believe he was smiling. He knew about it, too? Before me? It felt like such a punch to the gut, but I could see the whole thing. Harris got to Mike, told him about the deal so that my husband could pressure me into taking it.

This ambush had more courses than I realized.

I dragged Mike into the dining room.

"What is it?" he asked, still smiling.

"What the hell, Mike? You *knew?*"

"Well, sure. Harris told me. What's wrong with that? I thought you'd be excited."

"Why didn't you tell me?"

"And ruin the surprise?"

"*Surprise* and *ambush* aren't synonyms. You should have warned me. That was a long drive. I could have used it to think, to prepare, to be ready. Instead, I was blindsided."

His face changed. Became like the one he used on his tiptoes. An octave lower he said, "I was hoping you would be happy. That you would like the surprise."

"How long have we been together?"

He looked at me, struck dumb. "What does that—"

"The answer is *long enough that you should know a surprise is risky.* Remind me of our history there. Right? It's not good, Mike. And you know I like to be prepared."

"In the kitchen."

"In life!" The children could certainly hear us. Softly I added, "That wasn't fair."

I waited for Mike to say sorry. It only took him a second. Then he asked me what I told them.

"I said no."

I'd said *maybe*, but I'd been baking about it for hours and my internal cookies were burnt to a crisp.

"Why would you say no? You're not even going to think about it? Don't you think that's——"

"I said no because I was ambushed."

Again, his expression changed. But this one wasn't his tiptoe face. It was the one he usually went to next. His *heels in the dirt* face. The *I've had enough* face. The one that clearly said *we're going to have this discussion right now, whether you like it or not.*

His jaw was set hard, his eyes harder. "You've been obsessed with your restaurant to the detriment of this family."

"My restaurant has given this family everything it has."

"That's an overstatement."

"No, Mike. It's just a statement."

He stood like a statue, waiting to see if I would say more.

I did. "I've poured a lot of hours into the restaurant, and yes, that's taken time away from home, but I brought home a lot of money, too."

"That's not the point, and you know it. Who cares about the money?"

"We do, Mike. You don't get to do that."

"Do what?"

"The thing where you lob all the bad feelings over here and then get to feel innocent because you're better than me."

"I never said I was better than you."

I glared at him. "You act like you're better than me."

"I don't think I'm better than you."

I acquiesced, with a softness to my voice. "But that's how you make me feel. 'Who cares about the money?' is easy to say, and I get the appeal since it excuses you from feeling bad. But our lifestyle is to blame here, not me, and it took two of us to get here. You love this house and everything in it. You love our vacations and all the ridiculous meals. Probably more than I do. That culinary tour around the world we're always talking about? It won't be cheap."

"But I don't *need* any of those things. And I said we could start with A Taste of Peru."

"I'm not finished. You do *need* to pay for Constellation. That's much more important to you than me. That's eighteen grand for each of them per year, for *elementary school*. After taxes, that's your entire salary at A Fresher Sunrise. And it doesn't include all the extra expenses that come with sending our children to a such a fancy-pants school.

That's one example. And there are plenty. *We got here together,* so please stop acting like I shoved you into the oven at gunpoint."

Mike glared at me, but I could see in his eyes that he knew I was right, at least in part. He said, "You act like the restaurant is responsible for everything good in our lives. Like we'd be living in some shitty three-bedroom apartment if not for Arrivé."

"Our lives would be drastically different."

"Maybe that wouldn't be all bad."

"You're right. I'm sure it wouldn't be. And maybe it would be great. But so is this. The last year has been better, right?" I took his hands and held them. "Didn't we just celebrate that together?"

"Yes, it's been much better. Here at home. But what about at Arrivé? The restaurant's been bringing in less and less while our spending has gone up. You're right about everything you said, but this year we only managed to pay for Constellation because we dipped into my retirement. If we keep going at this rate, we'll have used our life savings before the kids get to college."

"Really, Mike? Where's the faith?"

"I've given you all the faith in the world. Been with you every step of the way."

"And now you're doubting me."

"I'm not doubting you. But we need to be responsible. You dropped ten-grand on a single dose of retail therapy while the restaurant was bleeding money, and we were cutting back on our household budget."

"I have much better coping mechanisms now, thanks to Dr. Jamison."

"I get it. But I also *get it*, Amanda. You need to at least hear me."

"I'm listening."

"We need to be smart about this."

"I promise, I understand that. That's why it's more important than ever that we make the restaurant successful again. I'll make a budget and stick to it. Just like at the restaurant."

"The problem is deeper than that. Or maybe it's that the solution is so simple."

"And what's the solution?"

"Saying yes to the Shellys. It's a good deal."

"You *know* the specifics?" That really pissed me off.

He shrugged. "I don't know how much of the picture I have, but I know they're offering $100K an episode. Plus a book deal worth millions. We'd be making money from the franchise without doing *any* of the work. They'd be licensing the name and recipes in exchange for big checks with many zeros. In contrast, Arrivé will always have a ceiling."

"So does the Sistine Chapel."

"Amanda …"

"Yes, Mike?"

"Play fair."

"How am I not playing fair?"

"Have an honest conversation. We're talking a lot of struggle versus an easy and lucrative win. Why isn't this at least worth a discussion without the unnecessary conflict?"

"Who says it's unnecessary? Do you think a soufflé is comfortable in the heat? Probably not, but it sure as hell doesn't exist without it."

"You know you never make your point as well when you personify food, right?"

Sure, I knew. But fighting wasn't going to get us anywhere. I reset my head and tried again.

"Let's say I made hand-blocked greeting cards. Designed every one, and carved each block myself. Inked them, rolled the things onto card stock."

"Okay …"

"Then some guy knocks on the door and says, 'Hey Amanda, we'd like to take your designs and print them in China, thereby bleaching every drop of art from your product and making it like

58

anything else you can get next to the Chiclets at the Circle K.' If that happened, I would have to say, 'No, thank you very much.'"

"I doubt you would thank them."

"That wasn't necessary."

"*None* of this is necessary." His voice was a volcano, lava already licking the lip.

"You're asking me to franchise my art."

Barely containing himself, he spoke low through gritted teeth. "This is the diva attitude that almost cost you the restaurant *and* your family. You have a responsibility to do what right for David and Chelsea, and you owe it to me, after everything I put up with while you were getting the restaurant started."

"That's blackmail."

Mike rolled his eyes. "Blackmail? Really? Why does everything in life have to be plated your way? Is the restaurant more important to you than me and the kids?"

He didn't understand. Never did. The restaurant wasn't just a restaurant, it was the obelisk of my professional success, and that monument was crumbling. If it were to fall, then I would fail as a human. Selling out didn't make that better.

"Why do you think I'm home right now, early

enough to say goodnight to the children instead of closing shop with the crew? I'm making a lot of effort."

"You are," he conceded.

"But Arrivé is important to me. And it's a pillar in our lives. We should be bonding over the restaurant's salvation, not casting it aside so we can move onto something else."

He shook his head. "That's not what we're doing. Maybe all the dreams in your head can be achieved an easier way."

"And maybe there is no *easier way.* Name a single chef that everyone knows who became a household name the easy way."

"Name one who wasn't miserable as shit in the process."

"I don't have insight into their personal journeys, Mike."

"I would argue the opposite."

We spent a half-minute glaring, collecting our breath.

He found his words before walking away. "Have a nice time saying goodnight to the children. I'm sure whatever you bake will be delicious."

That second part hurt more than the first.

Of course I was going to bake.

But for some reason, it still felt like Mike was reaching into my insides when he said that.

Which was the point.

I knew what I was going to make before I tucked in the kids, and I started the second I left their rooms.

Chocolate macarons with pistachio buttercream filling.

I was feeling dark and delicate. Soft in the center.

Just picturing the process on my way to the kitchen made me start to feel better. Sifting the dry ingredients, aerating the mixture, stirring in the pistachio flour until the rough texture turned smooth. Beating the egg whites — no oil, because even a touch could ruin the meringue. Folding the batter and counting each stroke of the spatula. Making perfect circles of batter on a silicone baking mat, then finally drying the shells before baking to develop the prettiest feet.

I pictured it all before I even started, and I couldn't wait to get busy.

My other aprons were all dirty — Mike hadn't

gotten around to washing them. Had he held off on purpose? I checked the laundry room, hoping there were some already folded or even still in the dryer, but I found them all in a basket with a pair of my yoga pants, waiting to be washed.

That should have made me feel okay with the alternative, but I still felt a well of guilt when I opened the kitchen drawer, fishing for the cheap fabric. When I pulled it from where I'd stuffed it, I wondered why the hell I never threw the goddamned thing away.

But then I put on the apron and began my beautiful work.

This was how I processed best, by losing myself in a complicated dessert. It was the best way to douse my sorrow, or at least muffle it long enough to meander into an answer that made sense for me.

I could sift through my thoughts with the flour and beat my questions and answers along with the eggs. The intense concentration required by all those fussy little details was the only kind of work that could ever keep me out of my head. Or at least in all the right places inside it.

There was a rhythm, meditative yet demanding, simple but repetitive, complex and elegant. Weighing and whisking cleared out the riskiest thoughts from my mind and eased my thinking from lumpy batter to artistic confection that eventually melted behind a smile.

The flour between my fingers. The blender in my ears. The unmistakable scent of sugar cooking, a fragrance to kill and die for. The experimentation — what tasted exactly the same to everyone else was slightly different to me every time I made it. Not necessarily better, but with a variant to teach me something new, because one of my biggest fears was having my talent go stale.

The cream was rich and required complications like boiling syrup and tools like a candy thermometer and a standing mixer. Perfectly-measured ingredients and perfectly-measured patience. Next to a preheated oven, it was easy for me to find. Then on to the bag of pistachios for my homemade paste.

But this time, it didn't work. Not like it should have.

The serenity was there, but none of the clarity. It was like baking something vegan — even at its best, it's only mostly there.

My head was still a mess, and I knew why.

But the reason was a butcher's knife between my ribs. The pain wasn't going to go away because

I squeezed dollops of creamy batter onto a cookie sheet, and I didn't want it to. This was necessary emotion. Something sweet was waiting on the other side of my inner heat.

Mike was an echo in my head, telling me I was a diva. Saying I had a responsibility to do the right thing for David and Chelsea, like I needed a reminder. Alluding to everything he 'put up with' when we were getting the restaurant started.

Soon enough, I was suffering through too many waves of emotion. I pulled a glass from the cabinet, then filled it with muscat. Should have started that sooner.

Mike was in my head because that's where he deserved to be. He was right, and in ways he didn't know. Yes, he knew I'd done some awful stuff, but he had no idea I had flirted with the unforgivable. Okay, I had fucked the unforgivable and allowed the unforgivable to fuck me right back, many times during the most regrettable month of my life. A personal Chernobyl that nearly destroyed my marriage. After realizing what I'd done, I came back home to where I should never have left.

And I was so deeply, deeply sorry.

But I didn't want to live in regret. Doing so wasn't good for anyone. I longed to feel as beautiful as the macarons. Making them was like having a vision board that dissolved on the tongue.

It wasn't a difficult decision in front of me so much as the most complex sort of concession. Saying yes to the Shellys' deal would open a lot of doors in our lives.

And the law of averages said we'd regret opening some of them.

I couldn't be binary this time. The offer wasn't good or bad, black or white, window or wall. This was the recipe that changed the entire cookbook. Whatever we decided to do next would impact the rest of our lives. Once we said 'yes' to any part of the deal, we put the restaurant behind everything else. A bitter but necessary pill to swallow.

Another sip of muscat didn't make it go down any easier.

I wouldn't sign for more than a season. But if we could get out after the first one was finished — or stay if we loved it, I suppose — then I couldn't say no. Even hard as it was, the last year had flown by. So would the next one. Mike's happiness would make it easier to stay centered. We'd have plenty of money for whatever we needed. A year's tuition for both kids at Constellation wouldn't even cost us half of what we'd be making per episode of our show.

We'd put away enough in one season for their entire tenure there, plus a lot of the other things we wanted to do.

By the time I was squirting pistachio butter-cream onto the bottom halves of my marvelous macarons, I was feeling surprisingly great about everything.

We would take the deal for one season, with anything after that to be determined. Arrivé wouldn't have to be franchised because I could design the menu for a new high-end restaurant that Harris could have all to himself.

I stared at my work with a smile, took out my phone, then snapped a picture for LiveLyfe.

Now that my work was done and my decision made, I nibbled the edge of the macaron. It dissolved in my mouth. Took another bite, then two fast ones after that.

I placed the last of it on my tongue, this time like communion, as I chanted a mantra in my mind.

*Only at our worst can we know ourselves the best.*

# SIX

## Noah

I was meeting Amanda's partner Harris for coffee.

We were given an intro bomb by Dominic, told when and where to meet and that we would get along famously the moment we did.

I was trying not to be nervous, but it wasn't easy. I'd gone from having no idea that any of this was coming to feeling terrified that the opportunity would evaporate out of my life without warning, despite a promise made otherwise.

Like Amanda had.

I didn't want to blow it. I needed her partner to like me.

We clicked immediately. Like kismet threw the two of us together. We were giggling in minutes. And not the awkward laughter that lays like a glaze over new conversation. This was familiar. Comforting. It wasn't that Harris was easy to talk to, or that I was, so much as that there was an undeniable ease to our exchange.

We ordered matching black coffees before even meeting. We shared both fury and contempt for pumpkin spice lattes and all the dairy- and diabetic-problems they caused. Both of us ordered a blackberry, lemon, and thyme muffin, and each of us planned to eat only half. Had we known, I'm sure we would have split one of the delicacies, with its buttery, crumbly, toasted honey finish.

Harris and I were both unabashedly still into Friends.

An episode was playing on the coffee shop's TV, which was too wide, especially in a corner that made it look backed against the wall like a man under arrest.

It was "The One With all the Rugby." Janice was at her most annoying in that episode, not that it stopped Chandler from going out with her again, just like never having played rugby doesn't stop Ross from playing the game to impress Emily. Shit got real when Chandler told Janice he'd been transferred to Yemen and was leaving the following day. She helped him pack, then took him to the airport. When she still wouldn't leave, he bought a ticket and boarded the plane. Harris and I both laughed the whole way through the episode as we sat there, eating that buttery crumble, sipping black coffee, and talking about our ripe opportunity. The episode had a goof where Joey says he saw *Dances with Wolves*, even though the movie came out in 1990, three years before he was in the group. I couldn't help but point it out.

"So, you're obsessed too?" Harris asked.

"I wouldn't say *obsessed*."

"What would you say?"

"Interested."

He smiled. "Have you seen all the episodes more than once, and have you ever watched them in order?"

"Yes. And yes."

"How many times have you seen your least watched episode?"

That got me laughing. "Four."

"Favorite episode?"

"The One with the Embryos."

Harris gave me an approving nod. "Great episode. Favorite friend?"

"Chandler, of course. I still laugh at some of his

lines, even though I know them all, so they can't ever surprise me."

"Same. I used to watch the show with my first girlfriend in college. It was our thing. I dropped out my freshman year, or at least I traded college for culinary school, and after that, my life was all sauces and listening to a lot of yelling. But I still always tried to catch *Friends*. Amanda always made fun of me for watching it."

"Really? She doesn't like it?"

I didn't know that about her. I thought everyone liked *Friends*.

"Not at all. That's probably my fault. Early on I started calling her Monica." Harris made a face.

"Ouch. I bet she really hated that! She is a Monica, though." It was a bit too familiar, so I cleared my throat and added, "Or at least, she seems to be."

"Oh, she is. You'll see." He looked at me, assessing, and I wondered if his next question was part of the interview. "How about you? Why do you love the show so much? It was a bit before your time."

"I don't think there is a *before your time* when it comes to *Friends*. It's the biggest sitcom ever."

"I think that might be *The Simpsons*."

"I didn't say *the best*. And I'm not sure cartoons

count. Anyway, I grew up with the show in syndication. *Friends* was always on. My dad was usually out drinking, and my mom was always … sleeping." I cleared my throat, certain that Harris could hear a whisper of the something within it I was hoping he couldn't. "The friends actually *were* my friends when I was little. And kinda like my only ones. It's where I learned about a lot of stuff, including sex."

"Ha, yeah. I didn't notice that when I was watching the show for the first time, but it's like sixty-four percent dick jokes."

"Is that scientific?" I asked.

"I've run many tests. But yeah, now that I have kids, I've been watching the episodes with a different eye." Harris changed the subject. "So, you were on your own a lot as a kid?"

I nodded, wondering how deep things might go, rubbing my thumbs against my pointers, as though nervously sanding my skin might keep us in the shallows.

"I was." Honoring the interview, if that's what this was, I added, "But it was good for me. I had to feed myself dinner a lot, so I was learning the basics of cooking in third grade."

"That's young."

I shrugged, then laughed, trying to lighten things up. "I would have gone hungry if I didn't."

"Shit. I'm sorry. So, culinary school was the great escape?"

"It was tougher than I expected, and I never imagined there would be even more yelling in the kitchen than there had been at home. But it was a lot easier to take, knowing that no matter how bad it might get, even if the chef was spitting on the back of my neck or right into my eyes, he was never going to hit me. I had to tune out the worst because the best teachers always gave you something, even when they were tearing you apart."

"True." Harris raised his cup for a toast.

We pretended to clink, not wanting to spill so much as a drop of our coffees.

"I didn't care how hard it was. For the first time in my life, I felt like I was finally doing something right. Finally on my way to who and what I was supposed to be."

"How about your current job?"

I laughed, but that time it was smaller. "The show is my current job. I'm quitting my old gig before my next shift. I would have already done it, but my boss, Emil, wasn't around after the Shellys dropped by the restaurant, and I need to do it in person."

"Of course. I mean the place you were just working. Before you got the offer."

"I was running the kitchen at a place called the Hotel Milano. You know it?"

Harris nodded. "I do."

"And?"

"It used to be nice."

"Exactly. Guy who owns it, dude named Emil? Not cool. I don't talk shit behind people's backs, employer or no, but I also don't mind calling out when someone isn't a quality human. The guy has some things that remind me of my father, he pretends to be more civilized. But I live for those moments, you know, when a customer compliments the food."

"I do," Harris said. "And how often does that happen to you?"

"Not often enough." Then I gave him a better answer. "It used to happen more, but Emil is making us use crap ingredients — frozen stuff where we have to use the microwave. I don't have a budget. You know the type of kitchen I'm talking about."

"Not personally. But, yeah. What's your toughest dish?"

"Swordfish. I can't stand cooking it. I never get it right. Too tough, a hundred percent of the time."

"Have you ever tried poaching it in broth, then searing it in a cast-iron skillet?"

I could feel myself lighting right up. "I haven't, but I'm going to!"

"Favorite dish? Not to make, but to eat."

So, this was definitely an interview. I laughed, enjoying it. "Fettuccini carbonara."

Harris looked surprised, so I explained.

"I know it's rich, but that's what I love about it. The ingredients are cheap, so you can make it even if you don't have much else in the fridge or your wallet. It's the kind of thing you appreciate when you grew up on ramen and PBJs."

"I can imagine." He stopped to take a sip of his coffee and a bite of his muffin. Then he asked me to explain the difference between étouffée and gumbo.

"Étouffée has a thicker sauce and usually only one type of meat. Gumbo often features multiple meats."

He raised his eyebrows and smiled. "This is great."

"What is?"

He smiled wider. "All of it. Tell me how you would make the perfect chocolate chip cookie."

It took me a moment to answer, some of it spent wondering if the question might be a trick, simple as it was. "Butter and eggs at room temperature, creamed together for at least five minutes to mix in tiny air pockets, because you want the cookies to bake evenly.

Harris shook his head in disappointment.

"What?" I asked with a sinking in my stomach.

"The correct answer was 'double the amount of chocolate chips the recipe calls for.'"

But Harris was obviously joking, so I laughed.

"You seem like someone who has the basics down and is eager to soak up as much as you can. That makes me feel like this is a great fit, at least for me. But we're supposed to be getting to know each other, and I'm hogging the questions. I'm sure there are some things that you're dying to know. Am I right?"

"No doubt. Can I start with what I'm dying to know most?"

It wasn't what I was dying to know most.

"That certainly sounds like the best place," he said.

"How did Chef Jacques spice his bouillabaisse?"

Harris laughed. "His Highness made his stock from a combination of fish and lobster, rather than just fish or just lobster."

"What makes the paella at Arrivé so savory? It's not better because it's different, it's better because it's actually better somehow."

Harris lit up enough to make me think the recipe was his. "We use Mexican oregano instead of the traditional Mediterranean version, and a mix of sweet and smoked paprika. Oh, and the onions and garlic are fried in bacon drippings."

"Well, that would make it a difference."

"Shhh." Harris puts a finger to his lips.

"Why did you give up being in the kitchen?"

"It was too much pressure," he admitted, "and honestly, not to talk shit about anyone either, but Chef Jacques was an asshole."

I said the next like it wasn't the big deal that my pounding heart knew it was. "What is it like to work with Amanda Byrd?"

A strange expression washed across his face. It was the first stiff moment I'd seen. Or felt. I wondered if it was because Amanda could be prickly or something else.

Then Harris made it worse.

"You'll find out soon enough, kid."

I couldn't stand the dismissal, and I really hated being called *kid*.

Still, I laughed like it was a joke. There was a truth here I couldn't ignore. The show was my ticket out of poverty, payment for the decades spent trying to work my way into a better procession of kitchens.

My gaze locked on Harris. "Thank you for this chance, and for letting me get to know you a bit today. I want to give you, Ms. Byrd, the Shellys, and this show all better than my best. But I can only do that if you're honest with me. I always want to know about the things I need to work on."

"And I'll want you to know them."

We finished our muffins down to the crumbs, though both of us knew we shouldn't. But it was like turning off *Friends* after an episode started. I felt compelled to finish, despite the empty calories.

But I left the coffee shop with a warm handshake that felt like we were withholding a hug for decorum. It also felt like I now had an ally to stand behind me. I was looking forward to seeing Amanda in person again, instead of occasionally breaking down to stalk her on LiveLyfe while sobbing to myself.

We weren't exactly peers yet, but things were now different than they were.

Soon we would be in the same room, and I would be pouring every cup of my charm into the mix.

Amanda would see that she missed me.

And that would make her realize that she should no longer resist.

Or that she didn't even want to.

I would be counting the hours until she was mine.

# SEVEN

# Amanda

Dinner — skillet chicken bulgogi served over rice — was delicious.

I made sure to let Mike know a half-dozen times, spaced out so he could hear it each time as genuinely as I meant it.

He made a lot of smart choices. I complimented those individually, as well. The carrot straws and sliced mushrooms, the peppercorn over black pepper, and peanut oil, I was almost positive. He even used foil to make sure it would cook evenly and keep the leftovers fresh while making the aftermath of his meal a breeze to clean.

I would have used less sugar and more garlic. I wouldn't have used soy sauce at all. A brown rice or fried noodle would have really brought out the flavors, for sure. But I didn't say any of those things and tried not to feel guilty for thinking them, seeing as they were part of both my DNA and vocation.

A second bowl on the table overflowed with a milder version of the same meal for David and Chelsea. It was thoughtful. I wasn't always willing to do that, telling myself I was teaching the children to like different kinds of food and helping to develop their tastebuds. But that was only partly true. Sometimes I just wanted to make what I wanted to make.

"Do you guys love it?" I asked.

They both nodded. David reached out to scoop more from the bowl.

"Great job," I said again.

He leaned into my ear and whispered, "I appreciate the compliments, really, but it sounds like you're working to hit a quota."

"I'm not—"

He stopped me with a subtle shake of his head and a kind look in his eyes. *It's okay, I get it. Let's finish eating in peace.*

So we did. Only after the meal was over and the table was cleared did we get into it again.

I wanted to make a dessert for our family, but Mike wanted to make enemies with my idea.

No matter what happened with all of this, I wanted to open my bakery one day. It was one of the biggest reasons for my agreeing to do the show. I needed the fantasy to keep me going through the coming year.

And yes, I could get a little obsessive, but this wasn't that. Baking made me feel better, feel closer to a dream I needed to hold tighter for a while. It helped me start grieving for the thing I was losing, while stoking excitement for the something I was working to win. A year from now we should have enough money to open my bakery, and every night in the kitchen until then was another chance to look for a little more of myself.

Besides, everyone loves dessert.

I didn't want to make just anything. I'd been imagining a new confection all day, and now I wanted to bring the baklava to life. Bake it in the oven to get it out of my system. Lavender syrup, orange zest, and macadamia nut honey. A baklava that would become a new family favorite.

If Mike would stop rejecting my idea.

"That sounds complicated," he said.

"It's really not."

"Is it less than fifteen minutes?"

I laughed, because of course it wasn't. "It'll take a little longer than that."

"Let's do ice cream instead."

"Ice cream is boring."

"Said the food snob."

"You're as snobby as I am."

He shook his head. "Not about dessert, and not tonight. We have things to do."

Then it hit me. Mike was in a hurry. A sinking feeling in my gut told me not to ask why.

Maybe it was on my face because he reminded me anyway. "It's your night to have mother-daughter time with Chelsea. I'm taking David to the art theater to see some weird anime thing."

"What weird anime thing?"

"I don't know. It's called *Grim the Reaper*."

"It sounds dark. Is it age appropriate?"

Mike nodded, a smile touching his lips. "Yeah, I looked it up on Common Sense. Apparently Grim doesn't like to end lives, so it's all about him saving people from their deaths, but with a lot of big eyes and drama. You do remember, right? We talked about this."

"Of course I remember."

I shouldn't have said that. Always tell the truth. It never works out when I don't. Only delays the inevitable. "I'm excited to have mother-daughter time with Chelsea tonight, and I totally don't have to make my dessert, so don't think I'm putting any of this on you—"

"But?"

"But maybe you could take Chelsea to go and see *Grim the Reaper*, too. Isn't she going to feel left out?"

"I don't want her to come see *Grim the Reaper*!" David bellowed from the other room. Apparently we weren't having a private discussion. "It won't be any fun if she comes."

David's declaration was followed by a little squeal from Chelsea, then a mighty howl from her brother.

"Ouch!"

"That's what you get for hurting my feelings!" Chelsea yelled.

"Are you going to do anything about that?" I asked Mike.

"She's being direct. And why should I have to do it?" Then, as a bludgeon for me, he whispered, "You're the one who doesn't want to spend any time with her."

"That's not true." And shit, that one really stung.

On cue, Chelsea ran into the room and made me a liar.

"Mommy, what is the special thing you have planned for us tonight while David and Daddy go to *Grim the Reaper*?"

She smiled at me expectantly.

Mike watched as I stuttered and fell.

I could have admitted that I forgot, and the two of us could have come up with something right there. Or I could have asked Chelsea what she wanted to do and called it *her choice*. I said something stupid instead.

"We're going to make your room look pretty by finding places for everything."

Awful as it was, part of me hoped Chelsea would pitch a fit in the kitchen and demand to see *Grim the Reaper* with the boys or anything other than having to clean up her room with Mom.

Instead, Chelsea looked up at me and mumbled, "Okay," through a slowly dissolving smile.

When had I turned into this particular breed of monster?

I looked at Mike, wondered if he was thinking something similar, hoped that he wasn't, then reminded myself I would certainly deserve it if he did.

I turned to my daughter. "I promise it's going to be really, really fun. Okay?"

Chelsea nodded.

"Now who wants ice cream?" I asked.

A trio of *I do's* rang out in unison.

Mike mouthed *Thank you,* and I gave him an *Of course,* but without the *Sorry* he deserved.

While the guys were at *Grim the Reaper,* I was determined to have a great time with Chelsea. My efforts weren't immediately rewarded because my daughter stayed suspicious. This was cleaning her room, after all, and being five years old didn't make her dumb. But she followed every direction, tentative at first, held back by her disbelief that a chore could be fun. But then I began to fake cry.

"What's wrong, Mommy?" Chelsea asked, petting my hair, overly dramatic because of course this was a game.

I wept imaginary tears as I pulled her to my chest. "I don't know what to do! My daughter doesn't want to play with me!"

Literal as always, and practical like her father, she said, "My mommy wants me to clean my room."

I thrust my pointer into the air, and like it was a brand-new idea striking like lightning, I said, "I bet your stuffies can help us!"

And they did. The two of us arranged her stuffed animals into storytelling tableaus. Runner the Rabbit hogged most of the glory, being the selfish hare that he was, but at least his narratives were bursting with color and the sort of character that kept Chelsea in stitches.

Soon enough, she seemed to be clueless that we were even cleaning her room, because when Owlexander asked her where the dirty clothes went, she answered immediately, and in a tone that told the old bird how much he deserved her answer. She was shrieking with laughter by the time her room was looking clean enough for a photograph, and not just because Mr. Penguin really was that hilarious when naughty, but because I had relaxed enough to have some fun with my daughter.

The time with Chelsea was definitely better than baklava, but I still wanted to make some sort of dessert. Sure, we had ice cream, and no, the girl didn't need another granule of sugar. It was all about me, and I knew it. But I really wanted it to be a night to remember, stretching the fun we already had as far as it could go.

"Want to make some caramel popcorn together?"

Chelsea squealed even louder.

We popped ten cups of popcorn on the stove, then removed all the kernels.

Melted butter in the saucepan, added brown sugar, lightly stirring as we brought the mixture to a boil.

I helped Chelsea add the vanilla and mix it in.

Her face lit with wonder when the caramel's color changed with the baking soda. She giggled when bubbles formed, aerating the caramel and making it lighter and lighter. When it was finally smooth enough to coat the corn, she was more excited than I was.

We drizzled the caramel atop the popcorn, gently stirred to evenly coat it, then spread the sticky mess onto a cookie sheet covered in foil.

Chelsea was sticky, and I was gratified. The boys would be over the moon when they came home.

It happened as our little girl was wiping her smiling mouth, after polishing the last of the popcorn out of her bowl.

"Go wash your hands," I told her.

We could hear the front door open. Chelsea turned to me. "They're home!"

"We're in here!" I called out. "In the kitchen."

I felt close to Chelsea and proud of myself. Exuberant, like a silly little girl. I couldn't wait for Mike to come in and acknowledge me, couldn't deny what I wanted.

Mike stopped in the foyer. David, scampering behind him, paused at his feet. My husband's gaze traveled from Chelsea washing her hands, to the oversized bowl of caramel corn sitting next to her much smaller empty one, then over to me with a smile I needed and knew I deserved.

He kissed the back of my neck.

Everything felt so wonderful. For a moment, it was so totally perfect.

Mike didn't have to ruin it, but he did.

"I told you. Paying attention to your family can be fun."

## EIGHT

## Noah

I still had to quit my job at the Hotel Milano.

I wanted to do it right after walking away from the Shellys, but I hadn't been able to find my asshole boss anywhere. Probably berating someone. Or maybe sneaking out to get some trashy food passed in a paper bag through his BMW window.

I couldn't stand bullies, and Emil was one of the worst I'd ever met.

He wasn't the most physically violent. By law he couldn't raise a hand to any of us, and plenty of people in my past had done that. Nor was he the most verbally abusive. But Emil was the first bully in my life who had no excuse. The man was in a position of power, had plenty of money, and according to Maslow's Hierarchy theory, his basic needs were more than satisfied. He was my boss, not my teacher like the bellowing chefs at culinary school. Emil never taught me a thing and probably couldn't if he wanted to.

Yet the man was a tyrant, filling his tank by siphoning from others, a swollen ego incapable of empathy. Surely bullied himself as a boy, the man now vented his impotence on victims weaker than himself through the force of his position.

I had to tell Emil what I thought before I left. The grit of a hard life made me who I was, scraping against my inner self since the day I was born. But that was like sandpaper on wood, and now my potential had a glassy polish.

On the other hand, Emil's adversity had turned him into an asshole.

My stuff was all packed inside my car, and I was milling inside the kitchen, wearing jeans and a tee, waiting for my old boss to show. Everyone wanted to know what I was doing, Leah the most insistent among them.

"Tell me what's happening," she demanded.

I was trying not to laugh with Leah standing there, my former sous chef with her hands on her hips, the corners of her mouth pulled down in a deadly curious scowl, no idea what she was about to see.

"You got mad at me for ruining the end of *Fight Club*, and that movie is twenty years old. Believe me, you don't want any spoiler alerts here."

She opened her mouth to protest again, but Emil walrus-walked into the kitchen.

He looked at me, noted my attire, turned that look into a stare, and then that stare into a scowl. "What do you think you're doing?"

"I'm giving you notice." My lips were dry, and I felt a compulsion to lick them. But I wasn't going to do anything until I saw Emil flinch.

He muttered, "Why aren't you dressed for your shift?"

"Like I said, I'm giving you notice."

It dawned on him. I wasn't just quitting, I was quitting *right that second*.

"You can't do that." He looked around the kitchen at everyone and realized that this was a show.

"I absolutely can." I smiled wide enough to show him all of my teeth.

"I don't have a chef. If you——"

"Leah is your chef now. She's excellent. Unfortunately, you've spent so much time either ignoring or diminishing her, that you don't even realize she's been your best asset for a while. It's been a long time since I've given a crap about this place, though I sure did at one point."

"You can't talk to me like—"

"Actually, I can talk to you however I want now. Watch: *You strike me as the kind of guy who shits through his dick.* See? It doesn't even have to make sense. If you were smart — and to be clear, you're obviously not — you would have fired my ass months ago when I clearly stopped giving a fuck and made Leah chef, since she seems to actually care, even though the owner of this place is a total fucking asshole."

"You better watch yourself, Noah Temple."

"You're full-naming me? Really, Emil Maldonado? I have been watching myself. And I hate what I see. It's easy to feel like a piece of shit here, working for someone who wants to cheat his customers."

"How dare you? I don't cheat my customers!"

But Emil was starting to sweat. I had never seen him so angry. Not a person in the kitchen was pretending to work.

"What do you call it, Emil? You charge top dollar, but it's always about the margins and never about the food. Notice how we're not a destination for *anyone?* We should be. Instead, our hotel guests are like hostages. *No.*" I shook my head. "*Your* hotel guests are like hostages. I'm out of here."

"I'll withhold your last paycheck."

I laughed. Shook my head. Looked into his eyes until I felt him flinch.

"Do you think I give a shit about your paycheck? It was the only thing you ever had over me, *Emil.* And now that's gone. So, what else do you got?"

"You're done, Temple. Ruined. You'll never get another job again."

I smiled wide, but didn't say a thing. Way more fun to make him wonder.

But he kept on threatening me. "I'll tell every hotel owner or manager I know that you're as incompetent as you are unreliable. You'll have to move to another state if you ever want to work again!"

I laughed and told him that he sounded like a cartoon villain, then I really let him have it.

"I hope you do make those calls, Emil. Not one of those people you talk to is going to take you seriously. You've probably met some of these other owners and managers at conventions where you were all glad-handing at the buffet before you took your hooker up to your room. But they'll remember a pile of shit who was clearly incompetent and somehow lucked into some money, either through birth or happenstance. One of the owners they ridicule in private for being too stupid and cheap to run a good show. They'll know it was your fault without needing a single detail. At the very least, they'll believe it was karma delivered to a small-minded man. Those who haven't met you will be able to hear it in your whiny little voice, so—"

Emil lunged forward and grabbed me by the arm.

I affected an expression reminiscent of the Joker and said, "Why so serious?"

My eyes dared him to do it. Whatever he wanted. It would be worse for him than it would be for me. A subordinate was being assaulted by his superior in a room full of witnesses. Didn't have to say the words. Emil could see the scoreboard for himself.

His entire face was scrunched enough to look like drying clay. He released his grip and took a heavy, begrudging step back. "You're a real piece of shit, you know that?"

"I couldn't forget it if I wanted to. Had it beat into me as far back as I can remember." I'm sure my smile had a million awful memories inside it. "Even once on my seventh birthday."

Emil straightened up and looked around the room again, his dignity shot. He tried to salvage it, anyway. "Get back to work. I see any of you pulling this shit, you're fired!"

He stormed off through the double doors.

Muffled cheers rippled through the room, getting louder as the seconds ticked, turning down-right jovial before a full minute had passed.

I grinned so wide, it cracked into a laugh. I couldn't make words.

"What the hell, man?" Leah punched me on the shoulder. "You wanna tell me what's up now?"

I started to rub it.

"Like that really hurt," she said.

It totally did.

"Now I have to finish rubbing my shoulder before I can give you your present."

"My present?" Her smile was delightful.

I reached into my back pocket, pulled out the envelope, then handed it to her.

She peeked inside, flinched, looked back up at me. "What is this?"

"It's three thousand dollars."

"Why are you giving me three thousand dollars?"

"So you can quit this job. Get another gig. I'll give you an amazing reference."

"Where are you going? What's happening?" Leah shook her head. "I don't understand."

"I got a job. It's a good one."

"Cooking where?" She paused. "Or for whom?"

"It's not like that. I'm not sure if I can tell you anything yet, and I don't want to violate any NDAs or anything. But it's good. Great. The best thing ever. And soon I'm going to have a shot at my own restaurant."

"Oh, my god! When?"

I laughed at the absurdity. "Maybe in a few months."

She shook her head. "This is a lot to take in."

"I know. But what's good for me is good for you. When I open my place, you'll have a home there. But until then, you've gotta get out here. And away from Emil."

"You just told him to make me chef!"

"He never will. He's too much of an asshole, and he doesn't care about running a great kitchen, so he'd rather hire a chef who thinks like him. And you're never going to get away from him by staying here. He's like human herpes. But he needed to be told publicly that you weren't getting the respect you deserved."

"Good point. He is like human herpes." A tear fell from one eye. She hugged me fast before I saw anything else.

When she pulled away, I was smiling ear to ear.

"What?" Leah asked. "There's something else. Tell me ..."

"I called in an anonymous tip to the health inspection department. You should really get to quitting." I looked at my watch. "Like, before the hour is up."

# NINE

## Amanda

I needed to bake.

Gillian had made an idiot mistake that would probably end up costing us tens of thousands of dollars.

I desperately, seriously, hopelessly needed to make something, taste something, and drink something while doing it.

Maybe I could bake something with a drink right inside it.

Beer brownies sounded perfect. I could make them for two; Mike and I could share. If he wasn't in the mood, I wouldn't be polishing off an entire tray by myself. I'm an Olympian of restraint, unless I'm stressed or sad, and in those cases, I might as well pour molten syrup down my throat.

Driving home, I felt stressed by at least a week's worth of bullshit crammed into an afternoon and sad because my dream had changed — not because it evolved in my mind, but because somebody decided to change it without my consent.

Beer brownies would bleed chocolate and alcohol into my psyche, pillow soft cake and a couple of tall ones.

The stress was receding from imagery alone. I stopped at a red light and began to imagine.

Heating the beer in a saucepan until it simmered and calmed. Beating the butter and sugar and melted chocolate chunks. Stirring in the eggs and vanilla. Mixing the beer syrup from sugar, butter, and beer — like rich and oily ambrosia on my tongue — then incorporating most of it into my batter before sifting in the flour, cocoa powder, baking powder and salt. I could smell them in the oven as I whipped the buttercream frosting, feel resistance on my knife when I sliced them. Sometimes enough to turn a bad day in the other direction.

By the time my foot kicked the front door closed behind me, I felt better. "Be right back!" I called into the living room before heading straight into the kitchen to set down my bags. When I returned to the living room, I tossed my coat and purse on the sofa, then flopped down beside them.

Mike was sitting in the recliner a few feet away, reading something on his tablet. He looked up. "Rough night?"

I nodded. "Terrible. I'm glad to be home. How were the children?"

"Ha." Mike actually said the word. "They were — a handful?"

"Yeah?"

"Yeah. David got Chelsea to play hide-and-seek, but he didn't tell me they were playing. He wanted to get rid of his sister for a while. So when I asked him where Chelsea was, he said that he didn't know. At least she was happy when we tracked her down. *Really happy.* She thought she'd found this amazing hiding place because it took us so long to find her, but then she was all clenched fists and crying after she figured out what happened."

"Where was she hiding?"

He laughed. "Behind one of the beanbags."

"You mean in the movie room? Right in plain sight?"

Mike laughed harder. "It would have taken, like, a minute to find her if we were looking."

"Was it bad?"

"It was a thing."

"What does that mean?"

"That I'm glad you're home." He set down his tablet, came over to give me a kiss, then settled next to me. "So, why was your night so terrible? Did someone complain that their raw carrots were cold again?"

I laughed, because fuck that guy. Two months later, I still wanted to tell him where he could warm them. I shook my head. "No. Worse."

Because I was leaning against him, I couldn't see his face. But I could feel him making one. "Worse, huh? Did someone complain that you didn't have any Sara Lee on the menu?"

"Do they still make Sara Lee?"

"Of course they still make Sara Lee. Why wouldn't they make Sara Lee?"

I shrugged. "I don't know. It seems so old-fashioned."

"That's why people like it. So, tell me for real, why was your night so terrible? Was it Gillian?"

I nodded. "Part of it."

"I'm listening."

Mike usually hated it when I bitched about work, especially right after getting home, but his invitation seemed genuine, and I needed to vent. He'd be irked with me if I went into the kitchen and got right to baking, which was what I really wanted to do.

When I still hadn't said anything, he prompted me again. "So, Gillian. What did she do?"

"She grabbed the coriander bottle instead of the cumin. It was for a Spanish chicken and rice dish."

"Okay, that's bad, but there has to be more."

"Of course there's more. The dish was for Gina Delicious."

"Oh."

"Exactly. We tried to make it right and got her another dish immediately, but she kept taking one picture after another. Laughing. Can you believe that? Actually taking glee in someone else's misfortune. I swear, she's worse than Micah Myles."

"I thought no one was worse than Micah Myles."

"That was before Gina Delicious posted some of her pictures to Instagram, and all of them to LiveLyfe with a little tease that said a 'full review would be coming soon.' Everyone reads her blog, so this is going to hit us hard." I was trying not to cry.

Mike pulled me against him.

I sniffled. "She hasn't been in the restaurant for

a year and a half, not since … you know. So this was a big deal, and now the review is going to be terrible."

"That sounds awful, honey. I'm really sorry."

"That's not even the worst part!" I pulled away from Mike.

His eyes were wide and wondering, waiting for whatever was coming.

"Harris won't fire her. He *forbid* me from doing so. She is absolutely untrainable, constantly in our way, and actively making mistakes. Unforgivable ones, like using coriander instead of cumin when we're cooking for Gina Delicious. She begged me for her chance, and this is what she does with it."

"Unforgivable is an awfully big word."

"She's making a *lot* of them, Mike."

His eyes were assessing yet no less a comfort. Finally, he said, "I'm impressed. You're making progress."

"We're getting a crap review online from a critic who seems to disprove the theory that people can't just go viral whenever they want to. Most of the times, it seems like she's being mean for the sake of being mean. How is this in any way making progress?"

"Because a year ago you would be having a meltdown over something like this."

I smiled. It was true. A year ago I would have been losing my shit. And sure, I yelled at Gillian a little, but it was a lot less than she deserved. Beer brownies and the brew to go with it, sharing the drinks and dessert with my Mike — those thoughts had kept me in a positive place.

Even agitated, that's where I was.

"Thank you," I said.

"Thank *you*. Isn't this better?"

"I don't know, is it? What if I've lost my fire? What if I can't bring the restaurant back, or ever open Bake it Away? What if I just haven't realized that I'm already giving up?"

"Maybe you haven't realized that you're *growing* up."

I looked into his eyes. "Want to make brownies together?"

"Okay."

"Guess what. They're beer brownies, and we can keep drinking as long as we're mixing and waiting."

His lukewarm consent changed into clear and present excitement.

We opened a couple of cold ones and toasted.

Then we talked about the old days, which weren't all that long ago, though they were still spoken about as the best and worst of times that they were, when the hours felt endless but the team was a family, and much more *all for one and one for all* than *every man for himself.* We'd been doing great work, and our customers had loved our menu.

"It was all about the food back then, and I miss it," I said in an echo I'm sure Mike was sick of hearing.

He didn't show it if he was. Looking up from his stirring, he said, "I know, honey."

"When did it become all about me?"

Mike looked into my eyes, silently asking me if I really wanted to know. "What do you mean?"

"I wasn't so shrill when we started, was I?"

He shook his head. "No."

"So, when did I start yelling all the time?"

"When you lost the space between you and your art."

"What do you mean?" So much of this conversation could be lived out on repeat, but that part was new.

Still expertly stirring the syrup, he said, "Cooking used to be something you *did*, but then it became who you *were*. You weren't an artist so much as you were your art. That meant that if Arrivé wasn't good, you were less as a person. These aren't conscious thoughts, but I'm sure they're inside you, whether you want them there or not."

"Okay." It was hard to hear, but fair and true. "But *when* did that start happening?"

Mike took a moment to think before he answered. "I think it was easier for you before the restaurant was a hit. You were always willing to work hard, but you were fiercer in maintaining your reputation than you were in earning it."

The truth hit home and made itself comfortable, despite its squirming like a worm and sitting like a splinter.

We sat in the silence, Mike knowing I'd need the quiet to process.

I owed him everything. He believed in me, encouraged me, and showed the patience of Job through the worst of my bullshit. I was grateful for the chance to spend a lifetime making it up to him.

He watched me spread the buttercream. Mike did a terrific job with most things, but it was too delicate a task for his unpracticed hands. Even though it was only for the two of us, I wanted the piping perfect and the slope of each heart to make his beat a bit harder.

It worked. I could feel his pulse pounding against me.

"Thank you," I said.

"For what?"

"You know for what."

"I want to hear it anyway. Before we shovel those brownies into our mouths."

"We're not going to shovel them into our mouths. We're going to eat them slowly. Savor every bite. Maybe even share one and save the other for later."

"Why would we want to do that?"

I looked into his eyes, hoping that mine were alight with mischief. Same for my smile.

"Because I thought you might like to fuck me in between dessert and dessert."

As promised, I showed up on set at six a.m. I've done one-hundred percent of everything I've been asked to do, and all of it with a smile. My makeup and hair were both a hassle, turning me into a person I barely recognize, but I understood it was part of the job and what I agreed to. So, all of that was fine.

But the wardrobe wasn't. I was doing my best to keep cool — no screaming, every word spoken with perfect measure — but the already too long conversation with my wardrobe person, Zoe, was running in ridiculous circles.

"Why would I cook in that?" I pointed to the low-cut blouse again, as if this time it might magically change from the neon cleavage enhancer to the sensible chef's coat I bought specifically for this occasion — gray and black with nice neat lines, a half dozen sharp looking black buttons running the length of each side, a high collar, and a perfect fit to consider comfort and mobility.

"We've been over this," Zoe said. "A bunch of times. What aren't you understanding?"

"I'm not understanding why this is my show and yet I get zero say in what I'm wearing."

It wasn't okay. My industry was dominated by males — a bone broth of an irony since cooking had been considered women's work for centuries. It was a constant. Condescending, patronizing crap. I'd had to curse more than I liked and had become less than I wanted to be, to claw for more of what was rightfully mine. I shouldn't be treated differently, not if I could do the same or more with some oil, ingredients, and an open flame.

"I understand," Zoe said, her voice finally starting to soften and lose its admonishing tone.

"Do you?" I asked her. "Can you?"

"Of course I can." Then she looked at me in a way that suggested she meant it. "You think I'm not expected to be some version of what everyone expects me to be?"

"At least your profession is filled with women. You don't have to feel so alone."

Zoe looked around dramatically, gesturing at her many invisible compatriots. "You're right. Hey, Matilda, you mind running out to grab me a latte?" She theatrically awaited the answer — one beat, two, then three. "Huh. She doesn't want to grab me a latte. Matilda can be a real bitch. Probably because she isn't getting any imaginary dick."

"I don't want to dress like a bimbo for ratings."

"I'm not sure a bimbo would wear this." Zoe holds up the blouse, looking at it again before turning her eyes back to me. "It's cute. Maybe you should give it a chance."

"What about my chance to be a role model?" I nodded toward Harris. "They're not asking him to cook with his shirt open."

"Who wants to see that?" Zoe made a face that got me to laugh. "Look, I'm just doing my job."

"I know, but—"

She held out a finger, and her eyes begged my attention. I nodded for her to continue.

"I'm sure a lot of people come to you and maybe doubt your recipes because it has some sort of ingredient that they've never heard of or some preparation that sounds a little weird. Am I right?"

I nodded again, knowing where this was going.

"But you know if they try it, they'll almost for sure like it, right? If they're willing to give it a chance?"

Another nod. If was being honest, I had no other choice.

"I'm the cook in this scenario, and in my professional opinion, this dish will look great on you." She smiled and offered me the blouse.

I tentatively took it. "Thank you. And sorry for giving you a hard time."

"I understand." She laughed. "I've seen it before. Plenty of times. Women think they're surrendering the cause if they wear something that makes them look pretty. But it's not an insult to your intelligence as a person or your competence as a chef. It's the reality of the television business. Viewers like it when the people they're watching are attractive, unless the point of the show is that they're not. A sexy host equals more viewers, and that means more opportunity for you. It's a good thing you can play sexy. You shouldn't feel like you have to apologize for that."

I didn't like it, but I also couldn't argue with the truth. Zoe was right, but I couldn't stand the loss of control and hated to be so powerless. The reality was there was nothing I could do to change my situation. Even after voicing my discomfort, I was still made to feel like there was something wrong with me.

The last thing I wanted was a meltdown, but I could feel one steadily brewing inside me. Maybe I wasn't capable of not having them, and the longer I went without one, the worse it would be in the end. Like Yellowstone. Apparently when that thing finally blows, it'll be the end of the world as we know it.

I finished getting dressed, then waited for the show to start, shifting my weight from one foot to the other while standing off to the side, watching the well-oiled crew as they scurried about. How long had they been working together? Everyone obviously knew each other. Maybe the Shellys moved them as a unit from one production to the next.

My attention continued to wander. Melinda finished talking to a man with a tablet.

She turned and saw me. Smiled and strolled right over.

"Is everything okay?" She sounded genuinely concerned.

"Do I really look that bad?"

"You look great, but not quite ready for the camera. What's wrong? And don't tell me it's no big deal or nothing to worry about. I don't want to hear that it doesn't matter, or any of the other bullshit women say that we shouldn't have to."

It's like Melinda was reading my mind. I would have hated myself for saying any of those things, but all three were crowding the tip of my tongue, and one was sure to wiggle out.

"That's it," I said, looking down at my blouse. "I don't like what I'm wearing. I mean, it's pretty, don't get me wrong." I laughed, because this was sounding like a terrible complaint. "I would never wear something like this while cooking, ever, and it feels dishonest to wear it."

She took my hands, and they felt surprisingly good in hers.

"I understand," Melinda said. "I know how you feel, and it really, really sucks."

Instantly calmer, I waited for more. And she gave it to me in a voice that wasn't quite motherly, but was rich with the warm silken comfort of a cashmere sweater. "Successful women are called *bitchy*. We get lower initial offers despite identical resumes because hiring managers are sexist enough to think of that shit and asshole enough to think they can get away with it. Put us in a group project, and watch the credit get picked from our pocket like we were strolling by an unlit alley off Bourbon past midnight. It starts when they're boys, but as men, they keep it going. We get promoted mostly for performance and rarely for potential. While men are articulate, we're too talkative. We're expected to be nurturing and kind, and we're considered emotional when angry, not because someone dropped the ball, but because it must be that time of the month for us. They don't want us knocked up, because then we'll have too much of our affection pulled out of their orbit or directed away from them. But if a guy gets his girl pregnant, well, cigars all around — because that man is now a provider!"

She paused for an overdue breath. "Should I stop?"

"No," I said, fighting a laugh that felt like a bark. "I'm enjoying this immensely."

Melinda laughed a little, too, making mine okay. Then she launched back into her tirade with the lilt of a lullaby.

"We're interrupted in meetings, especially if there are only one or two of us sitting at the table. We offer our ideas to silence, then wait for the echo a few minutes later when a man can lay claim to his brilliance. We're not invited when they gather, but we're resented when we get together ourselves. We're left in the corner and marginalized. Being ugly or fat is a strike. And you know the worst part?"

Melinda said that last bit for some much-needed breath.

But I nodded anyway, dying to hear it.

"We're scared. And we hate to talk about it. Because we don't want to be dramatic. Or worse, have someone think we are. All of us have heard it too many times before. We travel in packs, clutch our keys between our fingers, exhausted by it all. We get our tits and the whistling starts. It only ends to make room for the ridicule to begin. And the clothes. We stand in front of overstuffed closets fretting that we have nothing to wear. Thousands of dollars of clothes, tens of thousands in our cases." Melinda laughed. "More for me, I can admit it. But we don't stare into our closets because we have nothing to wear. We stare because we don't know what we should wear for *who we need to be* that day. Men get to roll out of bed if they want to. Does any of that sound familiar? Does *all* of it?"

"Yes."

"We can agree we're on the same side?"

I nodded.

"Let's be real, Amanda. You're pretty, and that's going to bring a lot of viewers to our show. Your wardrobe needs to play up your looks. That's the way it works." She paused, eyed my blouse, then finished. "But I agree, a woman your age shouldn't be leading with cleavage."

That's not what I meant at all, but I barely had my mouth open before Melinda was gesturing for Zoe to come over.

She started talking fast but not too fast, and then the wardrobe girl was gone before I could say a single word. The only thing I heard for sure was *Milfy, but not too milfy,* then Zoe vanished like a trick.

I didn't know what to say or how to respond. It happened so fast.

"Would you like to meet your new protege while we're waiting for Zoe to get back?"

"Sure." I still felt ambushed or coerced or something even worse. Because it wasn't about my age or my cleavage. It was about being seen as a person.

Melinda led me across the studio, gently stepping over snaking wires as we slalomed through an assembly of chairs, boxes, and clusters of people.

The new apprentice was standing next to the catering table, his head down, surveying the spread. I was curious about the food myself. What would craft services be like for a show about cooking?

He looked young, his mane full and body trim. He was in an Oxford and khakis.

We were nearly there when the apprentice started piling food on his plate.

He piled fast, finished up, then turned around.

I knew there was something familiar about the way he moved a moment before I saw why.

Noah Temple looked at me with his slow, sexy smile.

"Chef Byrd," he said, with the aural equivalent of him licking his lips. "You have no idea how much I've been looking forward to this moment."

# TEN

## Noah

I stared at Amanda, barely able to believe my eyes.

A shiver of delight rippled through me. Hopefully, neither woman noticed.

Until a moment ago, this was all still a dream. Something that couldn't possibly come true, despite the promise.

I had lived with broken faith, and the worst of those crumbling dreams had come from the gorgeous creature standing a few feet in front of me. She was staring back at me, eyes wide, full lips parted, pale cheeks flushed. I'd seen her like that before, but for a different and decidedly more intimate reason.

It was intoxicating, being back in her presence. The year had turned into an eon without her, like

I'd been six feet under the earth and had only now clawed my way back to the surface.

My body was returning to life, including a slight but insistent stirring in the one place I wanted to stay invisible for now. Until I had Amanda back where I wanted her. Where I knew she wanted to be.

Dreams can come true, but they're never handed out. Sometimes the person you love didn't feel the same way or needed to be reminded of what they'd recklessly thrown away. It took a year without Amanda for me to discover who I was. But even with that knowledge, I was incomplete. Now the final piece of my personal puzzle was staring into my eyes with a stew of emotions and a lip she was trying not to curl.

That made sense. I caught her off guard, and she hadn't been given a moment to ponder what she had lost.

Could Melinda feel something between us? She had to. The space was electric.

"This is Noah Temple. You're going to love him. He's everything you could want in an on-camera apprentice."

"What about off-camera?" Amanda sounded unsure, like she didn't even know what her question meant, and it was more that she was in desperate need of something to say.

Melinda laughed. "Off-camera too, of course. He has just enough experience to roll with whatever we give him but not so much that there's nothing left to learn. With the right support, you'll be able to mold his talents to your particular needs, and the audience will be learning along with him."

"Why No—" Amanda took a deep breath. "How did you choose him?" Her tone was as challenging as her words, suspicion practically radiating off her in waves.

"We considered two primary factors," Melinda answered without hesitation. "Aptitude and attitude. We were looking for someone with passion for the profession, a solid work ethic, and a fervent desire to learn new things and break new ground. We needed someone who would look great on camera and act natural."

"And how did you find him?" Amanda continued her interrogation, talking to Melinda and totally ignoring me.

"Oh, that was easy — Noah has a fantastic channel on LiveLyfe."

"He does?"

The way she said it, I wasn't sure if Amanda

was pretending or if she really didn't know about my channel — I started it after she left me, needing a new way to vent my feelings and frustrations. It hurt the same either way.

"I'll let him tell you all about it. You two should get to know each other a little better, since you'll be working so closely together."

Then Melinda left, the two of us alone, with the warmth of our history wafting between us.

Amanda obviously hadn't been happy to see me, but now with Melinda gone, she looked furious. "What the hell is this?"

"It's my big break." I enjoyed the way her rage made her fierce and imagined that same expression in a different context, like the one we'd shared nearly every day of the only month that ever mattered.

"You don't belong here."

"I would argue otherwise." I waited a beat while she glared at me, then added, "And the Shellys agree."

"That's only because they don't know about our history."

"Oh, right." I made my face serious. "Do you think we should tell them?"

"Fuck you, Noah."

"I'd love that, but we're going to have to wait until after taping. We don't want anyone looking for us, and it's probably not a good idea to throw the production into chaos on our first day of filming."

Her face was finding new ways to look angry, its full wrath like a sun about to swallow the sky.

"You need to leave."

I shook my head. "Not true. I need to stay. I quit my job to do this, so really, it's all I have."

"Why are you doing this to me?"

"I'm not doing anything *to you*. I'm only doing what you always encouraged me to do — nurturing my talent. Remember, Amanda? When you told me that I was one of a kind? That we would 'build something big together'?"

I waited for her answer, but both of knew that it wouldn't be coming.

So, I kept going. "I know you're happy for me because you feel a responsibility to cultivate talent on the rare occasions when you see it. Isn't that what you once told me?" Another pause. "Right after I fucked you hard enough in the pantry to make you cry."

Heat found her face and her body, baking the air in between us.

"You need to lower your voice."

"I'm not sure I do. Maybe there are a lot of things people around here would like to hear."

"This is a shit show," she said. "You can't be here. I'm not working with you."

I looked down at my plate. A mountain of eggs and bacon with a bagel to the side. Anything to keep my eyes away from her. Not that I didn't want to look, as there was nothing in the world I'd rather feast on, but I needed Amanda to know that I was in control of our relationship, for the first time ever.

"You don't have a choice." I picked up my bagel, took a big bite, then thoughtfully chewed as she glared at me. "People are starting to look at us."

With her back to the crowd and making no effort to look, Amanda said, "No one can hear anything. They're curious to see how we're getting along. We're blocking the food, and they don't want to interrupt."

After several long seconds, Amanda repeated herself, as though that next time might stick. "I'm not working with you."

Still chewing and talking through an ever-widening smile, I said, "And what are you planning to tell the Shellys when they ask why you aren't willing to work with me, a guy you just met a few minutes ago?"

That only made her glare harder.

"If you're not comfortable letting our benefactors know about the month you spent lying back, bending over, and begging for it fifty different ways …" I let that sink in as I stepped into her space. "You fucked the life right out of me, Amanda. Did you know that? I—"

"How *dare* you?" Amanda growled, then swung her head around to survey the risk, to see who was watching or pretending not to.

Melinda wasn't paying attention, and I didn't see Dominic or Harris. Other than the makeup and wardrobe people I'd just met while they were dolling me up, the studio was full of strangers. "How dare I, what? Tell the truth? I have nothing to hide, Amanda. That's your porn under the bed. You wanna keep it a secret?" I shrugged. "I'm cool with that. You want everyone to know, I see some benefits there, too."

"Fuck you."

"Okay."

"How dare you come in here and try to sabotage my career!"

"Your self-esteem was always inspiring." I laughed but made sure it sounded friendly. "I didn't come here to sabotage your career, Amanda. I came here because there was no way to refuse this opportunity. And don't act like you would have if our situations were reversed. I don't want to hurt your career, I want to help it. To be a part of it, if that's possible. You and me, back in the kitchen. Take the bedroom out of it, fun as that was, and our month was together was still the best time of my life. If you think we should tell the Shellys about our past, I'm game, but I—"

"Stop." Amanda shook her head, but she sounded calm, so I followed the order. "This isn't going to be a good situation. Not for either one of us."

I couldn't help but smile. "It will be a great situation for me."

"We can't—"

"And the Shellys, and Harris, and—"

"I love my husband."

Her words might as well have shoved me down a flight of stairs.

It felt like somebody stabbed a rod down my throat and started stirring the contents of my stomach. I held my ground even though my brain wanted my body to lurch back. The way she said that. Not *I have a husband*, which I'd heard plenty before and always irritated the hell out of me, but *I love my husband.*

Fucking Michael Byrd. Amanda wouldn't shut up about that loser when we were together, unless we were in the kitchen or the bedroom, which is why I made sure we spent so much time in those places.

But that man was awful for her, and I couldn't stand the sound of his name. Or to hear any of the bullshit he did to shut her down. As good as she was in the bedroom, Amanda was even better in the kitchen. And a brilliant mentor for those who knew how to listen. Her husband didn't appreciate her. He held her back, gaslit her into pumping the brakes on her career, heaped her with enough guilt trips to circle the world a few times. The SOB forced her to dilute the cream of her potential until it was pale and flaccid as watered down milk.

She made it a month — four buoyant, radiant, rapturous weeks — before Michael Byrd dragged Amanda back to a life of mewling mediocrity.

"Did you hear me? I love my husband, and—"

"I'm not going to tell your husband about us—"

"There is no us!"

People were watching. I laughed to maintain the facade of our friendly conversation. Amanda took the cue and joined me. But the air sizzled, the current in my body like live leaping wires.

"I'm not going to tell your husband about us," I finished, "because I'm not going to have to."

The surprise in her eyes was an early dessert. I wanted to lick my lips at the taste of her uncertainty.

"Once you remember what it's like when we're together …" I reached for her hand.

Amanda yanked it away and looked wildly around.

She would learn to trust me. I'd surveyed the area already and wouldn't have done that if we were in danger of being seen.

"Stop that," she said. "You have no right to touch me."

She was breathing hard, her face flushed.

"Once you remember," I said, voice low, words long and sweet, "and we're back in that place you were forced to leave, *you're* going to tell your husband. I'll never have to do a thing."

"That will *never* happen."

But it would. I would make sure of it.

# ELEVEN

## Amanda

It was the first day of shooting on *Chef Happens*.

I was holding a sauté pan full of onions, forcing my smile as I explained again, in yet another way, how to caramelize onions because apparently I couldn't articulate it in the right way even though I'd been detailing the process aloud for more years than David's and Chelsea's ages added together.

We were making pappardelle with caramelized onions and parmesan, but we were sure spending a hell of a lot of time on the middle part of that dish.

I smiled for the camera and started again.

"Done right, caramelized onions will add a sweet and savory layer to an already perfect dish. It's easy to do and always worth it. You'll need onions, plus butter, brown sugar or balsamic, and patience. You can't rush anything that you expect to eventually melt in your mouth. Too much heat and they scorch. Add the sugar or balsamic too early, and the rich savory flavor won't be there, even if your onions *look* the part."

I made another offering to the camera, a smile I desperately wanted to feel as I talked my way through the work.

"We're going to grab our biggest pan, put that burner on medium heat, and cook these alliums like we've nowhere to go."

I looked up at the camera instead of down on the onions where my eyes should have been.

"Onions are like people with all those layers, right? Well, at this temperature, we're trapping the sugars inside those layers. And the longer we can do this while keeping everything steady, the more delicious they will be."

I took a step back.

"Don't feel like you have to drop anchor in front of the onions. Stick around until you get them going, then you can check in every five or ten minutes to give them a stir and see how they're coming along."

This was the part I hated. The director, Anderson, wanted me to ad lib. Actually, he wanted me to follow the script, but I hated the teleprompter and everything I said felt wrong and unnatural, so Anderson — a man who could apparently grow twice as much hair on his eyebrows as he could on his face — suggested I "teach like I normally would."

But that was ridiculous, as I didn't teach like this at all. I taught by *doing,* not by explaining everything I did to an invisible audience, taking the time to go slow and show every step. And I certainly never used my kindergarten voice.

In my kitchen, I talked to the staff like they were assholes from a frat who needed to learn a serious lesson. In this kitchen, that would mean me making Noah repeat everything back to me, and at that moment, I couldn't even look at him. I would also want to tell him his nose and taste buds should be the judge of when the onions were finished.

But I didn't want to think about any part of his body, and definitely not his tongue.

I would talk about how every chef should taste her food, and that I love tasting onions straight from the pan. Awkward to say, though true.

But I would have to invite Noah to do the tasting, and I couldn't stand the thought of seeing pleasure on his face.

Next, I would advise the at-home cook to make more than necessary so a batch or two could be frozen for future use, then I would talk about the differences in onions — how all of them will caramelize, though each one seasons the dish with something slightly different.

Despite the accuracy of the information and the validity of the tip, every word felt wrong. Nothing felt natural.

Worst of all, standing behind the counter in that studio was the last place in the world I wanted to be. And that was a truth I wasn't hiding from anyone.

Again, Anderson yelled, *Cut!*

"What is it this time?" I asked, not defensive at all. Curious, like was trying to learn. Which I really was because I desperately wanted this to end.

Anderson spent a few moments searching for words.

I tried to save him some time. "I feel like I was doing what you asked me to do."

"Technically, yes." Anderson smiled, and I knew what was coming. "But spiritually, not so much."

I tried to keep my voice in check. "So, how can I deliver a more spiritual experience for our viewers?"

My smile felt like it's about to crack. I'm not trying to be a bitch, but this is hard. I've earned every eye in the room. The Shellys alone feel almost like an army. Noah, beside me, was a belligerent physical force. Heat radiated off him like a preheated oven with its door wide open.

Anderson looked at me patiently, which made me want to scream.

"You're coming off as patronizing rather than friendly. It's like you're talking to children."

"Before you told me that I sounded too aggressive. Now I sound too nice?"

"That's not exactly what I said." His smile went sideways, turned a little less certain. "You have to relax. You're too stressed out. That's why everything looks and feels so forced. It's supposed to be like talking to a friend."

"I can't imagine having any friend needing me to explain how to caramelize onions once, let alone ten times."

"You're right. Once *should* have been fine." He shot me an admonishing look.

I knew I was wrong, but that didn't mean I could explain how Noah was making me feel, with him standing there tight-lipped beside me, reveling in my discomfort, wearing a smile that seemed much too knowing for the diffidence it feigned.

Anderson turned to the room. "Why don't we go ahead and call it a day?"

Then he faced me again. "We'll try again tomorrow. I promise, we'll get this. The first one is always the hardest. Go home. Take a long, hot bath. Get your husband to massage you. Come back tomorrow fresh, and we'll do this again. Okay?"

His smile seemed genuine. And hungry for mine.

"Thank you."

Anderson went over to Noah and shook his hand, giving him a well-deserved *Great job!* for the little he got to do. I couldn't argue with what everyone else clearly saw — the man was a natural on camera.

Harris approached. He pulled me away from Anderson and Noah. His face matched the room — tense and brushing the edge of upset. It was well past dinnertime, and we still hadn't managed to get past the first day's shooting because I couldn't seem to pull myself together. This was harder than I imagined for so many reasons.

I could do the job if Noah wasn't right next to me or if I could yell at him and teach like I meant it. But this was neither/nor. I was trapped in a dressing of artifice, making me hate every word from my mouth or motion from my hands.

"What the hell is wrong with you?" Harris didn't just sound disappointed, he sounded angry.

"I'm sorry," I said, without a beat of hesitation. And I totally meant it.

"Are you trying to blow this?"

I shook my head. "I promise I'm not. This is one of the hardest things I've ever done."

He looked at me perplexed, really trying to get it. "What's so hard about this, Amanda? You're telling me you can't be genuinely warm for the camera for a few minutes? You either have to talk to our viewers like incompetent kitchen staff or like they're little children waiting to play Duck, Duck, Goose? I don't understand why—"

"Then you do it, Harris. You're the one who wants to be on TV. You and Noah can do the show together, the two of you. You'll be great."

"Amanda."

I didn't want him to be mad at me. It hurt to be trying my best and still feeling wrong, like I was paying old taxes on an ancient mistake.

"You know we can't do that. You're the star chef. People want to see you. They want to watch you cook and hear you talk about your recipes. No one is going to give a crap about my secrets to caramelizing onions."

"They're not secrets. There are 23,458 videos on YouTube that will show you the exact same thing. That was nothing special."

"Was that a real number?"

"No," I admit.

It broke the moment in just the right way, and Harris almost smiled.

"Look, Amanda, like it or not, you're the face of Arrivé, so this has to be you. And you'll be great at it if you give it a chance. You really will. I've known you for a long time now, and I know what you can do when you decide that something's important. So, I'm asking, can you please decide that this is important?"

"I know it's important, I promise. But are we always going to be talking about such basic stuff?"

"Yes," Harris said without hesitation. "Absolutely. But you need to make it conversational. As you talk about this stuff, you develop rapport with your audience. But stop trying to speak to everyone. Talk to *one person*. Someone you care for who knows nothing about cooking, and you want them to walk away with a solid understanding of who Amanda Byrd is as a chef."

I understood that and could do it a lot better without Noah breathing down my blouse.

Also, I was with Harris a hundred percent, so he didn't need to be a dick.

"You owe me, so you better not fuck this up," he said.

I was shocked, had no idea where that came from. Harris had gone from partner to opponent, an unexpected shot of vinegar into my milk. Sure, we suffered through some arguments, over and over, especially lately. But I'd agreed to the Shellys' proposal and was there as promised. We both knew I was too hard on the kitchen staff but acknowledged it was something I was both working on and making demonstrable progress in. And I was too much of a perfectionist — I would rather deliver a meal late than have it anything less than the diner deserves — but doing regular exercises to relax that less desirable part of myself.

Beyond all of that, despite our many differences, Harris had never yelled at me. Or cursed when angry.

"Why are you talking to me like that?"

"Because I deserve a better life."

"I'm not trying to make your life shitty, Harris."

"Don't get defensive."

"I'm not getting defensive. I'm responding to you saying that you deserve a better life and implying I'm somehow responsible for you not getting it."

He glared at me, his eyes doing more than implying.

"What, Harris? Say what you're thinking."

"It's taken a lot of patience to ride this roller coaster up and down with you, Amanda. I was fine letting you take the driver's seat, always deciding where we were going, jerking the wheel back and forth to suit your whims, even though I was getting jerked around in the passenger seat, with my head banging against the window."

"That's a little dramatic."

"It isn't just me anymore. I have Emily to think about."

"We've always worked things out, Harris. I'm on your side. I'm here, aren't I?"

"Barely."

"Thanks for that." I longed to offer him the explanation he deserved. Instead, I said, "I'm trying. I'll make this work."

"I need you to accept the reality that Arrivé is

failing. To compensate for that, you need to do your part to make this show successful."

"Okay and okay," I said, now fighting the tears.

Noah glanced over as his conversation ended with Anderson, and I felt a wretched corkscrew of hate. The emotion was too strong to contain, and as I couldn't unleash it on the subject of my ire, I took it out on Harris.

"You don't know what it takes to be the best. That's why you dropped out. If you had any fight in you at all, we could avoid all this and bring Arrivé back to where she deserves to be. I'm not sure I would have ever partnered with you if I'd known you were such a quitter. I guess that's all my fault. The clues were certainly there."

Harris shook his head and looked at me sadly. "That's fair. But since we're being so honest, you should know I'm not sure I would have ever partnered with you, seeing as I thought you were the best when both of us know you're really the worst."

# TWELVE

## Noah

My exchange with Anderson rattled its death cough.

After a final laugh, a shaking of hands, a "well done" from the director, and a clap on my shoulder, I glanced over at Amanda, who was doing her best not to notice me.

I wasn't close enough to hear what she and Harris were saying, and I didn't try. I needed to be fully present for the director. It might take a while for Amanda to find her balance, and I would have to pick it up enough for our little team of two. We were a team, despite her fervent wish to the contrary, and I had to do more than my part to get us both of through this rough patch.

But whatever they were discussing, it was deep

shit. Harris looked hostile — I didn't think he had it in him — and Amanda was obviously upset. Defensive and trying not to be. Mad but working hard not to show it.

Harris said something that made Amanda bite her lip. Then he stalked off.

She turned around, hiding her face as she hurried out of the studio and scurried off in the other direction.

I followed her outside. A flurry of wind began building up inside me when I lost sight of her, frantic I wouldn't find her before she left. The desperation kept brewing and brewing as I scoured the parking lot until it was like a cloud about to burst.

When I found her, the turbulence dissipated.

Amanda stood in front of her car, fumbling for her fob, obviously trying — yet clearly failing — to look like she wasn't crying.

I felt deeply sorry, seeing her like that. And like a devil for being the cause.

I'd enjoyed catching her off guard. I'm human, after all. I'd never been lower than where she left me a year before, so seeing her unseated made me feel like I was sitting slightly higher, in a spot I'd been working to earn all my life.

I needed to see her unbalanced.

Which is exactly what I got.

I'd been terrified of Amanda's indifference. That she would look at me with empty eyes and a vacant expression, because Michelin for me was a drive-thru for her, and that would kill me enough to keep me from going on.

But Amanda was a solar system outside of indifferent. Her passion was there, obvious beneath her knee-jerk reaction. As was her fear of our being found out. It would happen, but it also made sense that only one of us was ready. Not just because I knew I would be Amanda's apprentice before she knew about being my mentor, but because I spent a year with most of my thoughts simmering in a hearty broth of *her*.

It was my time to taste it, and the universe had brought me this opportunity to prove it.

Fate had finally taken an interest. The odds were too slim for me to believe in anything else.

Now I wanted to be her shoulder to cry on, offer her comfort like I did so well before. Softly, gently, I said, "Amanda ..."

She whipped around like a wounded cat anyway, keys like claws in her fist. "Get away from me, Noah!"

I raised my hands like a supplicant. "I just want to talk."

She jabbed her fist, like Wolverine about to pierce me, and growled a warning. "I'll hurt you if you try anything."

I looked at the keys like they were made of candy and said, "You can't hurt me more than you already have."

"Oh, please." Her fist was still raised, her body still ready to launch forward.

"I mean it. I've spent the last year feeling like a ghost of my old self."

She sneered. "I would, too, if I worked in that shitty kitchen."

My smile felt thinner than my patience. "Well, my ticket out of there disappeared overnight, without any warning. The opposite of what was promised."

"I never *promised* you anything, Noah. Don't lay that on me."

"Who should I lay it on? Let me know, I'm open to suggestions."

"How about yourself, to start?"

I was starting to get mad. "Maybe we should change the subject."

But Amanda said, "Why don't you let me go home? To my family."

She only added that second part to make me boil. I let the words do their work before I simmered down. "I'm not trying to keep you from going home. But we should talk, since we're going to be working together. We have a chance to make things better before——"

"Get to the point, Noah." Amanda lowered her fist, but her body and posture were both still on red alert.

"I wanted to see if you needed anything." I fought to keep my tone steady. Kind, even.

She looked confused. "No, I don't need anything. Thanks."

"You seemed upset. When you were talking to Harris. Are the two of you doing okay?"

Her confusion turned to agitation. "How is that any of your business?"

"Are you kidding me? I'm in this, too. So long as we're doing the show together, anything that threatens our partnership is my business."

Amanda scoffed. "We don't have a partnership, Noah. Maybe this really is a coincidence and you didn't somehow weasel your way into this, although I'm having an awfully hard time believing that. But I don't need to know because I don't care. I'll see this through because I have to. It's a job, not a partnership. You were hired without my consent, and I never would have hired you, or agreed if I'd known. Any history we have—"

"I wouldn't do that Amanda."

The tone in my voice made her pause.

"You know where my career was headed when you met me," I said. "This is my big break. You have no right to take it away from me."

"Do your job, and we'll both get through it. But there's nothing between us, and you better never ambush me like that again. Whatever happened in the past is totally irrelevant to our present, and dragging it into the studio won't fare well for either of us. If you really want to make the most of this opportunity, you better make damn sure you keep the bullshit to yourself."

"What's that supposed to mean?" All the humor faded from my voice. From me.

"What do you think it's supposed to mean? You're out here threatening me with—"

"I'm not threatening you!"

"—exposure, looming like salmonella on old poultry. Well, fuck you. Go ahead and—"

"I already told you, I don't want to tell anyone anything."

"—talk. See what happens to your career."

"I don't want to tell anyone," I repeated, in case she hadn't heard it the first time.

Amanda was panting from her tirade. I waited for her to calm down without saying another word. Finally, she asked, "What is it you want, Noah?"

"You promised me a big break. Do you remember that, Amanda?"

"No, that's not exactly how I remember it. But please, go on."

"You offered me a big break, before you went back to—"

"No way. I'm not taking responsibility for your inertia or poor career choices. Those aren't my fault. We all—"

"*You* made me think I had a chance. A genuine shot. Until you took it away, and I'm not going to let you do it again."

"Or what?"

It was hot enough to bake bread in between us. I stepped forward and reached out, wanting to squeeze her shoulder, complete the circuit.

But Amanda flinched, then gasped to prove her reaction wasn't an accident.

Bothered, insulted, and surprised, I pulled back my hand. "Why are you afraid of me?"

"You mean besides the fact that you're stalking me?"

"*Stalking you?* Why would you say I'm stalking you? We broke up over a year ago, and I never bothered you once!"

"You're bothering me now."

"The Shellys approached *me.*"

"Right, and I'm sure that was a coincidence."

"It was. It is."

"And you being out here now, that's because you were about to leave in your own car, right?

"I told you, I came out here to check on you, as a colleague and a friend. You looked upset, and I was worried—"

"You don't need to worry about me, Noah. And really, I'd prefer that you didn't. It isn't your place. You're not my colleague or my friend. We didn't break up over a year ago because we never had a relationship."

"You can't say that."

"I just did."

The loud chirp of a car unlocking cut through the silence. Amanda turned her back to me, climbed inside the car, then slammed the door. As she yanked the seat belt across her chest, she jabbed a finger behind the steering wheel to start her car. And without so much as a glance in my direction, she screeched out of the parking lot.

My heart broke another three times, all of them right in a row.

I thought it would be simple. That all I would have to do was stare into Amanda's eyes to make her remember that she loved me. That Michael Byrd had her brainwashed. Because that was the only way a person could ever forget her soul mate.

Romeo and Juliet, Robin Hood and Maid Marian, Harry and Sally — every great love affair had its ups and downs.

It was going to be a lot of work to win her back. More than I had imagined.

But that was fine. Some recipes took many tries and a lot of work to figure out. Like the very best dishes, Amanda would absolutely be worth it.

## THIRTEEN

# Amanda

*What the hell was that?*

I was reeling, but I had to collect myself before I got home.

If I walked into the house upset, Mike would know. He was so hungry for all of this to go well, and I couldn't stand the thought of letting him down.

But Noah was a surprise ingredient I didn't yet know how to handle. Sour, acidic, and bitter. Obviously salty, though it once was sweet. How could he say he wasn't stalking me? He'd appeared out of nowhere after a long year of nothing, first on the set of a show I never wanted to do, then out in the parking lot while I was trying to make my escape.

So many feelings came rushing back, and I needed some silence to sort them.

I wanted the quiet of my kitchen. Today's show wasn't anywhere close to cooking, no matter how many times I caramelized those onions. It was something else, and whatever it was had an audience. Nothing about the process was conducive to relaxing.

I needed peace. A little time to myself.

Maybe music would help. I turned on the classical station, played some Mozart to soothe my mood for a few miles until I got home. With some help from his old buddies Bartók and Strauss, I felt calm enough to fake it by the time my car kissed our driveway.

But I couldn't kill my headache, which was viciously screaming as I stepped onto the porch, my stress like a scythe, swinging in wild arcs through my psyche, each oscillation another assault in a rolling wave of regret, guilt, and shame like sea and salt inside me.

As soon as I opened the front door, I was bombarded by Chelsea, who clung to my legs like she once did as a toddler.

"You're home!" Her bellow was sing-song, like the ending lick of a nursery rhyme.

"Hi Chelsea!" I leaned down to give her a kiss and a hug, I said, "I missed you."

"Are you going to read to me?"

"Of course I'm going to read to you!"

It was the last thing I wanted to do. I didn't want to look at anything. My eyes were a dying fire and my head a beaten piñata. I wanted to close my lids, stare into the blackness of nothing, and hope-fully, mercifully, fall asleep.

Mike came into the room, and I met him with a tight-lipped attempt at a smile. Even though it was the best I had, I could instantly see the evidence on his face that he was hoping for something more.

And yet I felt so immediately grateful to see him. Deeply so. The guilt and shame were both still there, sloshing in all of that salt, but I knew that Mike could make things better, if I was willing to let him.

He gave me a big hug and a kiss on the cheek. Then he took a knee and met Chelsea's eyes.

"Hey, Magic Muffin."

"Yeah?" Her big eyes stared up into his.

"I want to talk to your mom real fast, so I can see how her day went. Will you give her a kiss, then go pick out your bedtime book and wait for me?"

"Okay!" Chelsea planted a juicy kiss on my

cheek with a *SMACK!* before saying, "Night-night, Mommy!" She scampered off to her bedroom.

"I'll read tonight. David already fell asleep in front of the TV." Mike held up his hand. "I know, I know, but I promise, he read plenty."

"I didn't say anything." But I did smile.

And he returned it. "Dinner is on the counter. I know it's not your favorite, but Chelsea wanted pasghetti." He laughed like it might be funnier than the last time, then left me with another peck on the cheek.

I knew what I was going to see ahead of time, but that didn't stop the gust of disappointment from blowing in when I saw it. Chelsea's favorite pasghetti came from this bullshit place called Bono's a few blocks away. The place was Italian only in name. I'd never been brave enough to order the calzones, but I wouldn't have been surprised if they put ketchup inside them. The place was an embarrassment for any family, but mine knew enough to be mortified. Instead, it was a regular stop. David liked the place less these days, but I could tell that was at least partly for my benefit. Mike didn't like Bono's at all, but he loved pleasing his children, so he didn't loathe the dive like I wanted him to.

I was sure with enough good food and time, I

could make them forget the place, but it was on the way home from David's painting tutor, and the children mentioned Bono's every trip past it.

No surprise, the food was terrible. The fettuccini was four minutes from al dente, the pesto had way too much parmesan and not nearly enough walnuts, the chicken breast was drier than the Mojave, and — sweet Jesus — did they really put sun-dried tomatoes in this thing? *The kind that come in a box?*

It wasn't even worthy of a plate. I ate it at room temperature in a Styrofoam container with the plastic fork that had been taped to the top. *Classy.*

The shit meal wasn't Mike's fault. If he was to say I was being picky, I would have to agree. Not every meal had to be outstanding, and if the children were happy with their dinners — which I was a hundred percent sure they were — and their father was happy enough, who was I to take everything so seriously?

It was sweet of him to get something for me. And out of all the things on the menu, it was the least objectionable choice. Saying anything other than *thank you* was an invitation to a fight that I would deserve to lose.

I ate fast, hoping I could drop the container —

and the remnants I didn't manage to gag down —
in the garbage before Mike was done saying goodnight to Chelsea.

All I wanted was to lie down. I was tired enough
to fall asleep immediately, which meant I could
avoid talking to Mike about my day. And right at
the moment, that was the last thing in the world I
wanted to do.

I dropped the food in the trash but was barely
out of the kitchen before I heard my name. So I
turned around. "Hey, sweetie. That was fast."

"She was totally tuckered. It's hard work waiting
up for you." He paused a beat, then added, "That
wasn't a complaint. Sorry if it sounded that way. I
just meant that they really, really want to stay up,
even when their bodies want them in bed."

"I understand." I smiled, shifting on my feet like
I do when impatient. "I'm tired, too."

"You want to go to bed already?"

I nodded. "Before I even got home."

"Great. Let's go." He took my hand. "Tell me
how everything went."

"It was fine."

"Fine? Come on, I need more than that." When
his foot hit the stairs, he let go of my hand.

I followed him up, two steps behind. "It was

very, very long. Can we talk about it tomorrow? After I've had time to process."

"Of course." But then he immediately contradicted himself. "Tell me one thing. I'll settle for anything better than *fine*."

"Well, now I know I'm terrible at this and it isn't in my skill set at all. I'm best in the kitchen and really shouldn't be anywhere else. This whole thing feels like a giant distraction."

We stopped in the hallway at the top of the stairs. Mike took both of my hands and told me to breathe.

I did, then in a quieter, softer voice, I kept on going, now needing to get it out rather than trapping it inside. "I just want to go back to the kitchen, but I can't. Because Harris thinks I'm blowing this on purpose."

"Are you?"

I'd expected some empathy, maybe a shoulder to cry on. My partner at work was being a dick, so I needed my partner at home to put in an extra shift. Instead, he levied a sick day.

He looked at me, waiting for an answer. His words weren't accusatory, or apologetic.

"Of course I'm not trying to blow this. It's been

made excruciatingly clear to me how important it is that I get this right."

"It's a fair expectation."

"So I keep being told."

"Ever since the restaurant began to decline——"

*AND WHOSE FAULT IS THAT?*

"——we've been tapping into our savings to keep up our tuition payments."

"Are you bringing this up to make me feel extra terrible at the end of a really long day?"

"No, Amanda. But we've gone through ten percent of everything we've saved in the last year alone. That means——"

"Do you think I need this reminder? Do you really think this is what's best, with all I'm trying to manage?"

"You don't have to manage that much, Amanda. Let the restaurant go, focus on the show, and everything else will fall right into place."

"I can get Arrivé back on track. I swear."

"Maybe so. But it has to come behind *Chef Happens*. Please. Can you focus on getting the show going strong before dividing any more of your attention? Give this project a hundred percent."

"I thought you didn't want me to give a

hundred percent to my career," I said. "So I could put our family first."

"This is giving a hundred percent to fixing what's broken, Amanda. That means it *is* putting our family first."

He couldn't know I was equating the show to Noah and hating it with all of my heart on the intruder's behalf. "You're asking me to be someone other than myself."

Mike stared at me for a while before he finally answered.

"Maybe I am." His jaw ticked, his eyes blazed. "Because if you're still this much of a prima donna, I have to wonder why you came back."

Things weren't working out for me at all, and it didn't matter how hard I was trying. I still seemed to be ruining things, both personally and professionally.

It wasn't enough that I meant what I said to both Harris and Mike. I was committed, happy to do whatever was asked of me, all out when it came to making the new show a big hit. But I'd been thrown too many curve balls.

I've always understood that success is about more than hard work. It requires a fierce dedication to your goals, knowing you can achieve them — regardless of what the odds might say — and staying focused even if the world appears to be falling down around you. Things can go to shit in the kitchen fast, but keeping ahead of your failures, or at least managing each one as it comes, is the best recipe there is when striving for anything.

No, the show wasn't my first choice, but I was committed to doing my part. But now, thanks to Noah, the Shellys were probably disappointed, Anderson likely thought me incompetent, Harris was flat out pissed and thought I was trying to sabotage things, and my own husband was having a hard time staying on my side.

All of that would have been more than enough, and I would have been hurting plenty. But Mike had stomped off after calling me a prima donna, and he left me feeling like my insides were scooped out with a melon baller.

I thought about following Mike up to our bedroom and trying to make up instead of medicating myself with a batch of maple pecan sandies, but I had zero confidence either one of us could keep ourselves from making things worse, so into the kitchen with a grimace I went.

My first stop was picking out a bottle to keep me company. Drinking was becoming as much a part of my ritual as baking. When my restaurant and life were both thriving, cracking a bottle of 2016 Patrick Piuze Chablis Premier Cru Les Butteaux was something I wouldn't be feeling so guilty about. Tonight, because I was feeling entitled, I wanted something expensive more than I wanted sweet. That particular pairing of wine and cookies might remind me that I used to have my shit together, and not all that long ago.

I had a pair of jobs to do. Baking would help to clear my mind. And by the time I had the sandies in the oven, things would be settling into place. I would feel better about the show and the Shellys, have a few strategies in mind to handle both Harris and Noah, and find the mindset required to help me kill it during the second day of shooting.

The wine was to keep the guilt from eating me alive, or at least help me to keep it at bay through the night.

I didn't want to think about Noah, but my thoughts were dirty rain on a freshly washed car. And there was worse stuff behind it. Memories of how easy it was to be with him, when things were at their best between us while scraping the bottom at home.

There was a warmth to those memories that I couldn't deny, but I also knew there would be nothing worse in the world than Mike discovering the truth — that I couldn't stay faithful to him during the one time in our lives when I was supposedly committed to finding my better self.

I started to bake, and drink enough that my tiny world began to incrementally improve.

That was how it worked. I kept my mind on the dessert while I marinated on whatever problem I had in the back of my mind. Baking and cooking were art and science, but the former was more of the latter.

If I had guests coming over in an hour and only a few items in the fridge, I could always throw together a quick meal. But it wasn't the same with baking, where everything had to be exact. It was chemistry, every element with a specific purpose. Flour for structure, eggs to bind the ingredients, baking soda and powder to make everything rise, butter and oil to tenderize, sugar to moisten and sweeten.

Recipes worked because the ingredients

followed certain proportions. Too much baking powder and an otherwise perfect cake cracked, too little and it became chewy and dense. Too many eggs turned a cake spongy and dense, but too few left it crumbly and dry. Baking was a better metaphor for life than cooking, because every part of the recipe had a specific job, and if it wasn't done, the dessert wouldn't be any good. You had to follow the rules, rather than improvising like you could over an open flame. Practice made perfect when it came to baking, or anything else in life, and every fresh batch of desserts increasingly helped me to feel like I was inching ever closer to some dreamy ideal.

I'd made the maple pecan sandies a couple of times before. David and Chelsea loved them, sweetened with real syrup and a couple of tablespoons of bourbon.

First, I browned the butter to give them an even nuttier, toastier flavor. I lost myself in the process, toasting the pecans, sifting the dry ingredients, mixing everything together. As I shaped the dough into perfect balls, I slipped into food-inspired memories.

The pecans reminded me of visiting my grandparents in Texas as a little girl, a natural grove rather than a planted orchard, often overrun with brush and weeds at the edges.

The browned butter conjured memories me of experimenting in the kitchen after Jacques had finished teaching us for the day, cooking the unsalted butter long enough to turn the milk solids brown while cooking out the water, then inhaling the rich and unmistakable scents as it turned from something rich and creamy into a nutty beurre noisette.

The syrup made me recall my father's big family breakfasts on the weekends — pancakes on Saturday and waffles on Sunday — that we'd drown in a flood of maple. And that memory was always chased by the one of me and Mike, sneaking away to a tiny B&B in Vermont.

As usual, the baking did its work. By the time the cookies were ready for the oven, I was feeling like my situation might be salvageable. My stomach had settled, despite the wine, and I knew what I was going to do.

I would take a quarter Xanax to loosen up before the show. Apologize to Harris first thing, remind him that we were on the same side and wanted all the same things — yes, salvaging our restaurant was still important to me, but I also wanted Harris to be happy and would do my part to see it through.

Noah wouldn't be a problem because the man was no longer an ambush. Now that I knew what I was dealing with, I could stow my old feelings and stay focused on the job. He would get the hint and stop harassing me as long as I stayed smart enough to give him the cold shoulder without falling into his manipulations or emotional traps.

Anderson would be happy with my smile and my delivery, blown away by how much difference could be made in a day. If Melinda was on set, she would be pleased with me, too.

I would come home happy, and Mike would be proud, knowing that I was following through on what I promised. And if I kept doing all that, he would eventually come around to supporting me in the one thing I really wanted — to someday open Bake it Away.

But first, I had some work to do to get us through the inaugural season of *Chef Happens* and away from the constant dipping into our savings. Mike had always believed in my dreams, but it was on me to pull us away from the edge of this nightmare waiting to happen.

As expected, the cookies were beautiful.

Perfectly round, each with the dusty yellow sparkle of desert sand and a giant hand-selected pecan encrusted in the cookie's heart.

I admired them as I transferred them from the pans to racks. Once they were cooled, I began slipping them into baggies for David and Chelsea. Each of them got a bag with two cookies for themselves, plus a second bag stuffed with cookies for their friends.

And my very responsible hubby had already prepared their lunches — sandwiches, nuts, juice boxes, fruit, and even personalized notes.

I added the sandies to their bags, thinking about how lucky I was to have a husband who took such wonderful care of our children.

As I took a long swallow to finish my glass, I knew I had to do better.

# FOURTEEN

## Amanda

I couldn't believe how tired I felt, especially considering the day that was waiting.

It wasn't because I stayed up too late baking. I went right to sleep around eleven.

The problem was that I woke up about an hour and a half later, then slept in fits and starts until I finally opened my eyes for good a bit after three. From that moment on, I lay still in bed, not wanting to wake Mike. He'd be a trooper. Instead of complaining, he'd roll over and ask me what was wrong. But I didn't want to talk about it.

I wanted to fix it instead.

Hair and makeup expected me to be on set at six. I gave up hoping to go back to sleep at four, so I got out of bed, feeling like a bag of defrosting meat.

Coffee helped a little, though not nearly as much as the early morning silence.

Sitting on the couch, I slowly sipped and stared out the window, waiting for the sun to start kissing the sky. More than an hour before Chelsea should even be thinking about getting up, she wandered into the living room rubbing blurry eyes.

I was about to start getting ready, but the delay didn't bother me. I genuinely felt happy to see her. "Hey there, sweetie."

"Good morning, Mommy!"

Chelsea and I cuddled up on the couch. She nestled into the crook of my arm and put her head against my chest, seeming to be even happier to see me than I was to see her.

"How did you sleep?" I asked.

"I slept okay. Are you going to work late tonight?"

"I don't think so. I wasn't supposed to work late last night, but Mommy didn't do a very good job."

"Did you burn things?"

"No. I was making a TV show, and—"

"Daddy told me!"

That hurt. Making a TV show was a big thing in all of our lives, and we hadn't even agreed how to tell our children as a family. Yet another sign that I was getting my most important recipe wrong.

"Can we watch it tonight?" Chelsea asked.

"It's not ready yet. Making the shows is like baking cookies. We have to wait for them to be done before we can enjoy them."

"How long will that take?"

"Longer than cookies."

"Like a day?"

"More than that." I laughed and squeezed Chelsea against me, soaking her up before having to let her go. The minutes were melting away, and knew I had to get myself going. After holding her too long, I stayed for another five minutes because I wanted to. Maybe even needed to.

After easing myself out of our embrace, I stood.

But Chelsea wasn't having it. She looked up at me with sleepy eyes and an uncertain smile. "Where are you going?"

"I have to get ready to make the show," I said. "And I'm running late."

"Can I come with you?"

"No, sweetie. I'm sorry, but you can't."

"Can you make me breakfast?"

"It's too early. Daddy will make you breakfast when he wakes up."

"But I'm hungry now."

"You'll be fine. Your tummy is used to eating later than this."

"I woke up because I was hungry. My tummy was like Pooh's."

"Okay. Let's get something in your tummy. We wouldn't want it to get all rumbly."

Chelsea smiled and took my hand as we headed into the kitchen. She climbed onto a bar stool while I grabbed a box of cereal.

"I want you to make me something."

"I can't make you anything right now, sweetie. I have to get ready."

"You always have to get ready."

"We just cuddled for a while on the couch."

Chelsea didn't respond. I set a bowl on the counter and opened the box.

"Wait!"

It was getting ridiculous, how long she was dragging this out. I hated to admit it, but half the time when I refused Chelsea outright, it was because I knew she would demand more than whatever I had to give her. A hug meant she'd want a kiss, and a kiss always meant a cuddle, then a cuddle plus a story, all the way to breakfast. Then clean-up, because our little girl was always a mess, especially when she insisted on doing things herself, which she did a lot more often than not.

I looked down at my daughter, waiting.

"I want to pour the milk."

I glanced at the carton. A half-gallon, two-thirds full.

*I don't have time for this.*

Her eyes were hopeful and pleading.

"Both hands!"

"Okay, Mommy!"

She started with the cereal, squinting as she used both hands to control her pour, stopping when the flakes were nudging the bowl's pouting lip.

Chelsea looked up at me, waiting for approval.

I smiled, kissed her on the forehead, then handed her the carton of milk. She took it with both hands and a grin, proud of herself as she gingerly tipped it into the—

*FUCK!*

"Sorry, Mommy!"

I wished she'd tried to recover the fumble instead of apologizing, but Chelsea gave up when the carton started belching milk, going nowhere near the bowl's interior, just everywhere around it, before she was surprised enough to let it go. The carton dropped to the ground, where it exploded into an alabaster spatter on the butter yellow walls.

"Jesus Christ, Chelsea! Are you kidding me?"

*Oh, no …*

She looked up at me, eyes welling, lip trembling, cheeks going flush, breath beginning to hitch as she tried her hardest to keep what was coming inside.

After a long, pregnant moment, Chelsea burst into tears.

Just as Mike came running into the room.

She scrambled off the bar stool, ran to her father, then jumped into his arms.

"What's going on in here?" His voice was stern.

Mine would surely be unsteady. "We spilled a little milk." I made the most feeble attempt at a joke. "No use crying, right?"

I didn't like the way Mike was looking at me. It was even worse than last night.

He tipped Chelsea's chin with his knuckle so that she was looking right into his eyes. "Everything okay?"

She nodded and put her head on his shoulder. "We were making cereal, but I dropped the milk."

Mike turned to me. "Is that why you yelled at her?"

"I wasn't yelling at her."

Glaring, but with Chelsea's head on his shoulder so she couldn't see either of us, he mouthed, *Apologize to her.*

That pissed me off. Like I wasn't going to apologize? I gave him a look.

He gave me one back that clearly said *now.*

I was standing there like a reprimanded child. I didn't mean to do anything wrong. It was only a reflex. I'm a different person in the kitchen, it brings out a separate part of my personality. And besides, seeing a carton of milk explode like that would make anyone react. This was perfectly normal.

Yes, I needed to apologize, but without being demonized.

"Mommy's sorry, Chelsea. Please stop crying."

My voice was stiff. Same for my message. Chelsea cried louder.

Mike carried her out of the kitchen, petting the back of her hair while shaking his head in a way that was clearly directed at me. So, I started mopping the milk.

He came back into the kitchen, literally less than a minute after the milk was all sopped up, walls patted dry, and the mop put away. I had to get ready forty-five minutes ago, but he started in on my anyway.

"You realize you're falling right into your old patterns, right?"

"Please, Mike, can we do this later?"

"I'm sorry good parenting isn't always convenient."

"I'm really late. That doesn't make me a bad parent. I'm not saying I don't want to discuss it. I'm saying that I *can't* talk about it *now*."

"Do you really want to scar our daughter's psyche for life?"

I shouldn't have laughed at him, but I couldn't help it. I was going on zero sleep, fueled by a terrible headache, betrayal — mine, but still — sabotage, and awful mojo with my partners. Work and life were in shambles, recovery, or on their way to one or the other, and it had been that way for a while.

He hated that I was standing there laughing at him, but I did nothing to diffuse it beyond stopping. "We can be dramatic later, but I'm running late for the thing you really want me to do. Chelsea will get over it. I'm sure Gordon's Ramsey's children are perfectly well-adjusted."

"That's great. Even when you're late, you still have time to compare our lives to someone else's."

"That's not what I'm doing. I was saying that talking to a little girl like I would an adult isn't the end of the world. I am sorry. I did just take the time to clean it all up without even trying to use it as a teachable moment, which we really should have done, and I took that time despite not having anywhere near enough of it to spare. Same for this conversation."

"She shouldn't have to get over being harangued by her mother."

"You're being ridiculous. She spilled the milk, and I had a natural reaction. Your response, on the other hand, is unnecessarily petty and drawn out. I will make it up to Chelsea tonight. I'll apologize and explain why I sometimes talk that way, so she has some context. We can do it at the Inside Scoop or get ice cream and make toppings at home. But *I have to get ready for work*."

I was careful not to yell that last part and to keep my voice pleasant the entire time.

But I still left Mike alone in the kitchen after I said it, passing by him without a second glance.

I had no time to get ready. I told myself that it didn't matter, that's what hair, makeup, and wardrobe were for. So I took a fast shower before dressing in yoga pants and a tee.

I didn't say goodbye, and Mike didn't seem to be looking for one.

While I waited for the garage to open, I looked into the rearview.

*Crap, I look terrib—*

It took me a second to decipher what I saw across the street, but my instinct knew it was something worth paying attention to immediately.

A car passed by as the door rolled high enough for me to see it.

The driver glanced over, wearing shades and a hat but not really hiding at all. He went by in a blur, but even so, I knew who it was.

Noah.

# FIFTEEN

## Noah

I had to laugh at the timing, driving by just as Amanda's garage door was rolling open.

How could I mind, when the danger added to the excitement? It was risky, driving by like I was. But part of me wanted her to see how much I cared, how much my life still revolved around her.

I didn't know if she saw me, though I was sure I'd find out soon enough. So far, she'd pretended to ignore me. But it was all a farce. I could see Amanda as well as I could smell her. All the tiny movements, the invisible gestures, things I'm sure she didn't even know she was doing. But it was all there, the invitations and evidence.

She wouldn't be able to keep this up. And when

she cracked, I'd be there to melt like butter in her nooks and crannies.

My job as the apprentice in the show was to stand off to the side and look like a goofy bastard, grinning like an idiot while watching the master cook. I was cool; it wasn't nearly as bad as the time Joey was in an infomercial on Friends, when he was playing the idiot Kevin facing the daunting obstacle of opening a carton of milk without making a mess. But at least Joey wasn't ignored by the host trying to sell that Milk Master 2000.

Harris and Amanda were going over their recipe list while I stood off to the side, watching them. She played the perfectionist like always, apparently unhappy with her sous chef's assembled ingredients, beautifully arranged for a b-roll shot before they were to be chopped, measured, and sorted.

Amanda clutched a fistful of parsnips and turned to Harris. "This isn't right."

"Isn't it right enough?"

"No. Why would it be right enough? Fresher Sunrise was supposed to deliver daikon radishes, not parsnips."

"We can make a substitution."

"It's a Japanese-inspired salad." She shook her head. "That's *why* we need the daikon radishes."

It was cute, listening to Amanda try hard to keep her voice level. I didn't want to stare, but I would've bet everything in my wallet and whatever was left in my bank account that she was chewing on her bottom lip.

Harris looked understanding, but not eager to concede. He seemed about to say something when the director came over, cutting him off before he started. "Can I help either of you with anything?"

"We have the wrong ingredients," Amanda said, her voice like raw sugar. "No big deal. We can call Sunrise and get the produce we ordered."

"What were we supposed to get?" Anderson asked.

"Daikon radishes."

"And what did we get instead?"

"Parsnips," Harris answered. It was said like a timer going off, a full stop at the end of his sentence. *Good enough,* his codicil seemed to say.

Anderson turned toward Amanda. "Can we use parsnips?"

She shook her head. "It's not the same."

"I realize that, but will they look any different when they're all chopped up?"

I dared to look, and sure enough, Amanda was chewing her lip like it was covered in candy. She was probably sweating under that pretty blouse. I bet she had clammy palms and perspiration beading between her tits.

My thoughts ran wild while she sifted through her head for a civil response.

"I understand we can do a lot with our language and the way we use cameras, and I'm willing to be a team player and do whatever needs to be done, but you're asking me to teach people how I cook, and to do that, I need it to feel authentic. The more ways I have for this experience to feel like I'm myself in the kitchen, the better it will be for the viewer. I promise you, Anderson. There's so much about this that's already unnatural. Please, let me use the right ingredients, if that's at all possible. This can be taken care of in five minutes. I'll call Mike myself."

Anderson nodded. "Fair enough."

Amanda smiled and clapped. "Thank you!"

The words were spoken in the highest voice I'd heard in a year.

I walked over to the director. "Excuse me, Anderson?"

He turned around. "Hey, Noah, what's up?"

"I'd be happy to make the run out to Fresher Sunrise. I can grab the radishes."

"That's cool of you to offer, man, but totally not necessary." Anderson laughed and clapped me on the shoulder. "Amanda's going to call her husband, and I'm sure he'll run it out as soon as he can."

"What if it takes too long and that delays shooting?"

"Jim will be back in a few minutes. He can run out to grab them. That's his job. I appreciate the offer, but you should stay on set."

"No one needs me here. It's my job to stir things while the chefs talk, then look uber excited once the dish is all done. I can run out real fast. I've been there a bunch of times and know exactly where it is. I'll be in and out before Jim is even back. Amanda will have her radishes, and everyone will be happy." I dared to give him a wink.

He rewarded me with a nod and a smile. "Hurry back!"

Eleven minutes later, I was swinging into a parking space at Fresher Sunrise, an all organic produce supply shop that furnished a few boutique restaurants willing to pay the premium required to say *farm to table* and mean it. I wasn't sure what Michael Byrd did at the place, but he was head honcho enough to have his own office in a place that couldn't have possibly had more than two.

I walked up to the receptionist and explained the situation, my voice full of worry as I told her that I was hoping we hadn't wasted anyone's time with the re-delivery already leaving.

"No way." She laughed. "Maybe if you were spinning saffron from straw and the show was about to end."

I laughed back. She was cute. "What's your name?"

"Nala. You?"

"Nala, like from the Lion King?"

She nodded. "It's my parents' favorite movie."

"Wow. That's either adorable or sad."

"In my life, I have chosen to see it as both." Nala smiled, then just like I was hoping, she said, "Let me go and get the boss."

She didn't keep me waiting long. A few minutes later, Michael Byrd came walking toward me, holding a brown paper bag with one hand and tapping at a tablet held by Nala with the other.

She circled back around to her side of the desk.

He stopped in front of me. "You're here to pick these up for Amanda?"

I tried to eye him without staring. "Yeah, we got

parsnips instead of—" I slapped my forehead like I had made a mistake instead of a perfectly strategic move. "Ah, I'm sorry. I forgot to bring them back and—"

"Don't worry about it. I'm sorry for the mistake."

"Oh, no big deal." I shrugged. "It's cool that the chef cares so much. I bet you get that with a lot of your customers."

"That's definitely the type of fish in this particular pond. But still, there's no one like Amanda."

"Do you know her well?" I asked, playing Michael Byrd like a banjo.

"We're married." He grinned.

"Really? You're married to Amanda Byrd?"

"I am."

"It's a huge honor to work with her. I've admired her for a long time and really appreciate the good word she was willing to put in for me with the producers. I don't think I ever would have landed the gig otherwise."

"She put in a good word for you?" he asked, tasting my bait on his tongue.

"I was shocked, too!" I grinned as wide as I could. "We barely know each other, especially now."

"What do you mean *especially now?*"

"Oh. Well, it's been a long time." I scrunched my nose. "I guess about a year?"

That really changed his face, cooked the blood right out of his raw meat. But he kept his voice friendly. "Where did the two of you meet?"

"Work. I was head chef at the Hotel Milano. She ate in the restaurant, like, a lot. So we used to talk, she even came back into the kitchen a few times, showed me a thing or ten." I laughed. Short, but sharp as an arrow. "Amanda was always a great teacher, and I suppose I made enough of an impression that she thought of me when the producers were looking for an apprentice chef. I guess in a way, the show is sort of like a sequel to last year."

"She never mentioned you to me." His voice was dry like jerky, bitter like dill.

I didn't miss a beat. "You know how she is when she's working on something. She gets *so absorbed.* It's like the rest of the world ceased to exist or totally stopped mattering." After another laugh, I continued. "What am I saying, of course you know!"

I held out my hand for the bag after he filled it with radishes.

He assessed me, waiting to see what I might say

next. The breezy rapport between us was gone. Now Michael Byrd knew that I might be his enemy.

But he also wasn't sure. His eyes were narrowed, though far from certain. He didn't know what to make of me. Obviously, he didn't care for my being overly familiar with his wife, though that might be explained away easily enough. His real problem was the thought now sitting in his brain. Right there on the front burner, where I had just started a flame.

The idea would eventually roll to a boil — the thought that maybe I was a part of whatever it was his wife was absorbed in, the thing that might make her ignore the rest of the world or forget that it matters.

It was hard not to smile wide or gloat out loud or punch him in the stomach.

I had to play it cool, let it be enough that Michael Byrd finally knew about me, even if he didn't yet know about all the times I'd been inside his wife, or any of the times that we tasted each other all through the night.

"I'll tell her you said hi." I turned to leave.

"You don't need to do that. We've been married for a while now. The greeting is implied."

"Okay."

I left without another word, holding the daikon

radishes close to my body, imagining the look on Amanda's face when I handed them over and told her who gave them to me, her eyes going wild with rage and arousal.

But an equally wonderful thought was settling next to that one — I was leaving Michael Byrd with more than a hint of suspicion and giving him a lot of time to marinate.

Amanda probably wouldn't talk to her husband until after we finished shooting for the day. She was good about not having her phone on set, same as she was in the kitchen, and he most likely wouldn't want to interrupt.

So Michael Byrd would spend the day alone with his thoughts.

Then he would spend the night questioning his wife in both subtle and obvious ways.

Amanda would see his true colors, realize she was better than the mess of yellow and green that always made her blue, then she'd come back to me.

I was laying a trail, breadcrumbs and petals, from her old life to a better one.

And that trail started today. Not with my interaction with her husband, but with the present I left her this morning.

# SIXTEEN

## Amanda

Apparently Noah ran off to Fresher Sunrise to pick up my radishes.

He was either a sycophantic little kiss ass or even more dangerous than I had realized. Of course I was nervous. That was the point. It was exactly where Noah wanted me. Off balance and borderline upset.

But I couldn't let him get to me like that.

Mike always had plenty to do and wouldn't bother to come out of his office to drop off a bag at the counter. Even if he did, it wasn't like he would recognize Noah. And while I didn't like the idea of that asshole getting close to my husband, standing around the studio fretting about it was pointless.

I went to my dressing room to relax. The best

guesstimate on Noah's return put it at least fifteen minutes away, so I figured I might even have time for a ten-minute nap. It was either that or find a trough of coffee to dunk my head in.

The dressing room was too small for a sofa, but there was a loveseat where I'd crashed twice for a short rest the day before. It was perfect for the ten minutes of comfort I needed now.

Halfway to the chair, I saw the blood red rose on the table. A small note, tied with a thin ribbon, looped from a small hole in the card to a bow around the stem.

I picked it up and read the neat line of cursive.

*Now that I've found you again, let us never be apart.*

With a yelp and a swallow, the note fell from my fingers. I glanced behind me at my dressing room door. Still closed, and Noah wasn't there like I expected him to be.

I went over to the rose, ripped off the head, folded the stem into several equal size pieces, and shoved the whole mess into my pocket. Next, I shredded the note. When I couldn't rip the pieces any smaller, the tatters joined the flower remnants.

Noah was obviously more dangerous than I realized, and if I didn't carefully control this situation and deftly navigate my way through it, I could lose everything. Mike had forgiven me for my all my bullshit last year, but only because he didn't know the whole story. If he were to find out about the affair — not just a one-night stand but sex more times than I could count and in ways that Mike hadn't enjoyed me in a while — it would be over.

There would be no putting Humpty Dumpty back together after that.

I thought Noah was a little infatuated, and if I was being honest, a part of me was flattered by such a depth of attention. But this was so much more than that. Menacing, threatening, and treacherous, from the pan of fixation into the fire of obsession. My life had a ticking bomb, and I couldn't let it detonate anywhere near my family.

Our time together had been short, but we went deep in the month we had. In some ways, our relationship transformed him. I could imagine what Noah might be thinking, and those thoughts were a threat to everything in my life. When he focused on something, everything else blurred into the background. Noah would play full out until the game was over, whether I wanted to play or not.

He was moving pieces on the board in between us. Several of my pawns had been caught unaware and were now laying on their sides. I had to study our positions, come up with a strategy. I couldn't let Noah waltz into my life and engage me in this game. I had to take control.

But that would be hard when he was doing such an excellent job in his role of the eager young student. Yesterday, he'd made a handful of beginner mistakes that he sure as hell would have never made before we met, let alone a month later. They were all intentional, part of his performance. This was Noah's mission, with me as his unwilling volunteer.

Staying silent was hard, and I'd never had a more salient muzzle. A few words could end my life, and it felt like he was daring me to say something with every fresh mistake. The more insulting the error, the harder it was for me to hold my tongue.

Noah knew to let the meat rest after cooking, but I had to stop him from cutting into the steak a couple minutes after I took it out of the pan. He chopped vegetables without a cutting board, which might be the most asinine thing I've seen anyone do in weeks. Noah had complained many times about one of the cooks in the Milano kitchen, who had constantly pissed him off by cutting on the counter, potentially causing cross-contamination. On camera, he wanted to know if wooden cutting boards trapped bacteria, but only because he was asking me directly and forcing me to answer his idiot question. So I told him that was only a myth, and that if you kept your cutting board oiled it was safe, and that's why wood was the standard.

But Anderson looked pleased with Noah's performance as the perfect student.

If the abundance of annoying moments and slights to my intelligence were bullets, his last analogy was a bomb. He'd said cooking and baking were essentially the same, and I nearly exploded. I'm still not sure how I stayed calm on camera while explaining the difference to that man as if he were a child.

Three light knocks sounded on my dressing room door, with a beat of patience in between each and a pregnant measure at the end. I somehow knew it was Dominic before hearing his voice.

"Can I come in?"

"Please do," I said.

The door opened, and I found myself sitting straighter as Dominic entered. I was dressed, but somehow his formality made me feel naked. Even though he exuded more power than anyone else I had ever met or been around — including a few of the biggest stars in the world when they'd dined at Arrivé — he did it with such an impossibly casual air. Dominic Shelly was excellent at life without even trying. He moved mountains without wiping his brow. Was intimidating, had an impenetrable character. Yet in one-on-one conversations, he still made me feel like I was the only person in the world. Or at least the only one who mattered in that moment.

And the way he looked at his wife would make any woman melt.

But as he stood in my dressing room, the look in his eyes made my heart want to stutter. He seemed to be trying to hide his disappointment for my sake.

"Mind if I sit?" He pointed to the seat at my dressing table.

"Of course not." I smiled and tugged at the ends of my hair.

He picked up the chair, turned it around, then sat facing me, eyes fixed to mine.

"Is there anything you'd like to talk about? Or anything I can help you with, to improve the early momentum of our new show?"

I would rather talk about how I sometimes fart when I'm alone, loud enough to embarrass myself, and how sometimes when the children or Mike come into the kitchen after I've cut one and they smell it, I blame it on cauliflower or eggs or whatever I can.

"No," I said, chirping like a bird but feeling like a bear. "Things are great."

"Are they really?"

I squirmed in my seat, hating the way Dominic's eyes were admonishing me, more like a loving father than the big boss bankrolling my family's future.

"I'm not comfortable on camera, that's all." I smiled again, wide like I meant it. "But I'll get better fast. And I'm ready for today."

"Anderson called me. He thinks it might be something else."

I held my smile. "And what does Anderson think?"

"He senses some tension between you and Noah. Is there a problem with the apprentice role? If so, now is the time to fix the problem. We're only one day of shooting in. Changing him now is a hiccup, but doing it later is whooping cough."

There it was, the perfect opportunity to get rid of him.

But he wouldn't go easy. He'd torch my life on his way out.

I was trapped. Maybe I could fix things, but not with Dominic, and definitely not right now.

I shook my head. "Noah isn't the problem. I mean, he has been asking some basic questions that I think even someone in the apprentice role should know, but maybe he's doing that for the viewer's benefit."

"I'm sure he is." Dominic paused, made sure I was meeting his gaze, then in a conspiratorial voice despite our isolation, said, "You know, I would be happy to get you something to relax, if you need it."

I didn't need drugs. I needed Noah Temple out of my life.

"That's kind of you to care, really. But I'm okay."

"We could get you an acting coach. Just say the word. You want to use the same guy we're using for Orson Beck?"

I hated the idea and didn't care who the guy had as his client.

I shook my head. "No, thank you."

"Will you at least thing about it?"

I nodded.

"Promise?"

"Yes," I lied.

Dominic paused for an uncomfortably long

moment. For a second, it looked like he was going to stand, but then his body settled. "Is there a problem, Amanda? Anything you'd like to talk about."

"No, sir. Really there isn't."

"Never sir, please." He laughed, though for the first time it sounded prescribed. "Do you know why I chose you and Harris?"

I had no idea, but it had been a constant wondering since the moment I met them. "I honestly don't know."

"That's one of the things that makes you so valuable to us." His smile knew a joke that I didn't. "You are precisely the type of talent that Melinda and I love to develop."

"And what type of talent is that?"

"We have a sixth sense for potential. It's our gift, and so we've made it our specialty. If I were to buy stock in people, I would want as many shares of Amanda Byrd as I could possibly get. And because we are in the position to do so, that's what my wife and I have done."

"That's flattering."

"I'm glad you think so," Dominic continued. "But it only works if you do your part. Our stock only performs if you do. Does that make sense, Amanda?"

"I promise to do my best."

"That's good to hear, but I'm going to want more than your best. We are asking for nothing less than your soul." He laughed, loud and boisterous. "But we will give you more than that in return. If you do what we tell you to, Melinda and I promise to make you the hottest chef in the world. You'll have more money than you can spend. Same for your opportunities."

"Can I open my bakery?"

"You can do whatever you want. We can make it happen for you, but you need to relax and do what you do best — cook. Just do it while the cameras are rolling."

"I can do that." At that second, I never wanted anything more. "I *will* do that."

"I know you will." Smug contentment crinkled his features, and again Dominic looked like he was about to stand. But he didn't. "One more thing."

I nodded, looking at Dominic expectantly.

"It isn't my business to pry, but Melinda and I have learned that if things are going well at home, they're usually so much smoother at work. Is your husband supportive of all that we're doing here at the show? Is there anything we can do to help you there?"

"Everything is wonderful at home. Mike is supportive of my career and really loves the idea of *Chef Happens*. He knew about our meeting at Bella before I did!" I chuckled, pretending that truth didn't hurt. "I'm very lucky to have him."

"That's excellent to hear. The last thing I want to do is disappoint your husband." Oddly, the way Dominic said it struck me as a threat I didn't understand, though I knew it couldn't be. "If you need anything, please let me know."

This time, Dominic did leave, and it felt like I could finally exhale.

I was trapped in something I didn't understand. Every action mattered. If I wasn't careful, I could end up having to chew off my own leg.

Time to face this thing head on. Reason with Noah. Acknowledge that he held all the cards and figure a way that maybe both of us could win.

We would talk after shooting, and I'd do my best to go with the flow until then.

## SEVENTEEN

## Noah

"If you put the tomatoes in now, you might as well be cooking for Olive Garden!" Amanda yelled at me.

This was a lot of fun, and getting more so by the minute, because she was taking all of this so personally. Amanda didn't realize I was just doing my job by pretending not to know things. It gave her a chance to explain it all to the viewers at home.

But nobody wanted to be yelled at. Not me, and not the folks who would one day be watching at home.

"I'm sorry," I said, looking at Amanda with wounded eyes. "I didn't know."

"Cut!"

Anderson marched over, his patience evaporating ahead of schedule. I expected him to blow up after lunch, but he looked long overdue already.

"What is the problem and how can we fix it?" Anderson asked, glaring at Amanda. "Whatever we're doing is broken."

"I don't know what you want from me!" she exclaimed. "You keep telling me to be myself, but you yell 'cut' whenever I am."

Harris stood between us. His body language was exhausted, almost defeated. "He's yelling 'cut' when you're being inappropriate, Amanda."

"It isn't just the attitude toward Noah, which we do need to fix." Anderson paused to offer me a sympathetic expression. "You can't disparage a national chain while yelling at your apprentice. Again, everything we're doing now is totally wrong."

He took a moment to breathe, think, and pace a small circle in front of me and my two mentors. Once he'd calmed, he said, "When Noah makes a beginner's mistake, it's your chance to teach the viewer something. Talk to him like you'd talk to one of your new kitchen staff."

"That's exactly how I would talk to my kitchen staff if they were making such an obvious mistake … seemingly on purpose."

Anderson clenched his jaw. "Okay, is that how you would talk to your children, if they made an error?"

Her face was flushed. "No." She waited a beat, then added, "I wouldn't let my children cook without knowing the basics."

Anderson said, "Why don't we break early today."

Amanda lit up like someone plugged her into the wall.

But he wasn't finished. "Why don't we take the rest of the day and use it to delve into some of those basics." His eyes were fixed on Amanda. "Spend it teaching Noah everything he needs to know for us to start catching up. We need to shoot a better version of this show. Tomorrow."

And it was like Christmas came early for one of us.

I couldn't have been happier, and even though it was exactly what I'd been engineering, I was surprised to get my way so easily. Now I'd be spending my afternoon with Amanda. If I played my cards right, and I was reasonably sure I could, the afternoon could melt into evening, and maybe if things got to cooking between us, I could parlay our time into dinner.

Once the two of us were finally alone, I could thaw our mood, fold the conversation over into something warmer, then garnish it with the kinds of compliments that were sure to weaken her resistance like they always had before.

Maybe I could manage a kiss. Get her to remember how great we were together.

How could she continue to refuse me then?

Our spark was immediate, that night we met at the Milano, and again when I'd awkwardly taken her into my kitchen — something I'd never done before and couldn't wait to do again.

The next day, Amanda came looking for me, and it seemed like she wasn't willing to leave my side.

That night, everything changed.

We waited until the kitchen was closed. Cooked, ate, and drank way too much. When we kissed, something inside me exploded. We barely stopped to breathe.

She took me to her room. Had sex all over the place. The next day, it was more of the same. We relived that day for a month. The two of us kept getting closer in the kitchen before diving back into bed.

But I still had plenty of work to do.

Amanda didn't have a drop of lust visible in her eyes, face, or body. And she spoke to me with a burning contempt.

After she looked around to make sure that no one was near enough to hear her, she said, "You're doing this on purpose. A year ago, you would never have made any of those mistakes."

"Thanks for the compliment." I smiled.

She refused to do so in return. "That wasn't a compliment. I mean it. You wouldn't have pulled any of this bullshit before."

"Maybe that's because a year ago I was still whole."

Amanda wouldn't acknowledge that truth.

So I continued. "You still hadn't broken my heart or left me trapped in that crappy job."

She rolled her eyes and shook her head. "I didn't have anything to do with that, Noah. I left you right where I found you."

I shook my head. "No way. It isn't that easy. You didn't leave me where you found me because I didn't know what was possible in this world until we met. You opened my eyes and showed me."

Amanda looked around again, obviously nervous that we'd be overheard. But we were still alone. "Can we please focus on *right now*, Noah? We have a show to do, and it's important to both of us, even if for different reasons. Why don't we keep our attention where it needs to be and leave the past where it belongs?"

"I'm glad that it's that easy for you, but it isn't for me." I wanted her to see my pain. "Our past *is* my present. And this last year has been hell for me. Everything fell apart without you. I had no idea how amazing life could be until you showed me. But then you left, and it was like living in Hawaii before getting banished to Detroit—"

"I have a job to do, and instead of helping me to do it like you were hired — and I'm sure over-paid — to do, you're standing in my way."

"I'm trying to resolve our issues so we can both move forward."

"It sounds to me like you're wallowing in the past."

"No, Amanda. I'm trying to understand it."

Her eyes softened, and her jaw finally relaxed. She shifted on her feet. After a swollen moment, Amanda turned ever so slightly closer to me, and in a voice that was barely more than a whisper, she said, "I'm sorry about everything, okay? You're an amazing person, and I did enjoy our time together. But we have to leave it in the past where it belongs. My kids needed me, and I'm not free like you—"

"*Free?* Are you kidding me? That's the opposite of what I am. A week ago, all I had in the world was unrequited love and six figures of debt."

"But now you have this show." Amanda sounded patient. Like the teacher that Anderson was begging her to be. "You'll be able to pay off your debts and start a new life. A better life. You're going to have tons of fans your own age throwing themselves at you the minute the first episode airs."

She looked at me expectantly, surely wanting me to nod along, thinking her logic was easy to agree with. But I refused to accept her flawed reasoning. It either heavily discounted or entirely ignored the fact that I loved her.

"I don't want a woman my age. I want you."

Amanda shook her head. "That's because you haven't found the right person."

"You don't know a thing about it."

"I know plenty, Noah. Because you know what?" She looked right into my eyes. "That's one of the things that comes with age, and—"

"That's why I need you. Girls my age have nothing to say. Most of them are totally vapid, always on their phone, more worried about what they're going to wear than anything else. They're fine for Tinder, but not for real life."

"That's ridiculous. This city is filled with viable women who are much more appropriate for you than me."

"You're perfect for me. And you can teach me so much. Think about all the things we could do together."

"I'm *married*, Noah."

That triggered my rage — an immediate heat, starting in my earlobes, then burrowing right into my brain — but I had to suppress it.

Instead, I gave her my sweetest, most patient smile. A cousin of the one that once melted her and surely still could, with the right mood and music and lighting. But the best dishes took time, and this one only just went in the oven. Pushing Amanda to leave her husband wasn't going to work. Not yet.

Softly, I said, "I understand that. But you can still teach me, right?"

Amanda shook her head, emphatic. "You don't really want to learn."

"I do. I promise. Let me be your protégé."

She almost looked scared.

It fueled my hope.

"I don't think that's a good idea."

"You left me with nothing, but this can be the something that makes it all okay. I promise to do my best, to take this situation seriously. I want to learn and won't let you down."

The old Amanda was back on her face. Barely a shadow, but even dawn is pure black before the sun shines her away.

"You're wasting this opportunity, pretending to be a beginner when you could be asking smart questions. Doing easy things wrong, so I have to correct you, instead of doing them right, so I can teach you advanced techniques. You could be growing as a chef instead of wasting my time."

"I can be what you want me to be." I gave her my best, most moderated smile and extended my hand to seal the deal.

She shook it.

I had to be beaming.

Because the oven was piping, and things were finally cooking.

## EIGHTEEN

## Amanda

After being a miserable little shit for the last two days, Noah finally surprised me.

We had a rocky start, but it was cake after that.

I didn't need to show him the basics like Anderson wanted me to, so we spent the day catching up. At first, I was worried he'd get weird and try to make a pass at me or something, but the air was surprisingly breezy between us.

When I left the studio, I felt better than I had in days. It was the right frame of mind to stop by Arrivé. I was worried about my baby and needed to check in and see how everything was going.

The restaurant was my second home. I opened the door and its scent hit me immediately, like a physical force pushing against my body. It still smelled heavenly, though I was in no way responsible for the restaurant's perfume.

Jenna, one of our most popular servers, smiled at me when I entered. I smiled back, both at her and at the Crème Brûlée French Toast, one of my signature dishes, which she placed in front of a lean, balding man at a table for one. No crusts, four layers, creamy vanilla and orange brandy. If it wouldn't be obvious, I would've stood and waited for the man to take a bite, so I could watch his eyes roll back into his head. They always did.

It looked perfect, and I could smell it from where I was standing.

I walked past Jenna and the old man. The kitchen door swung open, so I peeked inside before entering. The new chef was wearing my old uniform, and I thought I might erupt in hives. Instead, I ignored the lump in my throat and approached her.

Smiles spread amid the bustling. The kitchen hummed with a happy melody of frying garlic, boiling water, and sizzling meat. The clinking of utensils and clanging of pans were the harmonizing notes in the culinary symphony.

No one was yelling. Maybe that was why no one looked anywhere near tears.

Gillian was waving her arms like she was holding a wand, doing several things at once, and all of them seemingly well. I would have expected her to have been fired after all that time I spent getting nowhere, but under Chef Regina Long, the girl was obviously flourishing.

Harris had been adamant that he interview and hire our new chef, insisting that my emotions would only get in the way.

Arrivé was my restaurant, and yet I felt like I was standing behind enemy lines.

That probably explained the sweat beading down my back.

The kitchen staff, every one of them who seemed at ease only moments before, suddenly bristled. Their shoulders shifted into tense postures, then everyone started walking straighter and faster.

Our new chef approached me with her hand held out in greeting. "Amanda, hi! I'm Regina. It's great to meet you."

We shook. She had a firm grip. Her gaze never wavered as she looked into my eyes.

"It's great to meet you, too. How's it going so far?"

*A whole lot better without you.*

"Excellent," Regina said without deference. "It's been a smooth transition. Feels like a family already."

Was she baiting me? What was wrong with me? Would I really prefer a miserable transition? Discord among the staff? Things to fall apart without me? I forced a smile. "I'm so happy to hear that. Do you have any questions about any of the recipes? Or is there anything else I can help you with at all?"

"Would you like to taste any of the new specials?"

Specials, meaning her recipes.

"I've been eating all day, but I would love to hear about them!"

But that was like hearing about your lover's affair, instead of just seeing the video.

There were only two, but both looked outstanding. Fish with white asparagus, and a chocolate millefeuille for dessert.

"Those both sound wonderful. Really, I can't wait to taste them the next time."

And I totally meant it.

I felt relief that a quality replacement had

already been found, even as I reeled from the realization that another queen was making herself at home upon my throne. Regina was clearly a competent chef, and even better with people. The staff had been working with her for days and clearly loved their new boss. They were happy, and while there was a time when I believed that happiness equaled complacency, I couldn't find a fault in my kitchen. By all accounts, the entire operation appeared to be moving along with oiled precision.

Maybe Mike and Harris were right. I was a monster who chewed people up and spit them out in my quixotic quest for perfection. I left Regina with another compliment, this one on the state of her new kitchen, then went to see Harris in his office.

His fingers paused on the keyboard as he looked up from his monitor. "Amanda. Hello. What are you doing here?"

"I came to check in."

I was glad that I'd made up with Noah, but also a little jealous of Harris. After production shut down for the day, he got to spend the afternoon at Arrivé. I had to waste a day "getting Noah up to speed" because he'd been acting incompetent.

"So, I take it you met Regina?"

"She seems great."

"And you seem like you mean that," Harris said, his smile uncertain.

"I do. I'll admit to it hurting *a little*. It seems like I haven't been missed."

Harris shrugged, but he didn't look sorry at all. "It's been a smooth transition. And surprisingly positive."

"What do you mean by that?" I asked, still trying not to let the envy get me.

"I was hoping for less drama in the kitchen, but the changeover has already made a difference in other areas."

He was being vague and making me fish. "Like what, Harris?"

"Our revenue is up."

"It's only been a couple of days, that doesn't mean anything."

"It's demonstrably up," Harris argued. "And we can track where it's coming from. Word of mouth has exploded, and customers are talking. Go online and look at the reviews. Regina is already experimenting, and customers are loving her specials. Most importantly, the staff is happy, and I think the diners can feel that."

I had never felt more replaceable.

And I couldn't stand his smug expression, especially with him pretending it wasn't there.

"Are you trying to make me feel bad?"

"Why would I try to make you feel bad, Amanda? I spend an inordinate amount of time doing everything in my power to make you feel good. Probably better than you deserve to."

"You make it sound like managing my moods is part of your job description—"

"Isn't it?"

"—and like I'm not needed here anymore. Or wanted."

"I didn't say either of those things, or *any* of those things, even though whether you want to face the truth or not, managing your moods *is* part of my job. But I also can't pretend things aren't already easier, or that I can't see how easy it will now be to grow things around here."

"That hurts, Harris."

"I know, and I'm sorry. But it's true. Your heart hasn't been here for a while now. And I know you don't want to talk about it, but I'd still like to discuss the idea of buying you out of your half of the rest—"

"Absolutely not, Harris. We're not having this

conversation again. Arrivé is my baby. Would you like to buy David and Chelsea, too?"

"Being ridiculous isn't going to get us anywhere. It's a reasonable proposition, and I'll make a fair offer. You know me, so——"

"There is no *fair offer.* Arrivé is *my* restaurant."

"Our restaurant."

"Why do you want to change that?"

"Because our partnership is no longer working. I seriously don't even see why this is a problem. You could use the money to start your bakery. You've been talking about it for years, and if you really want to maximize your new venture's chances for success, you can't be struggling with trying to run the restaurant at the same time."

"So, the solution is for you to take my biggest success away from me?" I didn't mean to start screaming, but there I was yet again. "How can even think about doing that to me? The recipes are mine, and so is the reputation. None of this would even exist without me!"

"What about your family, Amanda? Don't you want to have more time with them? And if you're being honest with yourself, don't they deserve more than what you give? You can't work non-stop for the rest of your life. There is zero chance that you can make this restaurant what it needs to be while also filming the show. And getting Bake it Away off the ground. Not without your family falling apart. You have to stop and smell the roses."

"I haven't even seen the roses."

"Bullshit, Amanda. Eighteen months ago, your life was filled with them. You're the one who—"

"Are you ever going to stop throwing that in my face?"

"Maybe if it ever stops being relevant to every conversation." Harris glared at me and vented a harsh breath. "But this is my life right now — cleaning up after you or worrying that I'll have to. Knowing that at least half of our conversations will eventually turn into a fight unless I'm willing to pacify you or navigate through your increasingly unreasonable expectations. I want to be friends after this, but I feel like the longer we wait, the worse it will be."

"I've always loved your optimism. You should teach me to see the roses."

"Your face could be buried in a bed of them and you'd probably bitch about the subtle aroma of dirt."

I wished Harris was yelling at me, because his calm was making everything worse.

After a deep inhale, I strove for my most even voice. "I won't be pushed out of my own restaurant."

"Then buy me out. But we shouldn't be partners anymore. I want to move on from that era of my life."

Three sentences of blunt force trauma left me instantly dizzy. It would have hurt less if he'd slapped me. The air left my stomach, making my knees want to buckle.

It was an unimaginable pain, turning the theoretical into a proof.

Harris really did hate me, or at least, he was starting to.

Was I really *that* awful? I thought we would always be partners. What had felt like a constant was now clearly a variable that he was working to delete from his equation.

Spittle rained as I yelled. "You wouldn't have anything to move on from if it weren't for me, and no matter what happens, we'll both always know it!"

"Get out of my office, Amanda. And don't come back to the restaurant until you've gotten over yourself."

I glared long enough to let Harris know how I

felt, made an about face, then left without another word. I didn't slam the door behind me, and I was Meryl Streep on my way out, smiling and telling everyone what a great job they were doing, pulling Regina into a hug that seemed to surprise us both, and reminding our new chef that I couldn't have this next part of my dream without her and was grateful to the tips of my toes for all she was doing.

But I was burnt broccoli inside. My florets withered and crisp, the flavor reduced to a bitter char.

No one appreciated the sacrifices I made. The part of this restaurant that could have only come from me. I was the one who made it possible for Harris to be so successful. I raised Mike out of his lower-middle-class life and paid for our children to attend Constellation, which was one of the best schools in the state, if not the nation. I gave up everything to be the kind of chef that could be counted on to execute culinary perfection — not just the one percent, but the one percent of that. The splash of cream, the thing that finished the dish, while Harris saw me as unnecessary fat clotting his professional arteries.

But I wasn't a diva. This was what it took to be number one.

Harris thought he wanted something that he

didn't. Being irritated with me didn't make buying Arrivé the right decision. Even if he recovered, the restaurant would have nowhere to go. But that's the dream he was chasing. Same for Mike. The two most important men in my life were conspiring against me. There was poison in my blood and nothing I could do.

It would serve them right if I sold my share in the restaurant to open my bakery and left Mike for Noah. We could share custody of the kids. Maybe I'd be a better mom and a better business partner if I was with someone who believed in me.

And Noah was definitely that. He was also hungry, and in the same way I was. He had the same ruthless streak that somehow fueled the emptiest tank. It's what helped me finish culinary school, beat the odds on landing our Arrivé location — something Harris had doubted I could do, but he pledged his eternal allegiance to me the moment I did. It's what gave me everything I needed to turn Arrivé into one of LA's best restaurants, despite the long odds and fierce competition.

If I'd met Noah in my twenties instead of Mike, who knew what the two of us could have done.

But I wouldn't have had David and Chelsea, the

two accomplishments eclipsing all that I'd done with Arrivé.

There was no room for them in a life where I was constantly clawing my way to the top. Sure, balancing parenthood and my career wasn't easy, but I could never walk away from the children, and all such thoughts were like mold in a muffin.

I shouldn't have stopped at the restaurant.

It threw everything off, starting with my schedule and ending with my mood.

The visit ripped me up inside. Shredded cabbage in fermented sauces.

I felt worthless, unappreciated, and vulnerable — three emotions that brunoised my heart and soul, cutting both into julienned strips before finishing the destruction with the finest dice. I stayed in the car forty minutes longer than I should have, driving out to Longfellow Passing and back, to feel the bend in the road underneath me, the hard *BUMP!* after that scary steep dip before the sloping Pacific. It was the only way to clear my head enough to smile when I got home.

But my face didn't matter. Mike was still furious.

Not mad, *furious.*

Yes, I was too late to go out for ice cream as planned, and yes, I forgot about the promise altogether. Either one would have made him angry. Mike was over the edge because I didn't even call. I'd been home for six minutes. For five and a half of them, we'd been standing in the kitchen arguing.

"I'm really, really sorry."

"Except that you're not, Amanda. This is a regular thing."

"Stop saying that! I don't deserve it." I shook my head, not sure if I'd ever tried harder to stop myself from crying. The day — *the week* — was really piling on. "You can't spend a year telling me that I'm getting better then take that all away from me now."

But he went ahead and did it anyway. "Maybe not, but why don't I tell you a story and we can decide together. I'll tell you about the time you forgot you promised your daughter ice cream as an apology after screaming at her, then ignoring her, so that when you didn't show up and we went anyway, Chelsea wouldn't eat a bite. She cried instead. The entire time. David got a real kick out of it."

"Enough with the sarcasm."

"Would you rather I was yelling at you?"

"Those are my two choices? Your night sounds awful, and I'm sorry I caused that. Truly. But I don't want to fight. Let me say goodnight to the kids, then we can talk."

"No," Mike said, his voice chilled. "They're in bed, asleep. I won't be happy if you wake them."

"You're not happy now."

"I don't want to do this."

"I already said that."

He pointed to a bag on the counter. "I brought you dinner."

"Brought or bought?"

"Is that diva for *thank you*?"

I ignored him and looked in the bag. A burger from The Better Burger Company. I'm sure it would've been delicious if I wasn't sick to my stomach. "Thanks," I muttered as I put the bag into the fridge.

"I don't know why I ever bother to bring you anything. You can fucking cook for yourself."

"You don't need to swear at me, Mike."

"You don't need to swear at every person who has ever worked for you, but that's never stopped you."

"You're not in the kitchen with me."

"Do I need to be?"

217

"They're employees. We're married."

"Oh. Got it. So that means that we shouldn't swear at each other?" He scrunched his face. "But what about all the times when you've yelled obscenities at me? Do those count?"

"I'm not swearing at you right now, am I?"

"I don't want to get this wrong, so could you print a schedule of the different times we can curse at each other? That way there won't be any confusion."

"You don't have to be an asshole."

"There it is." Mike's smile looked ugly on his face. "So, are you going to tell me where in the hell you were?"

"Ask me nicely."

"Where were you, Amanda?" His voice was barely above a growl.

"The kid they hired as our apprentice kept making mistakes. So Anderson, our director, made me take the day to train him so that he'd be ready for 'shooting a better show tomorrow.' That was long and exhausting and not anything I should have had to do with someone hired for this specific job. I wanted to clear my head and not bring my shit home, so I stopped by Arrivé and met our new chef. Things seemed better than I expected, so I went to

Harris's office to compliment him. He was hostile, so we got into a fight."

"And I'm sure you had nothing to do with that."

"Do you want me to tell you or not?"

Mike said nothing, so I continued.

"I was really upset after leaving Arrivé. Harris is trying to force me out, and he said some really ugly stuff. I went for a drive out to Longfellow Passing, then looped back around before coming home. I'm sorry I forgot about the ice cream, but the day hit me hard and from two different sides."

Despite my efforts to keep from crying, the first tears were already spilling.

But Mike apparently had no sympathy inside him, judging by the way he was looking at me.

"Who the fuck is this Noah kid, and why did you pick him if he isn't any good?"

I wondered how Mike knew his name and replayed our exchange to see if maybe I'd said something that I shouldn't have. Even if I hadn't, Harris could have told him.

It's the most logical explanation. Maybe the only explanation.

But that made me wonder how often they were talking, how much they were conspiring against me. And why they would be doing that unless they were trying to lure me into some sort of trap?

I had to do something to keep the eggshells from multiplying around me.

"I didn't pick him. The Shellys did. I met him on the first day of taping. I have no line of sight into their hiring process, so I don't know why they chose him. It doesn't seem like the best choice given what I've seen, but I'm sure they know what they're doing. I'll also add that I liked what I saw today."

"I'm sure you did."

"What's that supposed to mean?"

"What do you think it means, Amanda?"

Mike's stare made me want to run into my room. "I don't know what you're getting at. Can you please be clearer with me?"

Even though that might be the most terrifying thing in the world.

"Why did you tell me that you met him the first day of taping?"

"Because I did."

"So, you had *never* met him before that?"

"Why are you asking me that?"

"Answer the question, Amanda."

"No, I never met our apprentice before the first day of taping."

"Why did he tell me that you had?"

"I don't know the guy well enough to understand his motives, but I can tell you that he's lying." The air smelled sour with the lie in my nostrils.

"He said he met you at the Milano."

"The Shellys hired him from the Hotel Milano. It makes sense that he saw me there."

"Seemed like more than a casual sighting." Mike's eyes bore into mine. "And funny that you didn't mention the connection a second ago. Before I brought it up."

I was keeping it cool, despite my panic. "Like I said, I don't know his motives, but any chef working at the Milano a year ago would have probably recognized me, and it makes sense that the new guy would want to ingratiate himself to my husband. But either he's confused, or you are. And I'm sorry for that, but I don't know what you want me to say."

"Sorry for lying would be a great start."

"That's rude."

"You should leave if you're not going to take this marriage seriously, before you hurt Chelsea any more than you already have. Last time was hard, but this time will devastate her."

"If you think it will destroy her, why are you even suggesting it?"

"Because if it's going to happen eventually, better that it happen now, and I'm not going to stay in a marriage where I'm constantly being lied to."

"I'm not constantly lying to you, Mike."

I couldn't stand the thought of Chelsea going back into therapy, or getting the calls from either Mike or her teacher telling me her tantrums were getting worse or that she couldn't be hitting the other children.

Like mother, like daughter.

"Whatever you say, Amanda." Without any anger but with enough defeat in his tone to unseat me, my husband went to our bedroom. He didn't slam the door.

I sat at the table, scrubbing my face into my palms, totally distraught.

I'd been wrong when I couldn't afford to be, and far too frivolous with my day. I thought Noah's crush could be contained, but now I knew it for the cancer it was.

The doomsday scenario was real. Noah was going to tell my husband about our affair, then Mike would kick me out of the house — this time for good.

The most important thing in the world wasn't the show or the restaurant. The crown jewel of my attention had to be keeping Noah away from my family at all costs.

I'd have to talk to him. Let him know I wasn't afraid and he couldn't intimidate me. Tell him our deal was off if he spoke to Mike again or even so much as coughed his way.

My husband would wake up in the morning to a basket of apology muffins. He'd forgive me, like always. I would continue to do better, keeping Noah out of my personal business, giving a hundred percent at the studio and at home.

I wanted to bake a batch of pistachio chai muffins.

But, no. I needed to put the children first, and they would want chocolate chip.

So, I cranked the oven to 400 degrees.

Flour, baking powder and salt, all in a mixing bowl.

Then sugar, milk, oil, egg, and sour cream in a smaller bowl. A touch of vanilla.

My hand made the mixer dance in the batter. Chocolate chips into the batter last.

The kitchen thickened with the rich aromas of my work. I sat with my back against the island, thinking about all the wrong I had done and all the right I could do to fix things.

There was nothing more important than my family.

And nothing I wouldn't do to protect them.

# NINETEEN

## Amanda

We had a publicity shoot for *Chef Happens*.

This was the sort of stuff I hated. I wanted to run my kitchen. Design recipes and cook. If my husband and my business partner insisted that I also teach in front of the camera, I supposed I could do that, too. But standing around and posing for still shots that would be airbrushed or Photoshopped, color corrected or touched up later — whatever they were going to do to nudge who I was just a little closer to who they all wanted me to be — was going too far. They said the shoot was supposed to prove that we were all a happy family in the kitchen. I somehow doubted even the best graphic artist could manipulate the pictures to make that happen.

I would have been uncomfortable at the shoot

even if I was allowed to wear clothes more suited to a chef, but I was dressed in another low-cut blouse to accentuate my inherent MILFiness. No one used those exact words that time, but they sure as hell all danced around them. The clothes selected for the promo were even more revealing than the outfits the Shellys had wanted me to don for the show. I'd been foolishly optimistic at first. Everything was baggy, loose. They got to work, turning my clothes into pin cushions, tucking and fastening the material until it was form-fitted. They made the outfit look better on my body than anything I'd have chosen if left to my own judgment and desire. It just wasn't … me.

Maybe someday I would feel comfortable with myself, no matter what I was wearing, from birthday suit to blouse and regardless of circumstances, but standing there holding an artificial smile that felt a hundred pounds too heavy was definitely not the time.

Bailey Frank, the photographer, was making it hard. Noah was making it worse.

She kept wanting us to shift positions. Smile. Hold our poses. Smile. Look at the camera like we meant it. And smile, of course. Just as the Shellys promised, Bailey was great, but that didn't mean it was easy. She understood that a photo shoot was an exchange between the photographer and the subject and she didn't want us to stand there while she demanded a parade of tricks without giving anything back. So she shifted and shuffled, posed as much as we did, and never lost her smile. She stayed engaging and funny. Worked hard to crumble our barriers.

But Bailey also kept yelling things like, "Tighter! Tighter!"

And Noah was hearing that as an invitation. It wasn't.

I was getting contorted into many different positions. The more awkward the stance, the longer it felt like I was expected to hold it. By the time we were a couple hundred shots in, my neck and lower back were throbbing only slightly less than the muscles under my shoulder blades, which were twisted like a knot of garlic. Though I would never wear high heels in the kitchen, they were required for the shoot, making it that much more difficult when Bailey asked me to lean back.

"Almost done!" Bailey said, still smiling. "You guys are doing great!"

I didn't believe her. Not about either part.

And if she didn't end things soon, there was a

chance I'd murder our new apprentice with my bare hands.

Noah had wisely chosen to keep his actions subtle, ensuring that I alone noticed his mischief. But boy, did I notice. He'd been handsy all morning, and Bailey had inadvertently made it easy for him by repeatedly asking us to cram up against each other.

That wasn't new. Men had been invading my personal space all my life. They rarely took the hint. Whether it was trying to slip out from under unwanted hands on my shoulder or away from an unwelcome hug, the opposite sex had always tried to take liberties. I had no sanctity of personal space, constantly suffering hands on my arms or shoulders or hovering at the small of my back, bristling the tiniest hairs on my body.

Stuff like that probably happened to guys occasionally, but it was a constant for many women. Men making a power play, even if it was subtle or something he wasn't aware of. Words, whispers, whatever. If I wanted someone in my space, I'd let that person know.

But Noah was touching me without my permission, and I hated how much the tiniest part of me actually liked it.

Couldn't stand how fast that small part was growing.

I needed human contact, same as anyone else. Our bodies and minds were designed to feel the comfort of skin upon skin. Touch had always been essential to our survival, and as tightly wound as I was, my body yearned a beat behind my brain. And since Mike hadn't touched me like that in too long, a small part of me was already screaming.

"That's perfect!" Bailey looked pleased as she lowered the camera from her eye to peer at its screen.

Noah knew exactly how to arouse me, and as I stood so close to him, I couldn't stop thinking about how we once were, for a short while, the two of us together in bed, all alone in my room with nowhere to go and yet so many places to visit. All the places Mike would never take me. My husband thought food in the bedroom was disgusting, but Noah saw life as emptier without it.

We started out messy. He drizzled chocolate syrup on my body like cursive, first with cocoa-colored hearts, then with actual words. Noah wrote *my whore.* He slowly licked it off. And I begged him to do it again.

I liked to dribble the syrup from nipples to balls, get it all over his shaft before lapping up every drop.

Making the syrup ahead of time was a rapture of foreplay, and the kitchen our playground.

Strawberries, bananas, cucumbers. Cherries, pineapples, and frozen champagne grapes. Heirloom carrots.

Brie on my nipples or all over his cock.

Ice cream on my clit a winter wonderland in his mouth, my pelvis bucking up against—

"Amanda!"

I snapped out of it and looked at Bailey. "Sorry. What?"

"I need you to scootch next to Noah. Just a little more." She waved me closer.

Harris had said less than two dozen cursory words since the day started, and he wasn't breaking the trend. Instead, he was glaring at me, letting me know yet again and in yet another way how disappointed I continued to make him. Fine by me. We didn't need to talk. But I did want to get Noah alone, first to yell at him for his inappropriate bullshit, then to lay my ultimatum on him hard.

His hand was on the small of my back, for the photo. But it was slowly slipping lower. And lower.

And lower.

Finally, it was an inch from my ass, and his fingers were flexing to palm it.

I smashed my heel down on his toe.

"Ow!" Noah flinched, pulled away, then started dramatically hopping on one foot.

"Amanda?" Bailey said, the camera leaving her eye.

Harris stared at me hard.

"I'm so sorry!" I said to Noah, before turning back to Bailey. "I'm starting to get a bad cramp in my calf from holding all of these poses. That must have been some sort of involuntary reflex."

Bailey pursed her lips, and she wouldn't meet my gaze. I felt bad for disappointing her, but I needed to stand my ground with the wolf breathing heavy beside me.

"I think we need a break," she said.

No one responded aloud, but our little trio broke like a cookie dropped on the floor. Harris strode from the room, already holding his phone and staring at the screen. He wasn't usually so rude and rarely had his phone out in public. But it was the easiest way to avoid me.

Which was fine, for now. It gave me time to school our apprentice.

Noah gave me a wink before walking over to the

catering table, the only place in the studio where a private conversation would be next to impossible. Apparently everyone was hungry. Except Noah. He wasn't even grabbing a plate. Just lording over the spread with his arms crossed, surveying the food, waiting to see if I would come over and say anything.

But I didn't want to talk unless I could at least whisper-yell and tell him what I thought of his crap.

I ignored his wink, spun around to head toward the bathroom. Maybe I could sit in a stall for a few minutes and pretend I wasn't dying in this paper-doll bullshit.

Only made it seven steps before Melinda intercepted me. "Amanda!"

I didn't even know she was in the building.

"Melinda. Hi." I had no idea what else to say. I never did. Not many people intimidated me, and after all the celebrities I'd seen dining at Arrivé, I wasn't exactly a panty sniffer. But there was something awe-inspiring about Melinda, and I always felt like I was either saying too much or too little.

"Are you doing okay?" She looked at me like she had x-ray vision.

Her intense stare prickled my skin and made me feel naked.

"I can't wait to get all my clothes off." My face flamed. "I mean, I didn't expect a photo shoot to feel so uncomfortable, but there are pins poking me *everywhere*, and these heels are killing me."

She gave me a sympathetic smile and glanced down at her own feet in bondage, courtesy of Alexander McQueen. "You'll get used to it."

*Or maybe I'll quit before I ever have to do another one.*

"There are a lot of people you need to meet at the Reception, so please do take whatever time you need to unwind after finishing here. We need you at your best tonight."

Ugh. The Reception. I kept getting reminded. An event I was expected to attend, whether I wanted to or not. And I definitely didn't want to. I would have to smile while Noah undressed me with his eyes and tried to do the same with his hands, because that was part of the job.

"Thanks, I will."

"I'm serious. It's important. I can have a masseuse here when the shoot ends. Giorgio's a miracle worker when it comes to releasing tension. Let him know how happy you want your ending to be."

I didn't know what to say. Didn't have a clue how I should respond to that.

*Thank you.*

*Thank you?*

Or, *What the hell? Are you really suggesting I screw your masseuse to relax?*

"I'm fine, thanks."

Melinda gave me a look. Almost sympathetic. "You're not very good at accepting help, are you?"

"I don't need help."

*I just need to get through this.*

"You're more than a chef now, Amanda. You're a celebrity, and that's a demanding lifestyle. It'll break you, unless you take care of yourself."

"I appreciate the advice," I said, stiffer than I intended.

She narrowed her eyes and made me want to shrink, the pins still nipping and my earlobes starting to burn. It was like I'd disappointed my best friend and mother, even though Melinda was neither.

"I don't need to remind you about the termination penalty if you break your contract, do I?"

A fair but awful thing to say. That was the last place I wanted my mind to go. It already had my heart beating faster. I agreed to the show for Mike and Harris, in that order. But now that I knew Noah was a part of the adventure, and perhaps even its maniacal captain, I wanted — probably *needed* — to escape.

But the cost was astronomical, and doing so would probably break my family.

"Of course not."

"Great." Melinda smiled. "Giorgio will meet you in your dressing room after the shoot."

## TWENTY

## Noah

My dream was coming true. But I wanted things to slow down.

All my life, I'd been waiting for whatever was next because it was surely better than whatever I had. Until last year, when I met Amanda. Everything changed, starting with the beating of my heart. I feasted for the best month of my life, then spent a year in the trauma of famine, endlessly waiting for life to offer me hope.

Then it did, the promise made and delivered like a blink with a sneeze.

Now it was happening too fast. I felt desperate to freeze it, particularly every time I inspired Amanda's annoyance or ire. Because this would be our story someday, and it was okay to have conflict now before our inevitable reunion later. Preferable, even. The salt on our caramel. At least I could see her, feel her, and know it was only a matter of time.

The photo shoot was uncomfortable. For her. I had the time of my life. As the tips of my fingers kissed her overheated skin, I knew I was stoking Amanda's fire despite her not wanting me to. And I fucking reveled in it.

She was probably dreading the Reception and the chance to see what still might be simmering between us. But I couldn't wait.

The Shellys weren't especially clear on what the Reception was going to be. That was apparently true for all their events. I'd done a lot of reading about the couple since we jumped into bed — a cornucopia of rumors, first-hand reports, speculations, and whispers. A site called *Hollywood Hunted* offered the most thorough posts with the most well-reasoned writing, but those articles also had the most damning things to say. *Hunted* definitely read like the author had an axe to grind. And so far, I'd enjoyed the hell out of every word I'd read.

I was hoping the Shellys would send the three of us — me, Amanda, and Harris — to the Reception in a single limousine. Instead, we each were picked up separately at our respective residences. I'd been wanting to talk to Amanda since I arrived over two hours ago, but I'd only seen her flitting by a few times, always with a different drink in her hand. But I hadn't been able to corner her yet. Each time I saw her, I was deeply engaged in an inescapable conversation.

Like the one I was having with Mason, who appeared to be the most naturally tan man I'd ever met. He looked like Robert Redford in the 90s. He talked too fast and was getting faster by the sentence, as he seemed convinced I caught his every word. I was lucky if I deciphered two of every five, but with the limited information I managed to grab, I determined the guy was a buyer. The kind of mover who could take a show like *Chef Happens* and get it on any streaming service who wanted it. "Or," he said with an almost alarming display of confidence, "even if they don't."

Same as the last several conversations, every word of this one was gold.

"Guys like you, they're making guys like me obsolete," Mason said.

I shook my head with a smile. "I don't know about that."

"It's true. A century ago, we were lucky to have the start of a film culture. That's what we gave to the world. Blockbusters and jazz. And it evolved, sure, but right now, it's going upside down. What kind of phone do you have? Never mind, doesn't matter. Point is, your smartphone has more power than yesterday's supercomputer and a full film studio if you want it. I'm not saying the Shellys are making crap that belongs on YouTube, at all."

He took a moment to sip his drink, then swallowed with a wince while shaking his head.

"I'm saying they understand where things are going better than anyone else I've ever seen. You're in good hands."

"That's great to hear. I love that about the Shellys. I've been reading up on them a bit, some good and some bad, as I'm sure you've seen. But even the bad stuff confirms they have excellent instincts."

"A sixth sense."

"Right," I agreed. "Good company."

He nods and raises his glass. "To the Shellys and *Chef Happens*."

We clinked, then sipped.

Mason held out his hand. "Let me see your phone."

"You mean my film studio?"

He laughed. "I'll be fast."

I had no idea what he wanted it for, but it wasn't like I was going to refuse, so I placed the device in his hand.

Mason looked like he wanted to roll his eyes as it sat like a brick in his palm.

"Oh." I retrieved it, unlocked it, then handed it back.

He started tapping. A few seconds later, he returned it to me. "My number is in there. You need anything, call me."

I couldn't imagine why, but it sure as hell felt good. "Thanks. For everything."

"Thanks for being worth remembering. That isn't always the case."

After our goodbyes, I wanted to look for Amanda. But I felt frozen, unable to move as I tasted the change in my world.

Hollywood wasn't all that different from the cooking world. The best chefs made themselves worth knowing. Relationships mattered, more than ability, because there was a trough of five-star chefs who seasoned every exchange with three-star charisma. You had to make an impression, one hundred percent of the time, and make anyone you talked to think you'd be the name on everyone's lips in a year, maybe less. If you got five minutes with the powers that be, you needed to make them want to offer you twenty. And if you scored twenty, you had to make sure that decision-maker left your conversation thinking the most humiliating thing in his or her shrinking little world would be getting fired for failing to give you a chance.

I wasn't stupid. Enthusiasm was free, and a little of it helped me make contacts that would launch me to stardom. Sure, I knew anyone could say anything, and the people I was talking to were filling their pantries, just in case. But it couldn't all be bullshit, and no matter what, I was still several classes better off than I had been a couple of weeks before.

Everything was fitting neatly into my long-term plan. I was well on my way to earning my own spin-off show — after I'd won over enough of the audience to make me the obvious favorite. The Shellys had already hired coaches for me, and I planned to do everything they told me, including playing eager apprentice to Amanda and Harris, kneading my style into the dough, and ignoring any of the more ridiculous requests that might interfere in one way or another with my goals for getting my Amanda back.

I looked over at Harris, who appeared more

animated than I'd ever seen him. It was the opposite of playing cool, but the style fit him. Harris struck everyone as an amiable guy. Not too ambitious, but determined enough. To me, he looked needy. I could never pant like a puppy.

It wasn't like the producer or whoever Harris was talking to appeared even remotely interested in what he was saying. The man's gaze was gliding right over Harris' head to survey the crowd. I couldn't place the starlet on his arm, but I'd seen her somewhere before. She'd been playing opposite Orson Beck. Hadley something?

Her eyes were glassy, but not quite vacant. Some people inched closer by mirroring another person's movement, but she did the opposite, frozen in boredom beside an exuberant Harris and the tolerant producer waiting for the show to be over.

And there was Amanda — the fourth sighting with a new drink to match. Fortune was still my buddy, because there she was, her back and ass facing me, a ruler's edge of black hair sitting neatly atop a perfect rack of toned shoulder.

I smiled and went over to join her, thanking Fortune yet again and begging him not to let her turn around.

She finished her drink and turned, two-thirds of

the way toward me. Then she sloppily walked to the bar.

Amanda was succulent. Too bad I couldn't let myself taste her tonight.

The first time I saw her at the Reception she seemed relatively relaxed, but she was clearly uncomfortable around so many people. That was the thing people didn't understand about Amanda that I did. Once you knew her, it was clear as a pimple on the end of her pretty little nose. Everyone thought she was an extrovert because she yelled. But Amanda was as introverted as anyone I'd ever met. She saw how something needed to be done and was intolerant of lesser chefs who couldn't keep up. Because I could, our kitchen was more like a ballroom.

Amanda needed to recharge after being around people, but that's what made me special. I helped her to recharge in both places. Or all of them. I'm not sure there was a space of hers I couldn't touch when she let me. Maybe as a dad to her kids, but I didn't see why not. How hard could it possibly be? Happy parents meant happy children. My parents were a matching set of miserable fucks. And not because we couldn't afford even the cheapest shit from Walmart, meaning we usually waited for our neighbors to buy what we needed.

They were plenty awful before my mother OD'd and did everyone a favor by finally dying. But my dad went from a raging asshole who used to wish his wife dead and beat her most of the way there, to a throbbing cock who deserved to swing from a rope or worse, and more every day that the monster drew breath.

To protect my two little sisters, I took most of the beatings and all of the bullying from my two older brothers. Lucky me, to have been born as the meat in my family's misery sandwich.

Amanda changed me. Now I was going to change her back.

I knew how horny she got when tipsy. And I'd made sure to get her started early. Thanks to the photo shoot, I'd had my hands all over her all day, and she'd responded to my touch. I doubt her reluctance affected her wetness. I'd bet both of my balls she was soaking. After feeling my hands on her skin and my breath in her ear, she'd had to get naked. More than once. And I *knew* how she'd feel with the air kissing her bare flesh, from nipples to very sensitive pussy. Then she'd taken a short ride in a long car, her shapely legs peeking out of a knee-length skirt, crossing and uncrossing, just to go back the other way with a squeeze that would only leave her unsatisfied. Then all the drinking tonight.

At the moment, her whole world was a lubricant.

This would be easy. By the end of the night, Amanda would be starving for me.

But I wasn't going to let her have what she wanted, no matter how much I wanted to. I had to turn her down. For us. It was the only way that she'd ever know what it was like to be denied. And she'd never get another chance once we were spending the rest of our lives together.

My hand slipped around her waist as she turned from the bar. I expected at least a little resistance, but she was giggling too hard to stop me.

I led her from the bar to a quiet corner of the yard. "Having fun?"

Amanda twittered with bird-like laughter for most of another minute while I watched her cheeks get redder and redder. When she finally stopped, she said, "I want to go home."

She had her own driver, same as I did. But a gentleman would see her safely home.

"What's so funny?" I asked.

Amanda looked at her glass, decided not to take

a drink, then delivered a secret in a hush it didn't deserve. "*Everything.*"

"Anything more specific?" I gently pried the drink from her hands.

"Wait! One more." She snatched her glass from me, the swallowed — no, *gulped* — for two long seconds before handing it back. Another giggle burst out as she wiped her mouth, and she covered her lips with her fingertips. "Thanks."

"Sure thing. So, what's funny?"

She dropped her hand. "Oh, a lot of things. Have you seen Superbad? I finally saw it after Mike made me, and it was *a lot* better than I expected."

*Asshhepted.*

"Mike is going to be soooo mad. He *really* hates it when I drink." Another secret shared, this one loudly whispered as she took a step closer to me. "And I haven't had this much to drink since—" She gasped, laughed, and pointed. This one hit her hard enough that she ended up doubled over and clutching her stomach. "That was with you!"

I knew exactly the time she was talking about. I'd had a day off, and Amanda was still in the dawn of her meltdown. We wanted to see how drunk we could get without getting sick. The day was spent cooking on a hot plate, moderating our alcohol, starting early and finishing late. We fucked a few times — once on the floor, another on the bed, and the last time in the shower because we both really needed it. She couldn't lick me clean, so she licked me dry instead.

It was a hard-fought victory, but I managed to avoid showing my distaste for Michael Byrd and ignore the two mentions in less than a minute. "It'll be okay. We'll explain to him that you did it for the show."

Amanda looked at me blankly. Had no idea what I was saying. She squinted at her half-finished drink, still in my hand. I signaled a passing server, met her halfway, left Amanda's glass on her tray with a thank you, then returned to the side of my partner in waiting.

I opened my arms and waited for Amanda to fill them.

It didn't take as long as I thought.

Her resistance was only a stutter.

I buried my face in her hair for a moment, surprised that she let me, right out in the open without looking around.

Amanda pressed into me.

How drunk was she?

She had to know what she was doing.

But no, probably not. I knew her body, and this wasn't responding to me so much as withering against me. I could have been anyone.

Except when she caught my eye, her hunger for me was obvious, especially after she exhaled through her tiny little O of a suggestively open mouth.

She wanted me.

And I could easily prove it. But as tempting as she was, my plan was more important.

I wrapped my fingers around her hipbone, making her gasp. "Let's get out of here."

Panic finally found her eyes. "I can't go home with you, Noah."

"I'm taking you home. To your place."

I dulled her uncertainty by taking her arm and leading her toward the exit.

"Wait!" She wiggled out of my grip, grabbed a wineglass from a passing tray, started to gulp it. Downed four or more guzzles before I took it away from her and set it on another waiter's tray.

Amanda walked like a baby giraffe with a quarterback's confidence, stumbling three times but ready for six. The worst and final time happened while she was climbing into the car, ending with a face plant against soft leather. A slurred excuse was out of her mouth before she lifted her face from the seat.

"It's these heels," Amanda explained, taking them off.

"Sure it is." I closed her door, circled around to the other side of the car, then slid into the backseat, thanking the waiting driver with a nod and a smile.

The door closed, but I didn't fasten my belt. Instead, I slid nearer to Amanda, as close as I could, and listened to the tempo of her breath so I could match its meter with my own. My arm looped around her, and she didn't brush it off, so I started tracing circles on her bare shoulder.

A shiver rippled through her as she looked up at me with wide eyes. In a surprisingly sober voice, she whispered, "We're not supposed to do this anymore."

Amanda kept staring, but it was in no way inviting.

Still, I could see everything seething beneath it.

"Oh, right, I forgot." I started making a new memory to share while reminding her of an old one, my breath light on her neck as I spoke. "I can't stop thinking about that time we made stracciatella. Do you remember?"

Of course she did. How could she forget mixing the chocolate flakes into the gelato and tasting shavings as they melted on our tongues?

"Yes. I remember."

Amanda was already embarrassed, and my dick was beginning to thicken against my leg.

"What about what we did once we finished. Do you remember that?"

She nodded, and her breathing was suddenly different.

I dragged my fingers slowly across her skin, like calligraphy in sand. "We went into the walk-in. What did you do to me when we were inside the freezer?"

"I don't want to say." She shook her head, but her blushing cheeks told the story just fine.

"You don't have to. We both know what happened. And what happened after that." I waited a beat before adding, "We both know you're wet right now."

"You don't know that." Amanda was only slurring a little, but she didn't sound the least bit convincing, and at the end of her sentence, she left a wiggling tail of a whimper.

I leaned as close as I could without being all the way there. "Do you think about it — what we did — when you're with Mike?"

She radiated heat like a cast-iron skillet. But she inhaled and exhaled without any answer. Finally, she whispered, "Sometimes."

"Me, too," I whispered back.

We stewed in silence the rest of the way, because that's how it had to be. She didn't live far from the small club where the Shellys had held their Reception.

But we didn't need to say anything. Amanda resisted for the first few seconds, but they were short. She was hungry for the brush of my finger-tips — a velvety creeping up her arm, across her shoulder, down the side of her neck.

Her breathing sharpened, and she closed her eyes. Maybe she was pretending I wasn't there, though my money was on her imagining something better than that.

Heavy breath, born from her diaphragm, plumed out of her open mouth. Amanda might be thinking about the times we played with food and each other. She'd always liked that, and Michael Byrd apparently and rather absolutely did not. The idiot had no idea what he was missing.

I needed to stop the pictures in my mind, the ones I conjured and especially the ones I thought Amanda might be imagining. I was already half-hard or harder and a few minutes from doing the gentleman's dance with Michael Byrd.

The driver pulled up in front of Amanda's. I gathered her shoes and purse. "Let me help you. I'll come around the other side."

Before she could protest, if she even wanted to, I climbed out, let the driver know I had it, then went around to open her door. On my way around the back of the limo, hands low so no one who might be looking out could possibly see, I slipped a clandestine condom into her purse.

I held out my hand to help Amanda out of the car, then with one arm around her waist while still holding her purse and shoes with my other hand, I led her onto the porch.

"Ring the doorbell," I told her, pointing.

She laughed loudly while shaking her head. Then she did it anyway.

I smiled up at the camera over the door, resisting the urge to wink, though not by a lot.

The door opened almost immediately. Michael Byrd stared at us, eyes angry, brow heavy, shoulders arched as if ready for combat.

It was a delightful surprise that he didn't seem astonished to see the two of us standing there. Had probably been watching since we pulled up. Must have been thrilled when I came around to her side to help his wife drunkenly stumble to her door.

The meat was thawed with my visit to his business, now it was grilling. And I knew what victory smelled like.

"Amanda had a little too much to drink," I explained. "So, Anderson asked me to please bring her home."

She raised her pointer and pushed it toward her husband. It stopped him from speaking. "You can't be mad at me," she heavily slurred, "because I didn't want to do any of this in the first place."

I could fry morning potatoes on his midnight face.

Seeing no reason to acknowledge it, I steered Amanda past Michael Byrd and into the house that we might or might not keep, once we both had our shows on the air and were sharing a long lease on our lucrative bakery.

Probably not, since it would hold so many memories for her. Memories that I would have to compete with.

"Where's the bedroom?" I turn around and

asked him.

"Put her on the couch," he answered in a voice that made it sound like someone was trying to choke him.

I led Amanda to the sofa, then gently set her down. "There you go, sweetheart. You're home now, and good old Mike is going to take care of you."

She looked up at me with wide eyes and in a stage-whisper said, "This is the part where we have a fight."

"I'm sure your husband understands." I set Amanda's purse and shoes on the sofa beside her, making sure the bag was laying on its side, with the condom displayed like the feature in a diorama. "See you tomorrow."

"See yourself out," said Michael Byrd.

The guy looked apoplectic, but I could have floated into the heavens with a lead balloon.

It got better.

His gaze landed on the condom, the sight kicking him hard enough to drop his jaw to the floor.

I closed the door behind me, then adjusted my recovering hard-on, ecstatic for the epiphany Michael Byrd was surely having.

## TWENTY-ONE

## Amanda

I was home before anyone else and cooking up a storm.

Crêpes. It wasn't baking, but I knew it would make everyone would be happy, and I was trying to make amends for … something, while also working to clear my head. It wasn't a recipe, and there was nothing to remember. Crêpes are simple enough to cook on autopilot. It's almost mindless to make them, so rather than distracting me from my thoughts, they helped me sink deeper into them.

I finished Mike's favorite, filled with ratatouille and cream, and stared at it, trying not to think about work.

It was the first time all day that I'd felt anywhere near centered.

My morning was hideous and got worse from
there. I woke with a serious hangover. That
never happened, so I must have drunk a gallon.
That tracked — I vaguely remembered starting
fast and not stopping. I'd probably be shocked to
discover what I'd done to my body. But it wasn't
just the alcohol. I woke with a head like nails
still waiting for the hammer. Something
happened, but I couldn't remember what. It
wasn't in my head so much as sitting under my
skin.

The house was asleep, and I wanted it to stay
that way until I was gone.

No breakfast meant no confrontation. Even if I
couldn't remember what happened last night,
Mike's silent fury as he put me to bed was still like a
pillow on my face.

I have this sense that I did something wrong,
even though I'm certain I didn't.

I couldn't ask Noah. Not just because I didn't
want to hand him that sort of power over me, but
because of the way he kept looking at me. But we
didn't have a moment of privacy, and it would have
been difficult to nab one without my being insistent.
The day was our most productive so far. Anderson
was happy and promised the dailies were great. So,

I couldn't afford to season the shoot with my moods or misunderstandings.

Still, I grew increasingly uncomfortable by the dish. The warmer Noah became, the colder I felt I needed to be. But I was always aware of the camera, and that turned every moment into a miserable march, making the hours as daunting and long as a long and yawning line of traffic.

He smiled all day, almost sweetly polite. Did great work both on and off camera. I kept catching him looking over at the oddest moments, with a tender expression that made me rattle and hum in all the wrong ways.

I vaguely remembered Noah bringing me home, enjoying the feeling of his arm around my waist as he helped me out of the car and up to my doorstep. But I didn't remember anything unseemly. And I was sure I hadn't done anything I shouldn't have, even if I'd wanted to.

Still, Mike's rage was a roast in the oven.

It probably had nothing to do with Noah, and that was me being paranoid. I'd come home thoroughly basted, and that was plenty to piss him off. It sure as hell had before. Some of our worst fights came after Mike got mad at me for getting a bit too pickled. But I never did it to get sloppy. Sometimes it was just part of the day, after I'd pushed myself a little too hard.

Problem was that stopping at a glass had become nearly impossible. The first started the unwinding, but the third would trigger the fight. So, I usually hovered at two.

I was sorry I'd come home drunk, but I hardly thought it was inexcusable or worth the way he put me to bed. That memory filled me with yet another sober chill as I looked down at the crêpe, ready to flip it.

No matter how plastered I might have been, Mike was making it worse.

And besides, all of this was at least partly his fault. I never wanted to do the show. I actively *didn't* want to do it. The Reception was a mandatory part of that original agreement. I had to go because I was doing *Chef Happens*, which I only agreed to do because it promised to make my husband happy. But now he was salty because I'd come home shitfaced, which I only did because I had no idea how else to cope.

I hate that I overdid it, but I was thoroughly fried from the moment I arrived at the Reception, so strung out in the aftermath of that photo shoot that I surrendered to Giorgio on the massage table.

I wasn't going to let him do what Melinda had implied, but I did expect a release of tension. Instead, he dug his fingers so deep into my tight muscles, the hour felt like a punishment. But I didn't stop him because I'm sure I deserved it.

By the time the party started, I was on the verge of a meltdown. Would my husband have been happier if I'd lost my shit at the Reception in front of every investor or decision maker capable of killing the show he insisted I do?

The door slammed. I jumped.

I heard marching a moment before Mike appeared in the doorway. David and Chelsea paused beside him, a child per side. He looked at them. "Go to your rooms. I'll be up to get you in a few minutes."

"Are we in trouble?" David asked, even though Mike had been perfectly gentle.

Maybe he could read his father's eyes. I could, and the story scared me.

The children seemed unsettled at best, but without another word from either of them, they both scampered away.

He stared at me for a few awful seconds while waiting for them to move out of earshot, then broke our rule about never starting an argument while the children were awake.

"Did you sleep with him last night?"

I knew he was pissed, but that accusation shocked me.

"You're kidding me." There wasn't a single note of apology in my voice, because fuck him for thinking that.

"This will go a lot better if you don't deny it."

"I didn't cheat on you last night, Mike. You're being ridiculous."

"Admit you were *prepared* to cheat on me."

"Again, you're being ridiculous."

"So, you're saying you never had sex with that kid and never would? That's your story, and you're sticking to it?"

"What are you actually asking me, Mike?"

I expected this argument to go one way, with me on my metaphorical knees, doing whatever I could to make this right. But he was in the wrong, accusing me of something I didn't do. Not last night, anyway. I could barely hold my temper.

Mike pulled something from his pocket but kept it in his palm. Squeezed it in his fist. "If you had no intention of sleeping with someone else, why would this fall out of your purse?"

He opened his hand, showing me a condom with *What's Cooking?* written on the wrapper.

"Cute, but that's not mine. I don't carry condoms in my purse."

Mike sneered, then turned around and stormed into the living room. Over his shoulder, he said, "Let's look, shall we?"

I started to follow him out, but he was already on his way back to the kitchen. He shoved by me in the foyer, then dumped the contents of my purse onto the counter.

No condoms.

He looked at me, incensed.

"Wow," I said. "What's next? Wanna guess what I wrote in my diary, rip out a page, and see if you get that wrong, too?"

"I found it spilling out of your purse last night, Amanda. Maybe you only had one, but that little novelty condom is yours. Since my dick doesn't need a wrapper, it's safe to assume you were at least thinking of having someone else's inside you."

I turned furious as it hit me, the sudden understanding of what was happening. Noah must have planted that condom for exactly this reason.

*How about a little benefit of the doubt, asshole?*

Except Mike was right, even if he was a year late.

I didn't know what to say, and if my cheeks were as flushed with anger as I imagined they were, it could easily look like the blushing of guilt.

"That's a terrible thing to say to me."

"Well, it's a terrible thing to do."

"What do you think I did, Mike?"

"I think you got drunk last night and fucked that kid!"

"Why send the children up to their bedrooms if you're still going to yell loud enough for them to hear you?"

"That doesn't sound like a denial."

"I've already done that enough. I don't need to keep insulting us both." I shook my head, furious at the entire situation. I hadn't done anything wrong, at least not last night. "So, let me get this straight. You found a condom on or near our couch, and you've been carrying it around all day so that you could confront me with it?"

I was disgusted with both of us.

But he looked at me like I was the only problem. "What am I supposed to think?"

"I don't know, maybe that it's Noah's instead of

your wife's? Couldn't it have easily fallen out of his pocket or something when he helped me inside?"

Mike wasn't listening to a word I said. "Is that why you picked him? After you met him at that shit hole hotel where you had to stay after you realized you couldn't be pleasant for more than five minutes at a time around here? Now you got him on the show so you could finish the affair you started back then?"

"Would you please listen to me for a second?"

Mike fell sullenly silent.

"There's nothing between me and Noah. And you know I'm taking birth control. I haven't even seen a condom since ... well, before I got pregnant with Chelsea."

"If you were cheating on me, you would make him use a condom to keep you from getting an STD."

"I'm not cheating on you, Mike."

"That kid brought you home drunk. Not buzzed or tipsy, Amanda. *Drunk.*"

"Can you please stop calling him a kid?"

"Why? Does it remind you that you're a mother with the children of your own? Does it make you remember that you have a husband?"

"Will you please stop being a jerk and listen?" Clearly, I meant *asshole*.

"I'm waiting for you to say something, *anything*, that might make you look better than you do right now."

"I've said plenty. You're not listening."

"Okay." Mike crossed his arms. "Let's hear it. *I cheated on you, because …*"

I didn't say anything because I wasn't taking his bait. We sat there in silence for thirty long seconds or so, neither one of us willing to break our stalemate.

Finally, I couldn't take it. "I didn't do anything wrong. Yes, I drank too much, and I'm really sorry for that. But I was nervous. *Really* nervous. We had to do these photo shoots all day long, and I was in clothes I wasn't comfortable in, posing and smiling for the photographer when that was the last thing I wanted to do. Melinda could tell I was upset, and she insisted that I get a massage."

"From Noah?"

"With Giorgio."

Mike opened his mouth in obvious protest, but I didn't let him get it out. "Giorgio is Melinda's personal masseuse."

That didn't stop him for long. "So, while I'm

home taking care of the kids, you're getting massages from Giorgio before leaving work, then getting wasted with Noah before coming home. How does this in any way make me feel better?"

I threw another ladle of batter into the pan and swirled it around as I struggled to get a handle on my anger.

"Tell me what I did wrong, Mike. Because the way I see it, I'm doing everything I was asked to do. You're the one who wanted me to do the show. To give it a hundred percent. That's what I'm doing. I didn't want to do the photo shoot or be at that stupid party. I never wanted the show. I never wanted any of this."

"That's why you're purposely trying to sabotage things."

"Why would I intentionally try to blow this? How does that in any way help me or our family?"

"I don't think it helps our family at all, but I can see how you would think it might help you, and I wouldn't be surprised if you saw that as reason enough."

I shook my head, skin on fire and nostrils filling with an acrid scent. "I think we should have this conversation later, after we've both had time to think. I'm having a really difficult time reconciling how hard I'm working with the accusation that I don't give a shit and am intentionally trying to ruin things."

He shrugged, another dickhead gesture. "Blowing this on purpose to prove you have more artistic integrity than everyone else absolutely seems like something you would do. But if you think you can quit the show and go back to your stupid restaurant—"

"My what?" I could hear my own fury and it chilled me.

"—I'll never forgive you. That'll be it. You never appreciated what I gave up so that you could have your own business and never had to lower yourself enough to work for someone else."

"I do appreciate it."

"That's the first thing I thought, when I saw the condom in your purse."

"For Christ's sake, it wasn't in my purse."

"Close enough."

"I'm doing the show, like I promised. After the first season, we'll have enough to open the bakery, then—"

"Oh, no. You barely have time for us with the restaurant. You can't add a bakery on top of that."

I smelled the smoke before I could respond. Even if I hadn't, the alarm screamed a second later.

My crêpe was burning in the pan.

A string of curse words flew from my mouth as I raced to the sink. Mike watched me scrape the skillet for a few moments before lazily going to grab a chair. He dragged it across the room, then climbed atop it to kill that racket.

The room was suddenly filled with the sound of running water.

By the time I turned off the faucet and spun around, Mike was already gone.

I ran into the living room, making it just as the front door slammed.

A second later, I was at the window, parting the curtain to peek out. I stayed there until Mike peeled out of the driveway.

I dropped the curtain, then raised it right back up, my instinct catching an echo of what my eyes must have seen.

A familiar car. It took me a moment to remember where I had seen it before.

In the studio lot. Noah's car.

Shit. What was he doing in front of my house?

The car pulled away from the curb, slowly, same direction as Mike.

Was Noah leaving because he knew I saw him, or was he interested in seeing where my husband might go?

There was a lurch in my stomach, strong enough to send me running back into the kitchen, right to the sink where I let it all out, first with the vomit and then with the retching.

It was so painfully obvious. Why didn't I see it before?

Noah was trying to ruin my marriage.

"Mommy?" David said.

I looked behind me. He was standing in the doorway with Chelsea.

"Are you okay?" she asked.

"Mommy's fine," I told my children.

Then I followed my lie with a smile.

## TWENTY-TWO

## Noah

I didn't expect Harris to take mentoring me seriously, but there we were sharing a beer and making a soufflé in his kitchen on a Saturday afternoon.

He kept telling me he wanted me to get better, insisting that he'd do everything he could to help me improve and apologizing for Amanda, without ever saying sorry or being specific. The man was too loyal for that. But accusations sat in the spaces between his sentences, anyway.

He was a different, and better, teacher than Amanda. Patient and willing, eager to pass on what he knew.

"The sides of the baking dish need to be completely horizontal so the soufflé can climb." He showed me that the bottom of the dish was greased while the sides were not, which allowed the soufflé to "climb" as it cooked.

When Amanda told me things I knew, we rushed right through them. Her teaching was like a flambé, but a lesson from Harris was more like a chowder.

*The eggs must be room temperature, even a little cold is too much when you're separating the white from the yolk.*

*Always heat the cream before adding it to your flour and butter.*

*Whisk the egg whites to eight times their original volume by using a separate metal bowl.*

*Cream of tartar or salt will stabilize the egg whites, but you have to add it at the right time — after they've started to stiffen but before they've peaked.*

"And for goodness sake, stop folding the egg whites into the base while there are still faint streaks of white in the batter." Harris smiled with this piece of advice. "If you over-fold, your soufflé won't puff up as much."

We were working on the third soufflé, having spent all morning on the first two. Harris was pleased with what he saw, so he let me in on a little secret.

"It's for a surprise segment."

"What do you mean?" I asked.

"That's why I wanted you to come over on a Saturday, and outside of the studio."

"To make a soufflé together?"

Harris nodded and took a swig of beer.

"Sorry, I'm still not getting it. Do you mean you want to teach me to make a soufflé in person because you're afraid that I might us look stupid on camera?" Because fuck that.

"No," Harris shook his head, lightly laughing. "That's not what I mean at all. I wanted to teach you how to cook a perfect soufflé so you could take what you know and make something else with it."

"You mean a new recipe?"

"Exactly." The teacher beamed, proud of his student.

Harris let me think, and by the time he asked me for my final answer, I was confident in my flash recipe — a gruyere-spinach soufflé seasoned with thyme and a hint of rosemary, topped with caramelized onions.

He wanted the show to be a juggernaut, same as me. And he knew that bringing out my best on camera would be better for all of us. If only Amanda felt the same way.

Once the soufflé was cooking and there was

comfort and quiet between us, I finally worked up enough courage to make the conversation more personal by starting it off in a deceptively professional place.

"What was Amanda like when you first started working with her?" I quickly changed my question to make it feel less immediate. "No, what was she like when you first met? When she was an apprentice like I am. Was she just as mercurial back then?"

Harris obviously didn't want to discuss it. He took a moment to think, and another to nurse his beer, but he never really answered me, even after he opened his mouth.

With a shake of his head and a shrug, he said, "I think the show will be good for Amanda. It's pushing her out of her comfort zone, but that's what she needs. She's been stagnating for a while now, and I haven't been able to convince her of it. This is the opportunity we've been waiting for."

He clammed up, like he'd said too much and was sorry for opening his stupid mouth.

"Arrivé's recipes. They're all Amanda's, right?"

I'd been wondering this for a while, and something about the moment made it seem the perfect time to ask.

"We developed some of them together, but yes."

"You don't mind her getting credit for your ideas? Doesn't that make you sort of like a ghost-writer in the kitchen?"

"I don't see it that way." Harris shook his head. "We're partners, which means neither one of us should ever be keeping score. We should both always be doing our best and bringing whatever it is to the partnership the other could never do alone. Arrivé is *our restaurant,* so we both make money and feel fulfilled when it succeeds."

"Like Elton John and Bernie Taupin?"

Harris laughed. "Yeah, I guess so."

"You don't think that ever pissed him off? Taupin, I mean? That pretty much everyone thinks that the music is all Elton John."

"No way," Harris said without hesitation. "I think Bernie has the better life. Enough of the money and all of the anonymity. He got teamed up with some random musician a half-century ago, and the two of them have been making music ever since. They're *still* making it, and enjoying each other. As long as the partnership is alive, that's all that matters. Or look at *Friends*. That show ran for a decade. Think about how well those writers must have had to work together. I'm certain there wasn't a lot of keeping score on who was getting the most lines to script."

"I'm not so sure." I laughed.

He did, too.

"Yeah, maybe you're right," I said. "I'm only asking because I've seen that sort of thing before, and it isn't pretty."

"Seen what before?" Harris asked.

"Chefs stealing recipes from other chefs. You know, like the way comedians steal from other comics."

I was hoping Harris had a story. But he didn't, so I cooked up one of my own.

"There was this guy I knew in culinary school, Damon Bryan. Two last names and three times more of an asshole than anyone else in the room. He got caught stealing a recipe for our final exam and got expelled, no questions asked. Damon said he didn't do it, but he'd also said a lot of things that pissed too many people off. Did that kind of thing happen when you guys were in school?"

I was digging for specific dirt. Once, while lying next to Amanda in bed, my face still glazed like a donut, she told me a story about a time when she cribbed an inferior recipe from a younger student she was mentoring named Clarissa. After her apprentice refused to take Amanda's advice, she fixed the dish and plated it as her own — salmon fillet, sautéed in browned butter, infused with garlic and honey, then grilled to a crispy, caramelized finish. It was the recipe she used to audition for her spot with Jacques, and thus the dish that ultimately launched her career.

Harris was too civilized to jump in the mud. "We all adapt from an existing body of work. All musicians have the same notes, same for writers with their words. Even with identical ingredients we have infinite ways to assemble them. The *self* we pour into each recipe is how we claim it as our own. The best chefs can leave any dish with their signature."

"Like Amanda?" I asked.

"Oh, absolutely. Amanda is one of a kind."

I was hoping for gossip, but this wasn't anywhere close. Harris was in professor mode, trying to impart his philosophy. He wanted me to be the best. I wanted that too, but with Amanda beside me.

"What's your favorite thing about working with her?"

Without hesitation, he said, "At her best, Amanda is perfectly calibrated from her brain to her palate. She understands a new recipe is a gift to the world because great food will even make the most bitter man smile. That happiness in others is her primary driving force — so long as it comes from her kitchen."

Harris was dancing around the edge of something, but he wasn't about to dish on his partner, and I couldn't get him there without being obvious. So I hid my frustration behind the demeanor of a grateful student and thanked the man enough to make him live it out loud.

When the soufflé came out, we each took a bite. Harris proclaimed it delicious, and the delight in his eyes promised that the man wasn't lying.

But the whole time, I couldn't stop thinking about Amanda.

I would have to find someone from her past who was willing to feed me a few spoonfuls of dirt.

## TWENTY-THREE

## Amanda
_____

Dinner was miserable.

And worse, it was awkward.

Mike still wasn't speaking to me, and because giving me the silent treatment was harder if he was engaged in even a shadow of conversation, he barely spoke to the children as they chewed on their chipotle sliders and sweet potato fries.

"How was your day?" I asked him. But I got no response. It was mostly the same for every other question I posed. At best, I got a few mumbles or single word answers.

I may as well have been mute.

David and Chelsea were unnerved by the silence, but too timid to kill it.

The children weren't ignoring me, but it would

have been easier to get them each chowing down on raw vegetables than it was getting them into a fluid back and forth. David appeared mostly preoccupied, and Chelsea sullen.

"Does anyone want to play a game after dinner?" I smiled and made my face hopeful. "Whatever you guys want."

"Chelsea and I are painting a picture," Mike said immediately. "I already promised."

"Unicorns and fairies," Chelsea added.

"And I need six dozen cookies for the bake sale!"

"Wait. What?" I looked at David. "You need six dozen cookies for a bake sale, *when*?"

"Tomorrow." His tone would have been no different if he'd said they were due a week from next month.

Mike sat back and crossed his arms, watching me without getting involved.

"How long have you known about this?" I asked.

David shrugged. "I dunno. A week or something."

"So, you want me to make six dozen cookies *tonight*?"

"Yes, please."

It wasn't the baking I minded. I was planning on doing that anyway. Maybe a salted caramel apple pie. But whatever it was would accompany an open bottle of wine. I was too on edge from my unresolved battle with Mike for anything else. I wanted to start baking immediately, but I needed to feel connected first. Our family was floating out of orbit, and we needed a return to center. Yet Mike seemed determined to undermine me.

And I still hadn't done anything wrong this time.

"What if we all play a game, and I make the cookies after you go to bed?"

"I've got this," Mike said to David. "Chelsea and I can paint our picture in the kitchen, and I can help you both."

She cried out, "I want to make cookies with you guys!"

"We can do that." Mike walked over to his lone kitchen drawer, which was always full of crap — his choice.

Mike was holding an old dogeared photocopied recipe. It looked like came from a 1950s Betty Crocker cookbook.

"Oatmeal cookies." He waved the recipe over-head. "A classic. We're going to have a great time."

"You don't want to make those," I said.

"And why wouldn't we want to make these?" He looked down at the paper as though it was the cookies themselves.

"Because we can do better." I was getting excited. There was no reason for me to bake alone. Mike was right, we could do it together. I looked at David. "You'll have the best cookies at the bake sale. I have a *very* special recipe. It's a bit like your father's, just as classic, but we'll add pecans, and two different kinds of raisins — golden seedless and muscat. Plus a dash of cardamom and nutmeg to really ground the spicy—"

"I want Dad to make the cookies," David interrupted.

"Me, too," Chelsea said.

"Dad should paint with Chelsea like he promised. And besides, baking isn't exactly his thing."

My son scrunched his nose, soured his mouth, and struck me with a stare I can never forget. He slid out of his seat, looking an awful lot like his father, then stormed out of the kitchen.

That wasn't my best moment, but I could still make it right.

I followed David to his room. He was turned

away from me, facing the wall. Ridiculous as it was, my son was pretending that he was already asleep.

After sitting on the edge of his bed, I gently shook him. "Sorry to wake you, but we were still talking about dessert."

I didn't want to scold him, or insist he explain his outburst. None of my usual stuff. I needed to know he was okay. Life was exhausting me, but nothing was more tiring than the fighting, first with Mike, then with David. And I was desperate to make it stop.

"David, sweetie." I lay my hand on his shoulder. "Will you please talk to me?"

He said nothing.

"I'm sorry if I've been making things difficult for you. That's never my intent. But I've been having a hard time, too."

He stayed silent. Didn't even look over. But still, I could tell he heard me. I was getting through to him. Perhaps I'd nabbed his curiosity, and maybe enough to make him listen.

"You know how I'm making a TV show?" I wasn't expecting an answer, so I kept on going. "It isn't going well, and there are a lot of changes happening at the restaurant that I don't like and I can't do anything about. It's been really stressful, and it's affected my ability to be the best mom I can be. I'm really sorry for that."

There was nowhere to go but the truth. I needed to be honest with my son in a way that I'd never been before.

David didn't turn around or acknowledge me in any way.

"I don't know why you're mad at me," I continued, "but I can tell you are. If you don't want to tell me why, I can't help you. I'm good at making things better when I know what to work on, so maybe you can tell me. It doesn't have to be about the cookies. We can talk about anything. I'm here to listen."

After another long and awkward silence, David said, "Why can't you be normal, like Jacob's mom?"

*Jacob's mom?*

Jacob's mom always did the least possible amount for any given task. She was a prime example of the term *bare minimum*. I was about to open my mouth and explain how no one ever climbed to the top of their field by accepting anything less than the best from themselves and others when I realized something both obvious and alarming.

Not only was I being ridiculous, I was the last in my family to know it.

There was no *top of their field* here. So what if the school was Constellation? We were still only talking about a third grade bake sale. Half the parents would probably grab a tray from the bakery in their nearest Provisions, then pretend they were home-made. Or worse, bake their batch from tubes of frozen cookie dough.

But in that context, did they really need anything more?

Wasn't the problem with me, that I had to prove myself better than everyone? Was I really that petty?

No. Absolutely not.

I suddenly wanted to know everything I could about Jacob's mom.

"Tell me about Jacob's mom. How is she normal?"

David shrugged. "She just does normal mom stuff."

Most of the families who sent their kids to Constellation were too rich for a word like *normal*, so I needed something more specific. But it might be as simple as her being home more. Like most of the moms.

"You mean, she doesn't work?"

David nodded. He looked like he might say something, but then pursed his lips in defiance.

"You know I work really hard so your father and I can afford to send you to a good school. The *best school.* You'll understand how great it is one day."

"You always tell me that."

"Then it must be true," I said, rubbing his shoulder.

"I'd rather have a real mom." David scrunched his face in an attempt to stop crying.

*A real mom.*

A trio of words like a rusty lance to my ribs, pushing upwards until I could feel it piercing my heart.

How could he say that to me?

"Your father works. Is he a real dad?"

"Dad came to parent-teacher night. And to the talent show. You're always busy at night."

"That's my job, David. I—"

"We only see you in the mornings, and only sometimes, and what about when you're yelling?"

"I don't yell at you for no reason," I said in my quietest voice.

"Jacob said his mom doesn't yell at all. And Dad doesn't yell, even when he's mad."

Dad also wasn't in labor for thirty hours while

bringing David into this world, but there was no reason to go there. My son was sad enough, and making enemies with his father wouldn't help at all. It was a bit like kicking a dog.

"You know I *wanted* to come to parent-teacher night and to your talent show, don't you?"

David shook his head but ended the gesture with a shrug.

My son couldn't possibly doubt how much I loved him, *could he?*

This wasn't fair, and I hated every second of it. Mike had the easier job, so it was easier for him to be there for our children.

But really, was it? Maybe Mike was just less selfish.

I pulled David against me, and to my surprise, he didn't resist.

"I'm here now," I said, petting him as he let me. "I want to make cookies. With the normal recipe."

"We don't have any normal raisins."

"We'll go to the store and buy the normalest raisins they've got."

David sniffed. "You won't be mad if they aren't perfect?"

"If we're making them together, they will be perfect," I said, pleased to know that I meant it.

## TWENTY-FOUR

## Noah

The place was a pit.

I couldn't really smell the grease trap when I got out of the car, but the look of the dump sent the smell right into my nostrils.

Through a combination of things I remembered Amanda saying and a handful of nuggets from Harris, I'd discovered the name I'd been searching for — Clarissa Martin. She was a former student of Amanda's, and thanks to LiveLyfe, I was sitting outside the place she worked, a dive called Texas Lucy's.

I expected the place to be empty, figuring the cars in the lot were for the overcrowded strip club across the street. But Texas Lucy's was packed, so I took the only seat left at the bar rather than wait.

Making small talk with my server got her to like me. Eventually, I asked if there was a Clarissa working in back. She gave me a *sure is*, so I left a twenty on the counter in front of my half-finished Moscow mule, then headed into the kitchen.

I spotted her immediately. Clarissa didn't look anything like I'd pictured from her tiny avatar, but the shiny black hair and crooked smile were similar enough.

"Are you Clarissa Martin?"

"Unless you're looking for money," she answered without looking up.

"You have a minute?"

"Does it look like I have a minute?" Her eyes were fixed on the skillet. "My prep cook called in sick and the place is packed."

"I used to run a hotel kitchen. I'd be happy to fill in. I'll do whatever you ask as long as we talk while I'm doing it. Deal?"

Clarissa finally looked over and gave me a curiously appreciative smile. "You can start by chopping some onions."

I didn't bother bringing up anything for the first several minutes, preferring to find our rhythm. As she cooked, I prepped, and soon we were playing as though we'd been sharing a stage for years, old and grossly out of tune as our instruments might have been.

We made a lot of awful looking garbage, but the clam strips were the worst, by far. The coating had more fat and sugar than a bag full of cookies — though none of the flavor, despite the illusion of eating something slightly better. The unhealthy batter covered lumps of mucus that were definitely not clams.

And unless the customer was planning to hibernate for the winter, there was no possible reason anyone would ever need anything even remotely close to the week's worth of sea trash and batter.

"So, what do you want, hotshot?" Clarissa finally asked.

"To know what you think of Amanda Byrd."

"Ha. That's a name I haven't wanted to hear in years, and yet I keep seeming to."

"I'm guessing you don't follow her on LiveLyfe."

"Fuck her *and* LiveLyfe." Clarissa turned and yelled something to someone behind her, then grabbed and scanned another order. "Amanda Byrd is a stuck-up bitch who thinks she knows everything."

I saw where Clarissa was coming from, but

didn't like anyone spitting venom at someone I loved. "Didn't she mentor you?"

Clarissa stopped cooking. "Is that what she calls it?"

"What do you mean by that?"

"Sure, Amanda was in her second year when I was in my first, and she was supposed to help me through the program. But that's not what happened at all. Instead, she made me miserable enough to quit. Criticized *everything I did*. If it hadn't been for her, I probably never would have dropped out. But after a while, I couldn't stand being around her anymore. Or people like her. And there were plenty."

Clarissa was describing every successful chef I'd ever known.

"Was she dishonest?"

"Dishonest? I didn't know her personally. It wasn't like that. She was a hard ass who always had to have everything her way. No one was ever good enough" — she slopped some hash or something onto a plate, then grabbed another order — "but that's not the same as dishonest."

"I heard a rumor that Amanda might have stolen some recipes from other students. Did you ever see or hear of anything like that happening?"

"That's not hard to believe."

"What do you mean?"

"She took one of my recipes once. Changed a few things around, but I know she got it from me."

"What was the recipe?"

Clarissa stopped cooking and turned to me, almost wistful. "It was a browned butter, honey-garlic salmon. And it was delicious."

The recipe that won Amanda the apprenticeship with Jacques.

"How do you know it was yours?"

"Because she told me exactly how I could make it amazing, and I didn't listen to a word she said. I kept thinking, *Fuck you, Amanda, thinking you know everything.* Turned out, she did. The garlic and honey infusion makes the dish. I never tried it until after she won, so good for her."

"That must have really hurt."

Clarissa shrugged, flipped a patty, dumped some frozen potatoes onto the grill.

"It's my fault. A hundred percent. She tried like five times, but I refused to change the recipe. She kept getting madder and madder. I think I liked that, getting under her skin. A lot of good it did me."

"So, you regret it?"

"Not at all. Amanda taught me I wasn't cut out to be a chef, and I'm glad I learned that lesson as early as I did. Who needs all that debt? I may be working in this dive, but at least I'm not up to my eyeballs in owing people shit. My Accord is eleven years old and paid for. I'm happy I landed here, making simple food for people who want to eat it."

I had no idea if she was serious.

"Really?"

She laughed. "I'm sure you think that's stupid because you think there's some hierarchy to food or something. But there isn't. I like to satisfy people, and a lot of what you probably make wouldn't do shit to put a smile on our average customer's face. I can make them happy in a way that you can't. It feels great, and people like what I make. Besides, it's kind of zen to cook the same things over and over. I get into a rhythm, and it's like my shifts fly by. Most of the time it's just me and the griddle. Then I go home and enjoy my life. No one yells at me. I used to go home burned the hell out and feeling awful about myself and my life. And that was at *school.* I wasn't cut out for it. This is great — except for when my prep cook decides to call in sick."

A timer went off. I pulled a basket of fries from the fryer, dumped them out, and made it rain salt.

"Thanks!" Clarissa said, surprised I'd done that without asking.

I gave her a grin to follow my wink.

"So why are you asking all of these questions about Amanda Byrd? And I don't want to hear that you're curious."

"Well, I am curious. But I'm also your old mentor's new apprentice, and in the same position you used to be. I wanted to know what I was getting into."

"You mean you're cooking at Arrivé?"

"No. I've literally been hired as her apprentice."

"I'm surprised she wanted to do that."

"I think it was her partner's idea."

"Harris? I'm surprised he got her to agree."

I gave her another smile. "Would you be willing to tell me your story about Amanda on camera?"

"Oh, no. I wouldn't want to do that."

"Why not? She gave you a hard time once. Drove you to quit culinary school."

"She saved me from something much worse, and between the two of us, it seems like you're the one with the ax to grind. The last thing I want to do is cross someone like her. And even if I wanted to, it would be my word against Amanda's. I'm a cook at the diner. Your new boss is a famous chef with her own restaurant."

"She's not my boss. Amanda is my mentor. And I don't have an ax to grind. But I think people should know *how* Amanda got to be that famous chef with her own restaurant."

"And to give you insurance."

"Yes," I agreed. "And to give me insurance."

"Well, that's a different story. Hard to argue with, too. I'd want the same thing. Will you settle for *I'll think about it?*"

"Sounds great," I said, still working.

I would finish out the night. Give Clarissa all the help she needed. Make her glad the prep cook being a no-show.

If Amanda was too pig-headed to recognize what we could be together, then she deserved what was coming.

I was shredding lettuce for more than a minute before I said, "Do you think that Amanda might have stolen any of the other students' recipes?"

She pressed down on the hash browns and looked over at me.

Judging by the curl of Clarissa's lip, I finally had Amanda by the tits.

## TWENTY-FIVE

## Amanda

The morning had been going reasonably well, and I was trying to maintain my middling mood by not getting into any confrontations with Noah or Harris. The former was trying too hard, and the latter wasn't trying at all.

I was futzing around on my phone when my blood went cold at a forwarded email with the subject line, *You need to read this.*

There was zero chance this was good news. Beneath the headline, I could see the author's name — Gina Delicious — and knew this was the full review promised after Gillian used coriander instead of cumin for Gina's Spanish chicken and rice.

I didn't want to read it. It was going to hit the

restaurant hard, and it would probably slap me even harder. Criticism had changed, and not for the better. All of these little review sites meant *anyone* could be a critic, regardless of what they knew or how well they were able to articulate themselves.

Problem was, few food critics were saying anything new, since so many of them were now stuck at the bottom and appealing to the lowest common denominator. There were too many voices out there, and the ones that earned the most attention didn't necessarily do so with intelligence. It was always easier to accomplish with snark. And Gina Delicious was one of the worst.

Whether it was an amateur critic with a blog or a professional writer being paid for a review, the critic was always writing about the restaurant, not living in the kitchen like I did. Both sides of those swinging doors had something to prove. Most critics wrote to impress their readers, so the lens of their reviews were often pointed in all the wrong places. It was now worse than it had ever been. Writers, full of apathy, often phoned it in, taking pictures of their meals with their phones and calling a single sentence critique posted to their LiveLyfe accounts a review, even if it was more like a drive-by.

I wanted to delete the email without reading it,

but I wasn't about to stick my head in the oven or in the sand. So holding my breath, I clicked the link and started to read.

*Reading This from Your Seat at Arrivé? It Might be Time to Depart …*

*Just because reportedly prickly chef Amanda Byrd thinks so highly of her restaurant, with its cluelessly on-trend menu and outrageous pricing, doesn't mean you have to. There might be something worthy of the spend here, but it wasn't served to me. Not the last time I ate there, or any of the times before it.*

*I started with the beef tartare. Let's call that one a* two-bite travesty. *At least it was better than the fig-and-olive tapenade which tasted like it came from a jar, or the bacon-wrapped dates stuffed with blue cheese — yes, I realize that blue cheese is supposed to taste a little moldy, but there are also supposed to be other flavors, too.*

*The rustic chicken flatbread deserves a mention, not because it was a saving grace but because it might have been the most insulting thing I've ever been served. The starter looked like someone had taken a pallid saltine, emptied a squeeze bottle of pesto onto the cracker, then swept up the crumbs from a neighboring table's chicken dish to drizzle on top.*

*The appetizers were better than my entrees, but I'd like to start by discussing the Spanish chicken and rice, a dish that's simple enough for my six-year-old daughter to make. She's not blind, but even if she was, my little Leslie would still know the difference between cumin and coriander. Sadly, the mess of chefs who spend their evenings ruining dishes in the Arrivé kitchen do not. I would like to say that this was the worst of the profoundly awful entrees, but alas I …*

I couldn't keep reading, nor could I stop myself. So I scanned the article to its brutal conclusion, only to discover Gina Delicious thought our staff was as worthless outside of the kitchen as it was inside. She asserted I'd lost my touch and might even be suffering from early onset dementia. Gina suggested that I apply for a job at Applebee's, where the recipes were sent over by Corporate and half the ingredients were frozen and pre-seasoned. She ended the article with a truly brutal statement.

*Any foodie worth her Peruvian ceviche would never go here, but neither should anyone sober or sane.*

I wondered if Harris had seen the review. But the forwarded email hadn't come from him. I had to share it, even though I wasn't sure how to thaw him. Harris was perfectly professional while we were filming, but he turned into Mr. Freeze whenever the cameras stopped rolling.

He was talking to someone on the phone and killing the call as I approached, looking up at me with disdain. "Great job on wooing Gina Delicious."

"That's what I was coming over to talk to you about."

"Oh, were you wanting to apologize for getting us this shit review that's now on the Internet forever?"

"That review isn't my fault! We both knew this was going to happen because Gillian kept fucking up in the kitchen. Including with Gina's dish."

Harris shook his head. "No way, Amanda. You don't get to do that."

"Do *what?*" I genuinely had no idea.

"Blame this all on everyone else. We're *all* responsible for that review."

"You have to be kidding me! I told you the night Gina came in that we needed to fire Gillian. She—"

"And that's what you're not getting. You're selectively reading that review. She had plenty of problems with the restaurant that had nothing to do with Gillian or her mistake—"

"But that was—"

"—and training Gillian well was your job."

"That's not—"

"She's been doing great under Regina's direction."

"Well, good for Regina."

"No, Amanda. Good for us. Good for Arrivé. Good for the restaurant we started together, and good for all the people who work there."

"That's what I meant."

"But it isn't." Harris shook his head. "And both of us know it. You want me to fire the incompetent person who messed up that dish when we should be focused on fixing the incompetence still bleeding from the top. I'm sick of the constant turnover in our kitchen. You need to put on your big girl pants and train our staff, instead of abusing them until they finally quit." He paused, probably waiting for me to respond.

But I didn't.

So he added, "Or you can buy me out, at which point I won't care if you fire everyone and end up with nothing."

When had he stopped respecting me? Everything was different between us now. Every conflict an immediate clash. The show a demilitarized zone, the restaurant a battle ground. I was breathing deeply in and out, trying not to burst, working to control a blistering temper I was moments from venting.

I couldn't afford to snap, but I wasn't sure if I'd be able to stop it.

This was the final straw on the back of a camel's truly shitty week. Mike still wasn't talking to me, unless he was forced to exchange a few dispassionate phrases while coordinating the handling of Chelsea and David. But he wore an expression that I hadn't even seen a year ago, just before our long month of darkness.

Things were even worse with Noah, or at least a lot more unsettling. The situation was a ticking bomb, and I was spending too much of my time wondering when it might go off. He bought me a gift basket with a giant red bow. Left it right on my dressing room table for all to see. It was filled with a feather, a flogger, and a bottle of orange blossom massage oil. I dumped it all in the trash but hadn't stopped thinking about the inappropriateness of his 'present.'

Nor the feelings it tickled inside me.

I was sleeping too little and drinking too much.

Working too hard and relaxing not at all. Being come at from all sides and having no safe haven.

It was too much.

Yet I suspected that wouldn't be an acceptable reason for losing it.

But lose it, I did. I screamed, "FUCK YOU, HARRIS!"

He stared at me, open-mouthed. Then he fell a step back.

Harris had seen me like this before, plenty of times, but despite our conflict now or in the past, this side of myself had never been directed at him. He was my friend and partner. The other half of Arrivé.

But he'd abandoned me. I was doing everything he asked me to do, and it still didn't matter.

And I couldn't stop. "You are a talentless hack who couldn't handle becoming a chef. It was too hard, too demanding, too tall an order for someone so small. You're a dropout, a burnout, a deadbeat. You'd be worse than a quitter if it wasn't for me. I *allowed you* to take part in *my* restaurant. Yes, that's right, *mine.* Because despite what it says on the lease, we all know that it's *my name, my recipes,* and *my reputation.*"

"Exactly. Your reputation is killing us."

"How *dare* you criticize me when you could never handle the work I've done to make the restaurant successful. The work I *had* to do because you couldn't. I did this stupid show, even though I didn't want to, to make *you* happy, like so many of the things I've had to do during the decade I've spent carrying you on my back!"

Harris stood like a statue as I railed at him, arms across his chest, expression neutral, shoulders starting to tremble, and weak knees looking a loop or two from the buckle.

We were inhaling and exhaling, equally out of breath, though I'd used mine to rob all of his.

Quiet like thunder.

Harris finally spoke. "Thank you, Amanda. For telling me how you really feel."

Then he walked out of the studio.

I finally looked around.

Everyone was gaping at me. Each face fixed to the scene, staring in hideous silence.

Only Noah had kind eyes and a tease of a smile that promised everything would still be okay.

All the blood rushed from my head. The air burned with sweat and tension. My neck was sweating, my eyes were stinging. I did everything I could to keep myself from crying.

Holding my head high, I went into my dressing room and closed the door, feeling like the world's biggest asshole.

## TWENTY-SIX

## Amanda

While baking a batch of chocolate-drizzled maple hazelnut lace cookies, I drank an entire bottle of rose. I hoped the combination might drag me back to a quarter of myself.

My insides were outside and flopping all over the floor. Harris was pissed at me, Mike didn't trust me, and I'd thrown my children into a prison of disappointment. My only ally was the interloper behind at least some of the discord.

I progressed through my evening like I was following a recipe.

Heat oven to 375. Take a sip.

Melt butter over medium heat. Take a sip.

Stir in the brown sugar. The coffee crystals. The maple sugar. *Sip, sip, sip.*

Heat to boiling over medium-high heat. That one was worth a really long swallow.

Refill my glass.

Stir while sipping.

Dissolve the sugar, kill the heat. Grab another refill.

Stir in some flour and cocoa, blend it with vanilla and hazelnuts. Guzzle.

Drip teaspoonfuls of dough three inches apart. Bake for five to seven minutes. Drink as fast as I can while I wait.

Take the tray from the oven. Empty the rest of the bottle into my glass.

Let the lace cookies cool, taking my buzz to a belligerent hum while I decorated them with white chocolate snowflakes.

I was deep enough into my drinking-and-cooking fugue that the doorbell made me yelp out loud.

After inhaling the cooking sugar scent deeply enough to taste it, I walked to the front door. I peeked outside, but no one was there.

When I opened the door, my jaw dropped. My heart fluttered.

I gathered the presents, then carried them all back into the kitchen.

There was a bundle of deep red roses, almost black and unbelievably beautiful. They looked like they cost a fortune, arranged as they were in an abundant cluster, blooming through a bed of blush-colored hydrangea. A small box of handmade chocolates, each one inside was unique yet equally stunning. I hoped he'd found a chocolatier rather than making them himself. Because while the first option would be sweet, the second would be a little too wonderful and more than I deserved.

I opened the envelope that had been neatly set between the chocolates and flowers, pulling out what looked like a ten-dollar card. On the cover was a big bed, with one side rumpled, empty except for some women's lingerie and a pair of men's boxers. The bed, covers, and discarded garments were all individually crafted pieces, expertly glued to the card. At the top was an Art Deco arrow pointing down toward the bed, and in bold block letters were the words WE GO HERE.

It might have been adorable if it wasn't totally disgusting. But my heart was pounding, my brow was beaded with sweat, and I felt unsteady on my feet with an uncertainty that started in my knees.

I was having a panic attack. Or was about to.

It was all so terribly reckless. Noah was

gambling with my life. I didn't understand how somebody who apparently saw a future with me actually believed he could get there by destroying my present.

What if Mike had come home before I had a chance to answer the door? What if I'd been in the shower and never heard the bell ring?

Or what if he knew neither was the case because he'd been watching me cook — and drink — through the kitchen window before leaving his dangerous gifts?

It would have ruined everything. Permanently. Mike wasn't speaking to me and hadn't been since the condom incident, which wasn't my fault and must have been perpetrated by the asshole apprentice. I couldn't stop thinking of it as my second strike. But it might have been my third, depending on who was counting. There was the time before we took four weeks apart, that fateful month, and now. That would make three strikes, but I preferred to see it as our month apart and now, which gave me yet another chance to make things right.

Looking down at the collection of presents, I wondered what to do. I couldn't toss them into the garbage, because I didn't trust Mike wouldn't somehow see the evidence and draw his own unfair conclusions.

I peeled back my curtains, looking outside to make sure no one was lurking. It was silly, worrying someone was watching me from the street — or maybe a neighbor from his house — caring about whatever I might or might not be doing.

But my most paranoid self was rearing her ugly head.

I stepped out of the house. Headed right to my car. Opened the trunk, then dropped chocolate, roses, and the envelope inside. Slammed it shut with a plan to the lot of it into a dumpster the first minute I could.

Back into the house I went, straight to the sofa. I sat there for several minutes in silence, rubbing my temples with my eyes closed, still inhaling the scent of the cookies and lingering sadness.

Knowing it was wrong, but feeling like the alternative was so much worse, I got up to grab another bottle of something.

It was a terrible idea, seeing as I was already drunk. But it was too painful to sit on the sofa doing nothing when it would be so much easier to drink my problems into tomorrow. If I was lucky, maybe even to the day after that.

I didn't know how else to cope. Mike refused to discuss it. He wouldn't hear me or engage in conversation. He didn't answer my texts or my emails. I even got a new email app that sent me a message as soon as he opened whatever I sent him. But the app had yet to message me.

Things had never been so bad. Even at their worst, when Mike was angry enough to kick me out of our house, at least he was willing to talk. But three days of his iciest shoulder had me truly fretting that things weren't going to work out. That we might be at the start of a long and ugly goodbye. I couldn't stand the thought, nor could I keep living like we had been much longer. So I kept right on drinking.

Fortunately, I didn't get too deep into the bottle before I heard Mike's key turning in the lock. When he entered, his face was neutral. But then he saw me, and it fell into a scowl.

David and Chelsea scrambled in behind him. Their faces changed, too. It was enough to break my heart a dozen times, the way Chelsea looked inches from crying.

Mike commanded their attention. "I need you kids to go watch cartoons or something."

David nodded and took his sister's hand. "Come on, Chelsea. Let's go see if *The Dream Engine* is on."

Neither of them gave me so much as a passing glance as they left the room.

I wanted to say something, call the children back, give them a hug, or anything else that would remind my babies how much I loved them. But I couldn't stand the thought of their rejection or the looks on their faces if they got close enough to smell my breath. I'm sure the stench of my shame was strong enough.

It was a terrible minute or so, the graveyard silence of our house while Mike and I waited for the sounds of the children's bedroom doors being shut.

Mike didn't waste so much as a second once they were gone.

"Are you kidding me, Amanda? You're drunk in the middle of the afternoon, and in front of the kids?"

Bitterness seasoned my words and their tone. "This is what progress looks like. At least now we know what I have to do to finally get you to talk."

"So, this is what you want?" Mike yelled, spittle flying from his mouth. "You like it when I talk to you like this?"

"I love it," I slurred. "Totally my favorite. It's the new black, you always being pissed at me. I don't know how I ever lived without it."

"What do you expect with shit like this?" He pulled a phone out of nowhere, then jammed it in my face.

"I don't know what that is."

"It's you going nuclear on YouTube." His voice was a low growl.

The video was titled, *Early onset dementia or congenital asshole syndrome?*

I was staring in disbelief, so he pressed play to convince me. Then the world as I knew it withered inside me.

*FUCK YOU, HARRIS!*

*You are a talentless hack who couldn't handle becoming a chef. It was too hard, too demanding, too tall of an order for someone so small. You're a dropout, a burnout, a deadbeat. You'd be worse than a quitter if it wasn't for me. I allowed you to take part in my restaurant. Yes, that's right,* mine. *Because despite what it says on the lease, we all know it's* my name, my recipes, and my reputation. *How* dare *you criticize—*

"Turn it off," I demanded, tensing myself to reach out and grab his phone if he refused.

"How could you Amanda? You promised you

were going to stop being a diva, but things have only gotten worse since you started this show. And I don't want to hear that none of that matters and that it's totally fine for you to act that way because you never wanted to do it in the first place. We didn't want to have Chelsea as early as we did, is that why you've been such a shit mom?"

"How dare you say that to me!"

"How dare you with all of this!"

More staring, more heavy breathing. Our chemistry was dead despite the live wire sparking between us.

"You wanted me to do the show and make it a hit, right? Well, there's no such thing as bad publicity, so maybe you should thank the Good Lord for answering your prayer."

"That's not—"

"I AM DOING EVERYTHING I CAN TO MAKE THIS FUCKING SHOW A SUCCESS WHILE PUTTING UP WITH YOUR JEALOUS BULLSHIT!"

Okay, that was way too loud.

Mike's withering glare made me melt back into the sofa.

He turned away in disgust and started narrating the comments under my meltdown, with analysis of his own. I watched him, saying nothing, knowing I'd start sobbing if I tried.

*Amanda's a fat skank.* "Despite her diva like attitude, I'd have to disagree. I think she's done an admirable job getting back in shape after having that matching set of children she didn't want. Especially considering all the alcohol and sugar she goes through when she's sad, which is most of the time since she has a bad habit of pissing everyone off."

*Wow. That bitch is mean.* "They're not wrong."

*She puts shit on her awkee mushrooms.* Mike shrugged. "That's barely even clever."

*Amanda Byrd is a whore bitch who needs someone's big fat cock shoved down her throat to keep her cunt mouth shut.* Mike looked up and into my eyes, gave me a crueler smile than I thought him capable of casting, and said, "Great publicity opportunity with that one. Maybe the network will make that the show's tagline."

*Amanda's a MILF I would totally tap … after I've smacked her up a bit to teach the bitch how to stay in her place.* "Sounds like a true fan, for sure."

*Early onset dementia? Ain't nothing early about it.*

"Please," I finally begged him, once the tears were already spilling. "We can fix this. I'll find out who leaked the video and get him fired. I can threaten to quit if they don't get rid of him."

Mike's expression melted from fury to something even more grotesque. Still angry, but now smoked with sorrow and disappointment in me. With the saddest little shake of his head he said, "I guess you'll never learn."

And then he walked away.

# TWENTY-SEVEN

# Noah

I'd been dying to see Amanda.

But this was a waiting game, and so far I was playing it well. Better than I ever had. Good enough to win.

And that would feel great because I sure as hell hadn't had enough of those in my life. After the front of my asshole father's body got turned into a bloody English Muffin during a drive-by, I brought my little sisters home to my crappy one bedroom. Slept on a futon in the living room so they could share the bedroom. Mina graduated high school, then went off to college on scholarship. Leah was in her junior year, working thirty hours a week to keep pace with tuition. I couldn't have been prouder of my sisters, but my deadbeat brothers could die after lunch and I wouldn't shed a tear before dinner.

Life didn't know how to smile for me. When it did it, it came in fits and starts. This time, I planned to make it last.

I went into the studio early, hoping to catch Amanda alone. I wasn't sure where we were at and wanted to ask her directly. She was probably feeling awful after that video went live. Chocolates and flowers, pasta and sauce — comfort for what was probably killing her. Yesterday I had to care from afar. Today I could do it up close.

But there was more I hoped to gain from the encounter. I needed to see if she had any idea I was the one to leak that video. Well, technically I'd paid a guy on TaskIt two-hundred bucks to get it going. That money would have been wasted if Amanda's performance hadn't virtually guaranteed a viral run. She wouldn't have any reason to think it was me, at least not outside our history. Certainly not from anything she'd witnessed, as I'd stowed my phone a moment before she turned. She wasn't paying attention to anyone other than Harris during her meltdown, and I was the only person in the room who'd looked at her with any compassion.

The presents on her doorstep hopefully helped to soothe things further.

I made certain that Michael Byrd and their offspring weren't home before I left them. Double-checked, then checked a third time.

Finally, I found her, but she wasn't alone. Amanda was yelling at Anderson, and I didn't need to be within earshot to know what the battle was about.

"—whoever is responsible for the link and fire them! I shouldn't have to ask you for this more than once, Anderson. You're right, there's nothing I can do about that video. It's out there, and I have to live with it. So I'm fine hating myself even more than I already do for however long it takes to live all of this down, which might be never. But you can at least show me that you care about what I'm going through by yanking the weed from our garden."

"Please Amanda," Anderson said in a perfectly level voice, "I want you to understand that I do care. And I'm showing you by making sure we leverage the opportunity presented to us."

"You mean an opportunity for you."

"For all of us. This is great publicity for the show. Definitely better than anything we've shot for *Chef Happens*."

"Thanks, Anderson. That feels great."

"You know it's true, Amanda. We've had one day of passable shooting, and it's still weird. There's the obvious crap between you and Harris, and then the other drama with your apprentice that makes a lot less sense. It's like you've forgotten how to be human."

Neither of them could see me from where I was standing, so I wasn't going anywhere.

Amanda said, "So I come to you with a problem, and your solution is to make me feel terrible about our show?"

"No, it's to assure that our show has finally found its feet. We'll figure out how to integrate the fight between you and Harris into a workable story line and into the promo shorts. Viewers are going to eat that shit up."

"You want to turn *Chef Happens* into a reality show?"

"It already is a reality show," Anderson said.

"You know what I mean. It's a cooking show. We're not *supposed* to have drama."

"I would have agreed before you proved you were only capable of creating that one kind of show."

"That's not fair," she argued. "Give me a chance to do better and——"

"You've had chances, Amanda. But you can't be counted on. Even if you have a great day, a bad one might be hiding right behind it. Same for your hours. If the situation is volatile, then fine. At least we know what to sell."

"No way. That was a discussion about Arrivé. Our restaurant. It has *nothing* to do with the show."

"What don't you understand about this?" Anderson took a moment to stare at Amanda, as if she might actually answer. Then he blew a gust of angry air through his lips. "When you're yelling at the top of your lungs in a room full of people, you lose all rights to call that a private conversation."

"I can't believe this," she said. "You don't care that someone on our set leaked that video? What if this had happened to you? Or someone else on the set?"

"That's the thing …" Harris waited a moment, looking at Amanda like he wanted her to get it. "That couldn't have happened to anyone else here."

Then he turned and walked away, giving me a vague nod as he hurried past.

Finally, my chance to soothe her pain. I placed a

gentle hand on Amanda's shoulder as I came up from behind.

She lurched away, whipped around. Her face said it all — she was clearly loath to see me. "What the hell do you want?"

"I wanted to see if you were okay." After a beat of nothing, I added, "So, are you?"

Amanda hissed like a cat, then snarled, "You went to my house. What were you thinking?"

"That you were under a terrible amount of stress and needed a little pick me up. You said nothing makes you feel better than chocolate, and the sadder you are, the more you need it. You also said good flowers are like good food, worth every penny although both are so fleeting. Said seeing them was a guaranteed hit of dopamine. The card was so you had a way to permanently remember the gesture."

"So that my husband could see it and totally lose his shit."

"It's not like I signed it."

"It's not like you needed to! What the hell is wrong with you?" Then Amanda lowered her voice, realizing this was already getting too loud, despite there being no one around.

She had missed me, after all.

"Noah, you're not stupid. So why are you acting that way? If a man puts chocolates, flowers, and a card on my front porch, then it means something."

"There was no indication of gender," I said, mostly to keep her hot. When she was angry, veins throbbed on her neck. And it turned me on.

"My husband could have found them first! What if I had been in the shower?"

"I can imagine that," I said, brushing Amanda with my eyes.

How could she still be in thrall with that man? He was everything I hated — slow-moving, complacent, and self-righteous about being a father. A guilt trip in Oxfords, dragging Amanda down, causing her to procrastinate on starting the bakery. Every time I'd tried talking about our future as famous pastry chefs, she'd changed the subject or said something non-committal. And it was always because she was cuffed to that fucker, Michael Byrd.

She'd left me with nothing and forced me to learn a new breed of patience. Now it was time to rise from the ashes.

"Your husband doesn't understand you. And Harris doesn't get you, either."

Amanda shook her head. "You don't understand me at all."

"But I do. And you can deny it out loud all you want, but we both know it's true."

"What is it you think you know about me?"

"That you're the best because you never let anything get in your way. That everything in life must follow your art."

"That isn't true," she protested. "At least, not anymore."

"But only because you're lying to yourself. Think about it. When did things start going down-hill for you? Last year, right after you traded me for a husband who doesn't appreciate you and started putting your restaurant second."

"Keep your voice down."

"It *is down*, Amanda. I'm practically whispering, and there's no one around. You're having a difficult time dealing with a few realities—"

"But my children—"

"What about your children?" I let the moment hang, keeping her curious. Everything was going well. She was only inches away from where I needed her to be. "What kind of example are you setting for your kids if you let yourself get dragged into a life of mediocrity by a selfish man who's terri-fied of getting lost in your shadow. Isn't it—"

"Don't you dare."

I hated the look on Amanda's face as her game went from defense to offense.

"You don't have any right to go there, Noah. *None.* You say whatever you need to *me.* But if you can't leave my husband out of it, then we're not discussing anything. At all. Ever. Do you understand me?"

Amanda looked at me like a teacher scolding a child, either not realizing or losing sight of the truth that I was the one with all the control.

"We should be together," I reminded her. "I'm better for you than he is in every imaginable way. I would never ask you to choose. Me and you, all the way to the top."

"You're crazy." She shook her head, but she couldn't keep me from seeing her trembling body.

I was finally under her skin, imagining what else I might grow there. I leaned in with a smile. "It's time to be brave, Amanda. To cut the dead weight loose."

Her posture straightened. Her hands clenched into fists at her side. "If you come anywhere near my family again, I'll kill your career and end your future in the same phone call. You're too ambitious for our own good. Go ahead and mess with my family. Then see what happens."

A smile, then, "So, can you help me out? Tell me what I'm doing wrong. I'm sure I can improve, though honestly, I'd rather not have to do it at all. Wouldn't everything be better if we got to the happily ever after right away, where the two of us are making nice like you know we eventually will."

"I'll call the police and get a restraining order. Put you down for good."

"That's a great idea," I said with a smile that she was slow to understand.

"I'll do it."

But then it finally dawned on her, the realization now appearing on her face. I'd known she'd have no leverage over me since scrawling my name on the contract. Even though she was clearly coming to understand what that meant, I spelled it out anyway, enjoying the horror of her sinking expression, the understanding like a shadow.

"A restraining order means we can't be on the show together, and I'm not planning on going anywhere. That makes it your forfeit, which means you'll have to give back everything you've been paid so far, plus a quarter million dollar penalty for breaking your contract."

She swallowed hard, her throat convulsing again, just like when she came.

Over and over and over.

I leaned close and whispered, "I'm never letting you go. There will be no one between us, not ever again."

And then I stood there in the silence, enjoying the timpani beat of her belligerent heart.

My heart was pounding so hard that Noah was sure to have heard it.

He was staring at me, daring me to say anything else. To challenge his authority or dominion over the moment.

I had to let him have it. Surrender the battle if I hoped to ever win the war. A terrible truth because a war would be hard to keep quiet. But that's what it was, and I could no longer doubt it.

Finally he walked away, leaving me frozen in place, terrified and alone, my hitching an echo in the empty studio. I needed to get to my dressing room. Hide inside so I could slowly recover.

I needed a plan. A recipe to make my way out of this. Problem was, Noah had claimed control of my kitchen. He had all the ingredients and controlled all he the burners. He could get to Mike, same as David and Chelsea.

An awful thought punched through my chest, pressing my heart into molé.

*What if Noah was willing to eliminate his competition?*

No. He couldn't possibly be that crazy.

Except maybe he was.

I was an idiot. I should have come clean with Harris already. I had my chance, I could have done it on day one, right in front of Dominic and Melinda when they introduced him as my apprentice for the show.

I'd made everything worse by not confessing it then, burying the problem until later so that it emerged from the soil, undead and festering, rancid and rotten. I could have explained the affair and told them I couldn't work with him because of our history. I would have been branded a cheater, but now I was something so much worse.

And I was trapped.

Unless I could come up with a quarter of a million dollars.

I waited an hour for Harris to show, still a good forty-five minutes before he needed to, waltzing on set with Emily on his arm. The studio was mostly full of its occupants for the day, and there was no way I could catch him or call out without making a scene. With things as brittle as they were between us, I waited for Harris to close his dressing room door before I looked around, made sure no one watching me, then walked right up and gave it my most assertive knock.

His fiancé opened the door.

"Hi, Emily, I was wondering if I could speak to Harris alone."

She didn't get the chance to answer before Harris was behind her, trying to shut the door in my face.

"I want to sell you my half of the restaurant," I blurted before he had a chance.

The door paused, halfway closed. "Why now?"

"You were right," I continued, grateful for the chance. "I've been a monster, and I'm sorry. I want to talk about you buying me out."

"So again, why now?"

Harris was listening and sounding reasonable. I finally had a chance. "Because I need the money."

"You don't need that much. You're a little upside-down, not—"

"No, I need it because I'll have to pay the termination penalty for quitting *Chef Happens*."

"What?" Harris never saw it coming, and he sure as hell didn't like it. "Why would you do that?"

"You and Noah can have the show. I'm done with it."

"No way," Harris said, shaking his head almost violently.

"I mean it."

Harris glared at me. "I'm sure you do. For whatever reason, you've found something better, and you're off to that. But you need my permission, and you're not about to get it."

"Why not?"

"Because as much as it pains me to say it, you're the one they want. I'm the sidekick, Amanda. Not the talent. There's no show without you."

I shoved my foot past the threshold to stop him from slamming the door in my face. "Harris, *please.*"

He stopped trying to shut me out but did nothing to slow his assault. "I don't need you to buy me out anymore, Amanda. I found someone to do it. Like I've been begging you to do for years."

"What?" I couldn't believe it. "You can't do that without my approval!"

"Fortunately for one of us, I checked with my lawyer. Turns out, I can. Got an offer from Micah Myles this morning, and I'm taking it."

"You've gotta be kidding me."

Harris offered me his coldest smile, which made me lose every ounce of my shit.

"What the fuck, Harris?" I screeched. "Why don't you just sell your half to Applebee's?"

"I am not going to miss this. At all."

"Let's talk this through. You can't seriously—"

"That's the problem, Amanda. You don't take anything I say seriously. You've given me none of the credit and all of the shit for the past fifteen years. No more. I'm done."

"But—"

"I'm contractually obligated to speak to you when we're on set. That doesn't mean I have to waste a second of my off-time on you."

And then Harris finally managed to slam the door in my face.

## TWENTY-EIGHT

## Amanda

I needed my restaurant to soothe me.

Worse than being trapped, I was stuck in someone else's kitchen as a fire raged out of control around me without any way out. Harris wasn't going to change his mind, though maybe that was for the best. If we couldn't be partners, then maybe that meant Arrivé could finally thrive. The place had been dying in a valley of compromise for years, with neither partner getting anything close to what we wanted. We weren't running Arrivé like my restaurant or like his, and so the place was a purgatory of concession for us both.

If Harris was really selling his half of the restaurant to Micah Myles, I'd have to build some heavy boundaries between us. Without having a plan in place, things would get even worse, fast. I had to claim control and maintain it. Show a new side of myself to the staff. Tap back into the me who'd made Arrivé a restaurant worth talking about, while heeding the lessons I'd learned throughout the last fifteen years of making mistakes.

But I was unsettled driving up to the restaurant. I could see the crowd from a block away, large and spreading. It looked like more than a hundred people, many holding signs suggesting a boycott of *Chef Happens* before it even aired. A trio of news vans were there to catch the demonstration on camera, so I could be humiliated later on TV.

Some of the signs had a point.

EVERYONE DESERVES RESPECT

YOU ARE NOT GOD, AMANDA BYRD

NO ONE WANTS A BITCH IN THEIR KITCHEN!

But others were mean and unnecessarily personal.

GET OUT OF THE KITCHEN AND INTO THERAPY NOW!

COOKED BY KARMA. AMANDA BYRD IS FINISHED.

WARNING: EVEN YOUR FAMILY HATES YOU.

When I told Mike there was no such thing as bad publicity, I couldn't have imagined this.

The old me would have confronted the entire situation with my head held high. Shamed the abominable crowd into leaving me the hell alone. Cut through the horde like a hot knife through butter, making it clear to anyone watching that I considered every critic beneath me, knowing the truth and throwing it in their faces — their biggest talent was casting judgment on mine.

But the old me was either dead or dying because I was gripping the steering wheel, white-knuckled, terrified even if I didn't want to admit it. There was no way I could get out of the car, let alone push my way through the crowd.

I wondered why there weren't any police. Surely there should be with a crowd already so large and obviously swelling. Maybe I should call them. I glanced at my phone on the passenger seat and wondered what I would say. The protesters weren't doing anything violent, holding their sings and chanting words I couldn't hear with my windows rolled up, though I could read a few lips and had to ignore the chills as they filled me.

I parked across the street like a coward, then killed the engine, grabbed my phone, and Googled *Arrivé.*

No surprise, the protest was all over the news, and it wasn't about the restaurant so much as it was all about me.

But not in the way I wanted.

Not in the way *anyone* would have wanted.

There wasn't much to the story yet, so every link I clicked was pretty much the same, each one claiming the kitchen staff at Arrivé was over the moon because Harris had removed me from my position as head chef. It was insulting and ridiculous. The articles were making it sound like he fired me, when Harris only hired Regina to cover my shifts while *Chef Happens* was getting shot. That didn't mean that I had been replaced and …

It had never been harder to keep from crying.

I cracked the window for air, sucked a gust of it through my teeth, still inches from the tears, staring out at the crowd and wondering what to do.

The thought of driving away in defeat carved my insides like a paring knife. But my knees were shaking and my breath was hitching at the thought of leaving my car and walking into the restaurant.

Was I in physical danger? Would the defiant

horde keep chanting their slander or part like a hostile sea allowing my passage? I turned from the window to my phone, clicking on something else to read. A new comment from Gina Delicious.

*No wonder my meal was so awful. How can anyone expect the kitchen staff to do a good job when they're stuck in such a hostile work environment?*

I sat in my car, thinking about how much a broken heart was like a bad tooth, rotting with a dull ache that refused to leave, barring a sufferer from smiles, keeping them awake, and filling their waking life with long echoes of inescapable pain.

Life as I knew it was over, and there was nothing I could do to salvage what I had already lost.

Arrivé was my biggest success, and now there was a large crowd loudly declaring it my biggest failure. My entire career had tanked because of one stupid video where I lost my temper in front of a crowd.

Our TV show was a nightmare. I thought I could stick it out a season, take the money to replenish our savings and open Bake it Away. But now I was buried beneath the brutal reality of what my life had become, rattling the bars of my cell without hope of ever seeing the other side. I had no way to get the quarter of a million dollars required to buy my way out of the situation — I didn't even have enough to repay what I'd already been given. We'd spent it all, clearing a few credit cards and next semester's tuition at Constellation.

Noah was clearly determined to ruin my marriage, and if I told Mike that I'd had an affair …

I couldn't keep it a secret any longer. Telling my husband about my unforgivable transgression was the only thing that might save me. Because it wasn't a matter of *if* Noah would spill the beans about our affair, it was a matter of *when*, and that meant that I needed the guts to do it first.

But Mike was so mad at me already, I could easily see this being the final straw.

From the corner of my eye, I saw someone who looked like Noah wading through the sea of protesters.

I looked closer, tasting something terrible in my mouth, drawing conclusions with the dull nubbin of a pencil in my mind, looking for the rhyme or reason amid the confusion and chaos.

Did he organize the protest? If so, I would probably kill him. That fucking little—

No, it wasn't him. Just another twenty-something with the same build and a similar thatch of shiny chestnut hair.

Willing to kill another couple of minutes before making a move, I checked my phone again. I wanted to leave without feeling defeat.

A firm knock on the window caught me by surprise. I looked over to see a cop with the corners of his mouth turned down in a frown. He motioned for me to lower my window.

"Yes, officer?"

"I'm sorry, ma'am, but I'm going to have to ask you to leave."

"Why?" I asked, even though I'd been about to go. "This is my restaurant."

"Yes, ma'am. I'm aware. You need to leave for your own safety. We're about to clear these protestors, and it could get violent."

"That's her!"

The first yell was followed by a second, louder one. "It's Amanda Fucking Byrd!"

The cop turned from me to the crowd, so I could only imagine his eyes widening at the approaching mass. Without another word to me, he marched forward, moving to intercept the nearest protestors.

Riddled with panic, I gunned the engine then

tore into the street. Dozens of angry objectors shook their fists behind me.

My heart wouldn't stop pounding, and tears fell fast from both of my eyes.

Was this what my new life was going to be like?

And was there any escape?

## TWENTY-NINE

# Noah

I never wanted to leave this place.

The Shellys had invited me over to their home. When I arrived, they led me outside. Dominic gestured to a trio of empty seats around a small table on a spare yet somehow elaborate deck, allowing me to choose. I sat with my back to their mansion so I could fix my gaze on the infinity pool and the dazzling vista beyond it, enjoying the most stunning back yard I'd ever seen.

"Thank you for meeting me," I said.

Dominic sat on my left, Melinda to my right.

She took a sip of her ice water, three glasses on the table and no server in sight, then set down the drink with a delicate little laugh. "Did you expect us to refuse you?"

"No, but I didn't expect to come here. To your house."

"That was Dominic's idea," Melinda admitted.

"It's where we're most comfortable. And besides, I always think it's a good idea to have business meetings someplace aspirational. My wife and I have never done anything in this life that couldn't have been accomplished by someone else. Seeing what others have earned always inspires me to think about what I could go out and get for myself."

Melinda playfully rolled her eyes, as though she had heard her husband's micro speech too many times before.

"So, what's on your mind? Are you happy?" Dominic picked up his glass, crossed his legs, and gave me a knowing smile. "Thinking about the things you could go out and get for yourself?"

"I guess you could say that." I laughed, a little uncomfortable. It almost felt like that was exactly what they wanted, despite their manners and pomp. "I mean, I love being on the show, and I'm grateful for the opportunity ..."

"*But*," Melinda prompted.

"But I could do more."

"Like?" Dominic said.

"I have a great idea for another show. A better show."

Melinda narrowed her eyes. "You mean better than the one we haven't finished shooting?"

"The one that has a lot more problems than either one of us would like," Dominic added.

Then another from Melinda. "Or expected."

Dominic nodded. "But go ahead and tell us your idea."

"It's a cooking show for singles." I waited a second to study their faces. Liked what I saw and continued. "I could teach single women to cook gourmet meals for one."

The Shellys were interested, both of them leaning ever so slightly forward.

"How is it different?" Melinda wanted to know.

"There are already plenty of shows on the air that women watch because they're tired of soup. *Chef Happens* is one among many. This show is something different."

"We've established that," Dominic said, starting to look impatient.

"Sorry," I said, trying not to get flustered, especially right before I had to spill the most important part. "We're not selling the food, so much as the sex."

Together, the Shellys said, "The *what?*"

"The sex," I repeated, much stronger the second time. "On the surface we would have a strong feminine message. *You don't need to wait for a man to take you out to an amazing meal. Sisters can do it for themselves.* But at the same time, we would have a show appealing to their baser instincts. Meals will be romantic, same for the setting. We'll invite attractive guests to cook with me."

"You think highly of yourself," Dominic said.

"Don't you want me to?"

"Absolutely." Melinda was beaming.

"This is good TV." I looked from one Shelly to the other, offering each mogul my most confident smile. "Most of my viewers will be lonely women who are more interested in fantasizing about having me as a meal than they will be in preparing one for themselves."

"Again," Dominic said, without sounding disapproving, "it's good that you're secure with yourself, but you'll want to keep that arrogance away from the cameras and turn it way the hell down if you're ever being interviewed."

I nodded. "I will."

Melinda turned to Dominic and started talking to her husband like I wasn't even there.

"It's perfect for Juke."

Dominic shook his head. "It's too early for Juke."

"There is no *too early*, Dominic. We can bank content."

"It's ahead of schedule. We're supposed to see how this plays out, not grab the next shiny thing. We've talked about this."

"And what was our conclusion? That nothing is definite, and the future is always in flux." Melinda turned to me without waiting for her husband's response. "What's happening with Amanda? We saw the video. Looks like you've done an admirable job of driving a wedge between the partners—"

"Like a devious little shit," Dominic cut in.

"—but we haven't seen anything in the way of a romance between you two for the first season, and we were counting on that as the hook in all of our promo."

Dominic shook his head. "No matter how viral that video might be, it isn't the same."

"Isn't all publicity good publicity?"

"There's a line, and we've yet to see if Amanda has crossed it," Melinda said. "The audience will let us know, but in either case, it isn't what we wanted."

"What went wrong there?" Dominic asked.

"I've been trying, but nothing seems to work."

And Melinda asked, "If you can't accomplish the first thing we asked you to do, what makes you think that you have any hope for the second?"

I had to pretend that the question didn't upset me. "It's apples and orange juice. In one situation, I have all of the control and willing participants. In the other, it's all stacked against me."

"At the risk of being painfully blunt," Dominic said, clearly about to be, "that sounds like something a loser would say."

Taking a sip of water bought me a moment to think. "I've been trying, but I don't have control over another person's response. Especially when she's married."

I waited a beat to see if either of them had anything to add, wondered if I should mention the ethics of what we were discussing, determined there were too many landmines in that particular conversation, then finally said, "It's been difficult getting Amanda to warm up. She's still always professional, even when I'm flirting with her. It's only a matter of time before she responds. I'm under her skin in a serious way."

I leaned forward, making the Shellys want to hear what I had to say next. In a conspiratorial voice, I added, "You didn't hear it from me, but Amanda's marriage is totally falling apart. You're going to have all the drama you want soon enough."

"What makes you think we want any drama?" Melinda asked.

"Isn't that exactly what you wanted?" I said, slightly confused.

Dominic shook his head, but he was looking at his wife instead of me. "He doesn't get it."

"No," she agreed. "I don't think that he does."

"I'm right here. What don't I get?"

Melinda said, "We want suggestion and innu-endo, not a marriage broken up because of our show."

"I'm sorry. I misunderstood."

"We do like your idea. For the new show, and where we can take it." She shook her head. "But we only have so much money allocated to this part of Shellter Productions. Every episode we shoot for *Chef Happens* means less money in the overall budget for your new project. All the money for this is coming from the same limited pool."

"So what are you saying?" I asked.

Dominic stared at him. "If you're serious about

having your own show, then you have some work to do."

"What do I have to do? I'll do anything."

"Step it up with the seduction, son." He grinned. "Whatever you're doing, it isn't enough."

"Tell me what to do and I'll do it."

"Really, Noah?" Melinda gave me a knowing smile.

It rankled that I didn't have a clue what she was suggesting. But I was left with no other recourse than to admit it. "I'm sorry, but I don't understand."

"How long have you known Amanda?" Dominic asked.

The words were trapped in my throat. Lying felt like my saving grace, and the rope I might swing by.

"Noah?" Melinda pressed.

"Since last year."

"Elaborate," Dominic said.

"We met last year while I was still working at the Milano. She and her husband were on a break, so she was staying there. I already knew her by reputation, so I couldn't believe it when she came back into my kitchen to give me a compliment. We got along well, and yeah, we had an affair. It started right away. We cooked together every day for nearly a month. But we're close now, and I have her on the ropes. I can close the deal in another three episodes. Once her husband kicks her out, and I'm certain he will, she'll be vulnerable again, like she was when I first met her."

I stopped. The Shellys were looking at me with matching smiles.

"Why are you looking at me like that?" I asked.

And Dominic said, "Because that's what we've been waiting for."

# THIRTY

# Amanda

Sitting in the principal's office was only slightly better than sitting out in front of my restaurants while a crowd of protestors rattled their pitchforks and let the world know exactly how much they hated me.

Chelsea was definitely my daughter, the way she was pressed into her seat two feet away from me, her heels hard on the carpet, arms crossed across her chest, an unrepentant scowl creasing her face and yanking the corners of her mouth into a serious frown.

Principal Kirk was the kind of smug, self-righteous person I could never understand. Yes, I had a temper and yelled in the kitchen. But I said what I meant, and meant what I said. People could trust that I was always honest, never dressed my insults as compliments, and despite my abundance of overly colorful words, I didn't enjoy taking anyone down just for the sport of it. Principal Kirk clearly didn't feel the same way.

She sat there, looking at me like I was a sweet and salty dessert. "We cannot tolerate tantrums here at Constellation. That sort of primitive behavior is simply not allowed."

"*Primitive behavior?*" I repeated. "Isn't that a little over the top?"

"No, Ms. Byrd, I don't believe it is. Being elite means we have a standard to uphold. I am quite sure that you understand what that means, to stand strongly for values and virtue." She took a moment to wrinkle her nose, just enough to let Chelsea and me participate in her displeasure. "Yet there is a code of conduct we must respect while in pursuit of those standards. Do you understand what I am saying?"

"I think so. But you're taking an awfully long time to say it."

Kirk took another moment to straighten the perfect rectangle of papers in front of her before gracing the Byrd girls with more of her admonishment.

"Chelsea threw a tantrum today because she didn't want to take a nap."

This was exhausting. "Yes, my daughter threw a tantrum. I'm sorry she acted like a five-year-old girl."

"Your tone is inappropriate, Ms. Byrd. Chelsea is clearly in the wrong here."

"And that's why I'm here. But I'd like to talk about the problem instead of being told that my daughter is primitive, while you sit there talking about her like she isn't even in the room. I don't believe she's the only five year old to ever throw a tantrum. So, is this about her temper or mine?"

"Interesting that you should ask. I believe it has to do with both." The principal gave me another thin-lipped smile.

"What's that supposed to mean?"

"Chelsea referred to her teacher as an incompetent moron who 'doesn't have the sense to grease a gimlet.' So you can see where I might fairly make an assumption about where your daughter has learned her behavior."

Principal Kirk was clearly delighted by whatever variety of shock was painting my face. She neatened her razor-straight papers again, cast a withering glance at Chelsea, then continued. "After her outburst, she threw her pillow at Mrs. Rasmussen. Then she ran from the room, kicking another student who was lying down on the way out—

"That was an accident, dummy!"

I gasped. "Chelsea! Apologize to Principal Kirk."

But Chelsea said nothing.

"*Now.*"

"NO!"

Mortified, I leaned over and whispered to Chelsea. "*Please don't embarrass me. I need you to—*"

"Stop talking to me!"

Chelsea yanked herself away from me then scooted her chair an inch or two from mine. She crossed her arms even harder, then started growling through her teeth like a feral dog.

I took a deep breath and turned to the principal. "I'm so sorry. I don't know what's gotten into her. I'll make sure she gives you an apology tomorrow. Same for Mrs. Rasmussen, and everyone else who had to be around my daughter's awful behavior. I promise to do a better job. Pay attention to the ways I'm being a negative influence. We'll fix this. You have my word."

"I'm afraid it isn't that simple, Ms. Byrd."

"What do you mean?"

I knew what she meant, but dammit, I was going to make her say it.

"When I explained to Chelsea that speaking to other people like that was wrong, she told me it wasn't. She said that her mommy told her that was how you got to the top." Kirk leaned forward. "I am glad you understand your role in this, Ms. Byrd, but I am also afraid you are unclear on how deep it has gone."

"It's not like I teach her to throw tantrums. I said I was sorry, and I promised to fix this."

"By now, we've all seen the example you're setting for Chelsea at home." And the principal offered yet another smile to slay me.

The video. Of course.

Defensiveness wouldn't make the situation any better. So, I looked Kirk right in her piercing green eyes. After a hard swallow, I said, "I sincerely regret my outburst. I had no idea I was being recorded."

"So, you're sorry you were *caught*."

The way she said *caught* made me want to see Kirk catch herself falling off the end of a dock.

"No, I'm sorry about the whole thing. That was supposed to be a private moment between my partner and myself."

"A private moment? In the middle of a crowded room?"

I was really trying not to lose my shit. "I guess I got carried away."

"Is that how we can assume you would have behaved if you were behind closed doors with your partner, then?"

"Who's *we*?" I couldn't help it.

Principal Kirk continued to stare at me.

Chelsea stayed in the seat next to me, arms like a pretzel.

"My partner and I have a long history, and things haven't been going well between us. Clearly they were spiraling out of control."

"Or perhaps they had already spiraled." The principal pursed her lips and primly shook her head. "Here at Constellation, we only accept a certain caliber of student. When we admitted Chelsea, we believed she belonged here.

"You can't punish Chelsea for my mistake. That isn't fair."

"Chelsea will be suspended for three days. Then, if she returns to school with a full recognition and acknowledgment of where she has erred and who she has wronged, she may have another chance to prove she's Constellation material. And I believe that is *more than* fair."

I was floored. She was a kindergartner, and they were giving her a sentence and probation on the first offense? This was the last thing I needed. Same for Mike and our marriage. I might be looking at the one accidental ingredient that ruined the dish.

"We've given you well over a hundred-thousand dollars for elementary education in the last few years alone. And it'll be almost half a million by the time we're out of here, if you don't raise your rates. So—"

"I am sorry to interrupt you, Ms. Byrd—"

No, she wasn't.

"—but you have given us exactly the same amount of tuition as every other non-scholarship student here at Constellation." Then after a priggish beat, the principal added, "The same amount that everyone on the waiting list for this institution is also willing to pay."

I couldn't fault her for any of that. It was how I would have responded to anyone bitching about the prices on my menu. It was everything else I had a problem with. This self-important puritan wanted to put the point of her witch's boot up a five year old's ass for having *one tantrum?* It wasn't like we'd ever been called into her office before.

Mike's voice rang through my mind. His disappointment was too bitter to let him yell at me. Instead, he used his crestfallen drawl to tell me it was all my fault. I was turning Chelsea into a monster and ruining her future with my treacherous present.

No, I couldn't say any of what I wanted to say to Principal Kirk. Even if I trusted myself to keep my temper in check, articulate myself perfectly, and get out every word without raising my voice or saying anything wrong, Principal Kirk didn't want to hear what I had to say, so any attempt I made would only make things worse.

I held out my hand for Chelsea and looked over with eyes that begged her to take it.

She filled my heart when she did.

Then I turned back to the principal. "Thank you for giving my daughter a chance to apologize."

But then Chelsea muttered, "I'll never apologize."

My stomach dropped, the tips of my toes started grinding into the floor of my shoe, and my fingernails dug crescents into my palms. I looked at Kirk in defeat. "We'll see you in three days."

I scooped a thrashing Chelsea into my arms, carried her to the door, opened it with one hand, then left the principal's office before my life could get a molecule worse.

Even though I recognized my part in the matter, Chelsea had me so furious, I couldn't talk to her or even look at her. I turned on some Beethoven and let him try to convince me that everything was going to be okay.

"Can we make cookies when we get home?"

*No, we can't make cookies when we get home. Are you fucking kidding me?*

"We're not going home."

"Where are we going?"

*I'm dropping you off, then I'm screaming my goddamned head off in the car from Krystal's all the way to the studio before I buckle up for more bullshit.*

"I'm taking you to Krystal's. She needs to watch you until I'm done at work."

"No! I don't want to be babysat. I want to stay with you!"

I took a deep breath, then got it over with. "Did you see the video of Mommy yelling at Harris?"

*Did you see the video of Mommy being a total fucking cunt?*

"Yes."

"I was being mean to my friend. I was doing a bad thing that I never should have done, and that got me into a lot of trouble. A lot like the trouble you're in at school."

"Did you have to apologize?"

I felt like rotten meat when I told her the truth. "No, I didn't. But I will, because when we're mean to someone else, it's our job to make it up to them."

"Why is that our job?" Chelsea asked.

"Because even when we disagree with someone, we still have to be reasonable."

Mocking laughter, like church bells in shadows, bonged and echoed between my ears.

*When have you ever cared about being reasonable?*

*You've always used your drive as an excuse to roll over whoever you wanted.*

*You think being the best means behaving like you're better than everyone else.*

*And all the people in your life are sick of it.*

*Now,* I told myself. *I cared about it now. And would forever.*

"Chelsea, we both need to say we're sorry to all the people we were mean to."

"If I have to."

She was too much like me in all the wrong ways,

so no one in the world could do more than me to make her better.

"You do." I put a hand on her shoulder. "Me, too."

"Then can we make cookies?"

"Yes," I said, surprised to feel the smile on my face. "Then we can make cookies."

Chelsea clapped and squealed like the happy little girl I had kept her from being. "I wanna eat pecan sandies!"

*Sounds great. But first, we have to eat crow.*

THIRTY-ONE

# Noah

I was almost outside myself, looking around the room.

The mood was thick enough to slice and serve on a bed of mashed potatoes. Me, Harris, and Amanda. Anderson and the producers. Dominic and Melinda. Key staff. We were all sitting around a table, and not a single person looked anywhere near happy.

Normally in situations like that, where it feels like I can sort of see outside myself, I'm more in touch with who I am. It's in life's most terrifying moments where we discover ourselves, and it's a place I've always been willing to go. But I'd never felt like this, skirting the edge of something so unexpectedly awful.

Falling from the lip of enlightenment into a pit of despair.

And that's where I was, drowning in liquid disappointment, gasping for a breath of hope.

Dominic drained the final drop, summing it up in a single, devastating sentence. "We've run the first few episodes through a focus group, and the reaction is nowhere close to what the network was hoping. The show is totally broken, and if we can't find a way to put it back together, then the project as we know it is dead."

He looked to Melinda.

She added, "And we should also ask ourselves if we want to. If the juice is worth the squeeze."

Dominic nodded.

I was thoroughly unnerved. Raw batter refusing to cook.

The show's success was supposed to be a sure thing. Everyone agreed. It had the perfect ingredients and a foolproof process. Amanda's previous success with Arrivé, her relentless pursuit of perfection, and her unwillingness to settle for anything less than the best, not to mention the Shellys, who were apparently architects at building successful careers. Even after Amanda's meltdown, Anderson said it was something they could use. And he was still desperately fighting for it now.

"Isn't there any way to repurpose the footage? Maybe as a documentary of a project gone awry?" Anderson buried his forehead in his palm. "I'm not even kidding."

"We could repackage it," Dominic said, "But why would we do that? Hey, here's a bunch of shit that nobody liked with a different coat of paint."

Anderson looked up. "We can tell any story in editing that we want. So let's tell a different story. Have you ever seen that documentary about the first cut of *Star Wars*?"

"Who hasn't?" Dominic scoffed. "This is hardly the same thing. *Star Wars* was a game changer by putting old things in a new context. This is only a game changer in the context of something else."

Anderson sighed, sounding exhausted. "I don't even know what that means."

Neither did I, nor anyone else in the room judging by the looks on everyone's faces.

"Dominic means we need to make a hard right or crash into a wall," Melinda said. "We had hundreds of protestors show up outside of Amanda's restaurant. Not commenting trolls online, but real people, who had to get in their cars, drive across town, pay for parking, then spend their time protesting. It takes a lot to inspire that kind of ire, and any time you have one group so deeply rattled, you have another ready to yank their chains. We can leverage this attention, but not until we start thinking in different direction."

Amanda looked miserable and ashamed. Completely deflated. But she didn't open her mouth or protest at all.

"So," said one of the producers, "any ideas for how we can *start thinking in different direction?*"

Dominic and Melinda traded an almost imperceptible smile that I managed to catch while the room traded ideas ranging from decent to terrible.

One of the nameless staff suggested themed episodes.

Anderson wondered aloud, "What about celebrity recipes?"

Versions of *that's been done* rumbled around the room.

He continued, "Well, yeah, it's all been done. But we can make it more personal. Because we still have the Byrd name brand to incorporate if we can. It can be a sort of chef-to-the-stars thing. We'll have celebrities tell Amanda what their favorite recipes are, then she'll cook her version of them. If she doesn't know how to make a certain dish, she can make something up. Then our celebrities can taste and review her version of the recipe."

"Absolutely not!" Amanda finally spoke, obviously offended.

Despite the room's mood, the live show was admittedly fun to watch.

Melinda asked Amanda what she didn't like about the idea, her voice an indication that she actually cared.

"*Chef Happens* was pitched to me as platform to highlight my recipes and what made them special, not as a forum for C-level celebrities to critique my cooking."

"Who said anything about C-level celebrities?" asked one of the producers.

"Have you seen any other kind on a cooking show?" said another.

"We can help with that," Dominic offered, "but only if the idea is solid, and I'm not sure that this one is."

"Agreed," Melinda nodded.

"I don't like it." Amanda shook her head, but she sounded like she was trying her best to be reasonable.

"You don't get a vote!" Anderson snapped,

probably more bitter than he meant to. But he repeated himself. "You don't get a vote. You're the reason we're all in this room looking for a way to change things!"

Amanda looked furious, but she bottled her response.

I said, "How about we turn it into a reality cooking show?"

The producers and miscellaneous staff all seemed interested, and Anderson leaned forward in his seat.

"What do you mean, specifically?" Dominic asked.

"I'm not sure, *exactly*, but it seems like we can all agree that our strength isn't in cutting this like a regular show. For better or worse, there's definitely some volatility on-set, and a public perception of Amanda that we should be leaning into."

I took a moment to glance at my mentor. Sure enough, it looked like she wanted to kill me where I stood, though chewing her bottom lip to raw sausage was about as close as she'd come to making a stand in this room.

"Does that mean we would have to do the show live?" Harris sounded curious more than concerned.

"We wouldn't have to," said one of the producers, "but I love the idea. We could make the show a little rough around the edges. Because sometimes things go wrong in the kitchen, and this is how a fast-thinking chef like Amanda Byrd is able to fix them on the fly."

"I could definitely see that working," Anderson said. "Are we talking about a season arc where we're following the story of Harris, Amanda, and their apprentice? Or do we think the show would be better shot an episode at a time and see what happens as we go along?"

Someone, I wasn't sure who, said, "Same as any other reality show. We shoot the whole thing at once, then find the through-line once we're finished."

"I have an idea." Dominic took a moment to revel in the room's immediate silence. Everyone watched him expectantly, though Amanda was the only one who had any terror on her face.

"No disrespect whatsoever," Dominic gave an apologetic glance to Harris, "but I see this working best as a two-person show. We never address what happened between Amanda and her partner behind the scenes. Let the press and viewers speculate. Wondering is chum for ratings. But we can definitely crank up the chemistry between our apprentice and her mentor."

"There isn't any 'chemistry' between us," Amanda said.

But Dominic ignored her. "That's what people will want to see, so let's give them that. We can call the show *The Mentor Chef* or something like that. Noah can be her apprentice this first season, but if it works, she'll get another one for year two. The focus is always on the student in a show like that, but we'll put our emphasis on the teacher. We give Amanda highly qualified students, then we see if she pushes them into being the best or breaks them into pieces."

The room was definitely interested, as twitters and questions were rippling through it.

Amanda looked like she was about to crack in half.

I was beyond elated. There might have been a better way to reveal our affair to Michael Byrd than on live television with millions of people watching, but I had no idea what that might be.

Amanda's public death would be perfect.

Then our private life could begin.

THIRTY-TWO

# Amanda

We were filming our first live episode, and I'd never been more miserable.

I never wanted to do *any* version of the show, but especially not one where I was so obviously the punchline, where the purpose of each broadcast was to humiliate me in some way.

We were supposed to be making a pan-roasted fish fillet with herb butter. A relatively simple recipe with a straightforward execution.

Pat the fillets dry.

Season on both sides with salt and pepper.

Put a cast iron skillet on high heat then add the oil.

Place the fillets into the skillet, skin down and kissing the metal.

Lower the heat and let the fish sizzle until golden and caramelized around the edges.

Flip the fillets, adding butter and thyme to the pan, tilting it to let the butter pool at one end.

Use a spoon to baste the fish until it's fully cooked through, crispy and golden and ready to plate.

Something was seriously wrong with me.

I was scorched rice at the bottom of the pot. Parmesan in a can. Burned garlic. Over-boiled eggs.

Because I'd been floating through life for a while, secrets fermenting inside me and dying to get out while their host was too petrified to let them, I was now unable to focus. Might as well have been the apprentice and Noah my mentor. He radiated confidence beside me. Repeated my directions in a velvety voice then executed them perfectly, taking turns between throwing his smile at me and the camera.

Anderson asked Noah to suggest a recipe he wanted me to teach him, as leading with his selection might make for a better first show. But the director had no idea that the pan-roasted fillet with herb butter that we were making was the dish I'd been eating at the Milano when I went back into the kitchen, complimented the chef, then pulled the trigger on the biggest mistake of my life.

Either one of us could make the dish with our eyes closed, but I was nervous and screwing it up. My hands were shaking so badly that I over salted the fish, then I nearly dropped the salt shaker while I was setting it back into place on the counter.

I should have been demonstrating for the audience I kept forgetting we had, and Noah smiled wider every time he had to pick me up live. Meanwhile, I pretended I couldn't hear the quiet cackles from the crew. Told myself that they were laughing at someone else.

Noah asked me a question, but I didn't quite catch it, so he grabbed the skillet, flipped the fish, then tilted it so the camera could see how golden his fish was getting.

"That's what we want, that gorgeous golden brown." And then, as if Noah remembered I was supposed to be the boss, he turned from the invisible viewers to me. "Isn't that right, Amanda?"

Noah didn't wait for my answer. He started dramatically sniffing, first with a light twitching of his nose, but then a deep inhale followed by a clear look of sudden panic.

Then he was like a cartoon, leaving the ghost of a dust cloud in the shape of his body behind.

Noah bolted to the oven, threw open the door, then pulled out a pan of smoking potatoes.

Because *of course* I forgot to set the timer.

So much for roasted — the reek of burning potatoes filled the studio. Hot and earthy, like yeast and cigarettes.

The cameras were all still rolling while the crew suppressed their laughter and I stood there like an idiot.

Noah was still in motion. He put the hot dish in the sink then ran cold water into it, making a flamboyant sizzle and a plume of steam. Then he turned to the camera. "Well, at least now we know how *not* to make roasted potatoes."

If there had been hemlock in front of me, I might have grabbed it. Dropping dead sounded like the perfect dessert to this moldering feast of a day. Of a week. A month. A year.

And all of it my fault.

I had never been so humiliated. And would have probably sold my soul for some Stoli.

An eon stretched between *potatoes* and *cut*.

The floor manager made the signal with his hands, taking us to commercial.

Assistants rushed in to arrange the bowls of ingredients we'd need for the upcoming segment — a chocolate-blood orange mousse with pistachio-studded shortbread. Did I still have time to die before we started rolling again? I would live in a one-bedroom studio and let the children have the bed if there's only one. If Mike would have me, I'd sleep with him on the couch.

I'd ruined everything, and I had no idea how to save this dish.

I didn't think it could get any worse, but then Noah's hand fell on the small of my back. I was too defeated to shrug him away. I felt overcooked and undernourished. Limp lettuce in rancid ranch.

How had it come to this? Everyone was avoiding my gaze, pretending they were busy and I wasn't trapped in my exhibit, a bitchy chef in her human zoo. The only one who wasn't feigning indifference was Harris, who took a few minutes to give me a glare icy enough to keep his shoulders permanently cold. He wouldn't acknowledge my presence, and I hadn't managed to get him alone so that I could apologize.

Noah, the man who was aggressively working to ruin my marriage, was the only one in the entire studio who wasn't either ignoring me or being actively cruel.

"Breathe." His voice was like cream in the cracks of my skin. Then softer he added, "You'll get the hang of it."

I was blinking back tears, as I couldn't afford to let a single one fall. "No, I won't."

It was barely a mutter.

Through a watery blur, I saw what might be salvation approaching — Dominic, a kind smile lighting his way.

"Would you mind giving us a moment?" He clapped Noah on the shoulder and waited.

It didn't look like he wanted to, but Noah said, "Certainly."

Dominic took me aside, into the shadows. "What's wrong?"

There was no accusation in his voice. He was concerned, his solicitous eyes piercing mine with obvious kindness.

"I'm sorry." I wiped my tears before I went on. "I haven't been sleeping well in the past few days, barely at all, and I've never done live TV. I thought it would be hard, and it's even harder than that."

"But there's more, isn't there, Amanda?"

"What do you mean?"

Dominic sighed, small and patient. "How are things at home?"

I took a breath, bit my lip, then let it go. "They've definitely been better."

He nodded knowingly. "I'm sure that's getting in your head, all of that judgment."

I might have flinched.

Dominic put a gentle hand on my elbow. Thoughtful more than affectionate. "You're terrified of being live because if you make a mistake, it's out there forever. Everyone will see it. There are no do-overs. And for a perfectionist, there are few things more frightening. No wonder you're paralyzed!"

It was like rain after a drought to know that someone understood.

"Everyone is going to hate this show. The ratings will be terrible."

"Oh, not at all," Dominic said, sounding as surprised as he suddenly looked. "This is gold. Ratings *and* conversation. People are going to love watching this show, just to see what you're going to screw up next."

He didn't say it to sound mean. It was perfectly matter of fact. But my humiliation was complete, and I couldn't pretend that it wasn't a slap to the face. A swift and vicious kick to my ego. Deserving or not, it had stolen my wind. I was a punchline. The best possible scenario for my show was that I kept viewers tuning in, not to see what they could learn from me next, but so that they could laugh at me.

I was supposed to be a teacher, but instead I was a clown.

"Please, Mr. Shelly, if we could go back to recording the show ahead of time, I promise that I can—"

"Dominic, please, Amanda. And that isn't going to happen. We know what this show is now."

"But I can't sleep!"

"That's not a problem. Would you like a prescription for Ambien?"

I looked at him blankly, unable to believe what was happening.

"Something stronger?" Dominic looked at me back, neither one of us blinking. "Let me know."

The floor manager yelled, "Thirty seconds!"

Dominic winked and walked away.

I stood there, staring out at a sea of contempt and indifference.

Except for Harris and Noah.

Harris was glaring. Noah's lips looked freshly licked.

My entire life was on fire.

Maybe that explained the taste of ashes in my mouth.

I was in my dressing room, taking off the clothes that made me look like someone I wasn't, while trying not to cry.

I'd never wanted to franchise Arrivé because that always felt like selling out, and yet I had somehow ended up with something much worse. Reality TV represented a lot of what I thought was wrong with the modern world. Nothing but empty calories. I hated it deeply, and now I was a part of it.

Television was for entertainment, I understood that. And there was plenty to be entertained by. I couldn't keep up with the stuff I really wanted to see. I had no idea how anyone would ever make time for reality TV. The little I'd seen was terrible.

The Shellys had an eye for quality film and television, and by all accounts were putting together one hell of a portfolio. Not only did they work with some of Hollywood's finest, they nurtured some of its most promising careers. I had no idea what they were doing bottom feeding with this particular bullshit.

Every show needed an enemy and a village idiot. Now the Shellys were building a brand around both.

Reality television had to be over-dramatized because otherwise there was no reason for people to watch. It degraded society because society wanted to watch the most degrading parts. Now I was the butt of this joke and part of the cancer.

Down to my bra and panties, I ran out of energy. It was the first I felt like me, even if just a little bit, and I needed a moment to cry. To get it all out before getting dressed.

There was a knock on my door. It swung open without my consent.

"What the fuck are you doing?" I yelled at Noah.

I was already breathing too hard. What if someone saw him coming in and told Mike?

Or filmed it and put it on LiveLyfe or YouTube?

"I wanted to talk."

I grabbed my shirt and covered myself as best I could. "Get the hell out of here, NOW!"

"You probably don't want to scream. Someone might come in and get the wrong idea."

"I'm not kidding, Noah."

"Does it look like I think you are?" Then, smirking — and maybe leering — he said, "I don't see what the big deal is. Nothing I haven't seen before."

"You have five seconds. Five ... four ..."

"It doesn't have to be like this."

"It's your fault it's like this!" I wanted to spit, throw my T-shirt at Noah, slap him, tackle him, punch him bloody. But I sat there heaving instead, impotent, powerless to do anything in my bra and panties, terrified that at any moment someone would walk in and ruin my life even more than it already was.

"Really, Amanda?" He looked at me stone-faced. "It's *all* my fault? You don't see any way that you might be even the teensiest bit responsible?"

Without giving Noah an answer, I walked over to my robe, grabbed it, then tried but failed to maintain my dignity while slipping it over my shoulders.

Even after tying the belt in a knot, I still felt just as naked.

"What will it take to make you go away?"

"What will it take to make you want me to stay?" Noah countered.

His smile tickled something else on its way to my repulsion.

"Nothing." It came out flat. I didn't want any emotion in the room. "Promise to go away forever and I'll give you whatever you want. Within reason. I'm not sleeping with you, despite what I'm sure you're thinking. That isn't going to happen. I'm sorry it ever did. Now tell me what you want in exchange for leaving me alone."

"There's nothing I want more than you." His voice dripped with suggestion, but I was miles from where he wanted me to be.

"You can't have me. I'm never leaving Mike."

"So, you're choosing him over your career?" Noah's voice said that he didn't believe me, that the idea was ludicrous.

"Yes."

He inched forward, eyes on fire. "You said you loved me. That you were going to help me. But then you left. Are you a liar? Is that what you're saying, Amanda?"

"I'm not a liar, Noah. But things change, and they changed between us. I'm sorry about that. I made a mistake. I hurt too many people. First my husband, then you. You being in here is threatening to hurt him again. I'd give anything if I could take back what happened between us."

"But you said that you would give anything to live the way we did during our month together." His voice was brittle. "And you said it a lot."

I was crying, so the words stuttered through my tears. "I was lost, Noah. And really sad. You were there for me, and I'll never forget that. But it wasn't a real relationship."

He stood straighter. "Are you saying you never loved me?"

I looked into his eyes and told him the truth. "No. I didn't. I'm sorry."

His expression turned to concrete. "Take that back."

"I wish I could take it all back, but I can't. I'm sorry that it happened. I didn't mean to ever lead you on, or—"

"You said I would be famous one day. That *we* would be famous." Noah was actually snarling.

"I'm sorry that I said that. What I did, it wasn't fair to either of us."

"TAKE IT BACK!"

I stumbled and found myself suddenly sprawled on the couch, looking up at a frightening image of Noah, glowering over me. He seemed to be battling every one of his demons, barely keeping them from lighting his eyes and making him rip me to pieces with his claws.

"Calm down, Noah. *Please.* If you'll stop for a moment and listen, we can talk."

Barely controlling his breath, he growled, "Now you want to talk?"

"Yes. Please. I wanted to talk earlier, but I didn't want to lead you on."

"Again."

I gave him the moment he needed to glare, then apologized yet again. "I'm sorry."

But he wasn't having any of it. As I looked up into his eyes, I finally knew it. Finally saw him for who he was. The love-crazed stalker who couldn't live with rejection. He'd studied me, taken his time. Gained strength from the closed door behind him, enjoyed the tease of fabric held by a barely-there belt.

"What are you sorry for, Amanda?"

"I'm sorry I led you on."

"Wrong answer. Try again. *Why are you sorry?*"

"You want me to say I'm sorry we're not together." I shook my head. "But I can't say that. Because I'm not. I wronged my husband, not you."

Noah kneeled so we were eye to eye. In his

chocolate silk voice, he said, "You're going to leave that pathetic excuse for a husband, or I will ruin you. All of it — the show, any hope of anything like it in the future, the restaurant, and your reputation. Good luck with your bakery or getting anyone to fund your cookbook. Everything you cared about will be gone for good. It will be one insult too many. The world will have seen every ugly side of you. The Shellys won't represent you. You'll be bankrupt. And I'm sure once that happens, you'll find out your husband doesn't love you nearly as much as either one of you likes to pretend he does. Because money and children are the only things keeping you together. You said so yourself, Amanda. Go ahead and say you didn't mean it, but I'll never forget the look in your eyes when you said it."

Still looking up at him, I swallowed hard. It floored me, how much I had underestimated my adversary.

I didn't see him that way soon enough, and that might be my downfall. I thought of him as a kid who was infatuated with me. A part of me liked that, acknowledged that it felt good.

But his expression now was a horror show. I had no doubt he would tell the entire world about our affair on live television. And it would ruin me, just as he promised. Not my career — I couldn't care less if I never cooked or baked professionally again. But he'd cost me my family. And anything was better than losing Mike and my children, even if it was what I deserved.

I could still figure out a way to save this, but surrender could never be part of the plan.

He seemed to be awaiting my reply, but with no idea what to say, I said nothing.

Noah finally sighed, like someone had turned on the burner on his emotion, and suddenly I was a recalcitrant child. "You have until we start taping tomorrow to decide."

"There's nothing to decide."

He caressed my cheek like the lover I never should have let him be. "Someday we're going to look back and laugh at how hard I worked to win you back."

Then he turned around and left.

I covered my mouth to keep from screaming.

## THIRTY-THREE

## Amanda

I stood in front of Mike's office door, willing my body to stop shaking.

This was the worst, most terrible, most necessary thing I had ever done.

I was about to stick my head in the oven and see how long I could stand it. Look death in the eye without flinching. Hold my breath without screaming until I was seconds from death, then I would finally exhale.

This was gloriously difficult, but so was everything worthy in my life.

I knocked on the door. Turned the knob. Two steps inside then I'd be halfway to finished, the truth out of my mouth before I could stop it, melted cheese clinging between the slices in our sandwich.

I waited more than half a minute before I finally thought it had been long enough to knock again.

Mike still didn't answer, but I opened the door anyway.

"I was knocking. Didn't you hear me?"

He was sitting on his desk, studying something on his tablet. Probably doing inventory. "I heard you."

"We need to talk."

"I'm sure that means you have something to say and require a captive audience. So here I am. Dump it on me."

*Dump it on me?*

It's like he wanted to fight, but I couldn't let that happen.

"I need you to look at me."

"Fine." Mike looked up from the tablet and met my gaze. His eyes were sad and hostile, suspicious and angry. He wasn't going to make this easy, hands folded on the desk and feigned patience creasing his mouth as though I were an employee waiting to issue a complaint. "Well, then?"

I shifted from one foot to the other. I knew what I needed to say but had no idea how to start.

"I was in the middle of something, Amanda. I'm not in the mood for whatever this is."

"I'm sorry."

"Sorry for what?"

"For everything, including all the stuff you don't know yet."

He narrowed his eyes. "And what don't I know?"

I couldn't wait another second, I had to rip the Band-Aid off. "I slept with Noah. After you kicked me out."

The first sentence barreled into the second. I was dying to get it out. He had to know I never did anything like that before I left, nor at any time since.

Mike suppressed a flash of fury, but not fast enough to fully obscure it.

I felt like a piece of garbage, putting my caring, committed husband through this. It felt selfish to tell him. I would rather worship him to pieces for the rest of my life. *Show* him how sorry I was. But Noah would take the entire pot of beans and dump them on the floor in the morning. Whatever was happening to Mike right now couldn't compare to the torment he'd feel finding out who I really was.

"Do you love him?"

I gasped because the question surprised me. "How could you think that?"

"I don't know — maybe because you were willing to risk our marriage to do what you did."

"I wasn't thinking. I was in a terrible place."

"Clearly."

"Mike. I'm sorry. Like I said, it was never before, or since. I don't love him and never did. I hate him. Almost as much as I hate myself." He didn't say anything, so I kept on going. "Do you remember that day you came by with the children?"

What could have been the worst day of my life turned into one of the best. Certainly, the one that saved me. Mike dropped by for a surprise visit with David and Chelsea, nearly walked in on a scene that none of them would ever be able to unsee.

I broke up with Noah immediately. He threatened me even then, said he'd tell my husband about the affair. But I wasn't about to take that and told him if he breathed a word, I would use my connections to get him fired from the hotel and blacklisted from every reputable restaurant in LA.

I didn't feel good about it, but it wasn't fair of Noah to blackmail me. If he ruined my marriage, I would destroy his career.

But now his career was better than mine, and my marriage was in his way.

Mike nodded, still staring at me.

"I realized I couldn't live without them. Or you. I ended things with Noah the moment you left, and without a second thought."

"And then you suckered me into taking you back."

"No, Mike." I shook my head, ignoring the tears as they fell. "Nothing was more important than getting you back. I would have wasted away without you."

"Instead, your restaurant began to wither. Then you went back to resenting me, and I suppose that sent you right back to your little apprentice, down to your recommendation."

"It isn't like that!"

"You must think I'm a real moron, Amanda. What was the phrase you taught our daughter?"

"I didn't—"

"Too stupid to grease a gimlet, right?" Mike looked defeated. "Why now?"

"What?"

"Why are you telling me now?"

"Because Noah's going to tell everyone. On air. Probably tomorrow."

He stood and gestured toward the door. "Well, then, I guess there's nothing left to say."

"I don't deserve your forgiveness. I know that, and I'm not asking, I promise. But we have children. David and Chelsea didn't ask for any of this. For their sakes, will you please hear me out?"

Mike glowered at me, but then he finally relented. He sat without saying a word, folded his hands and waited for me to try to talk my way out of this.

But I didn't want to talk my way out of anything. I wanted my husband to know I'd thought this all through and had a solution. I swallowed the lump of mucus and whatever else was stuck in my throat, dared a few steps into the room, then sat on the other side of his desk.

"I have a plan."

"A plan? Wow, that's …" He shook his head, sounding incredulous. "I feel so much better now. Thank you for sharing that with me."

"Harris is selling his interest in Arrivé to Micah Myles. I'm going to ask him to buy out my half, as well."

His jaw dropped. He stared in disbelief, looking like he was cycling through an unlikely selection of words before finally settling on the most obvious four in the world.

"You hate Micah Myles."

"Yes, but I hate what I've done to you even more. I hate what I'm doing to the family. And most of all, I hate who I've allowed myself to become. I can't just say that I'll do whatever I can to make things right. I have to be willing to do it, too."

His face softened. He shook his head. "You don't have to do that. There are other ways. You can't lose the restaurant. It means everything to you."

"I can lose the restaurant, if it means I still have your respect. Or can gain it back." The tears weren't about to stop, soaking both sides of my face, while my chest kept hitching. He watched me cry without trying to comfort me.

"I'll pay the termination penalty and quit the show. It's a quarter million dollars to do it, but my share of the restaurant should be three times that, at least. I'll give the rest to you, for the kids. If you invest it, it'll cover both Constellation and college."

"But you hate Micah Myles," he repeated, as though I hadn't heard him the first time.

His anger felt like a hammer, and his astonishment like an ax. I didn't know what to say, how to respond, or what I should be feeling as an icy uncertainty slithered right through me. I wanted to please him, make this all go away, devote myself to making everything right with the world.

I was diced, grated, and minced.

This was the only way I might ever be whole again.

"Right now, he's my only hope." I trembled as I said it.

He shook his head. "You're really going to sell the restaurant?"

"I can't let Noah hurt you or the children. Not any more than he already has, thanks to me. It was my mistake, I'm the one who should have to suffer. I only want what's best for all of you."

"So you sell the restaurant and quit the show." His voice fell to a considerate whisper. "Then what?"

"It doesn't matter." I shrugged. "As long as you'll still let me see David and Chelsea."

Mike looked down at his hands, still folded on his desk, as if suddenly surprised to find them there. He took a while to speak. This time, it didn't seem like he was looking for the right words so much as deciding whether he should let them out.

"I put a PI on Noah," he finally said.

I gasped and did some fast math in my head, wondering what Mike might already know. "What?"

"I hired a PI after Noah came to my office. He rubbed me the wrong way from the second he came into Sunrise. I had a feeling, and I couldn't sit with it. I got his report this morning and was planning on bringing it up tonight."

I was mortified, trying to imagine what the PI must have seen. What Mike knew, and what he must have suspected.

Because how did the worst of it look from my husband's perspective? Noah leaving me flowers and chocolate, playing the protective boyfriend while bringing me home drunk. I know what I'd think, if our situations were reversed.

"Don't you want to know what he said?"

*Yes. Not at all. Absolutely, okay. Please no, anything but that.*

"It doesn't matter," I said. "It's already done."

"I think it does matter. The PI me told me that Noah is exactly what he appeared to be — a broke twenty-something working in a crappy hotel restaurant, dying for his big break."

I shrugged. "I still can't figure out how he

wormed his way onto the show or back into my life."

"My PI spoke to some of the restaurant staff. They told him some married guest broke Noah's heart about a year or so ago."

I swallowed but said nothing, because how could I possibly make this any better?

"Apparently the kid was a total disaster until about a month ago, when a couple of big-shot agents came to see him at work. He told off his boss and quit on the spot, even—"

"Wait. *What?* You mean, they came to him?" I couldn't believe it.

"Pretty amazing coincidence, right? Except before my guy showed up, these two agents hired a PI of their own. He was also nosing around, asking all the same questions."

My jaw was on the floor. "Dominic and Melinda knew I'd had an affair with Noah? *Before* they hired him?"

"Interesting, right?"

But if they'd known that, they must also have known that Noah was determined to win me back. That he intended to ruin my marriage. Instead of warning me, they helped him.

"This was a setup."

Mike shrugged. "I had my guy look into them, too. Wish I'd thought of that when they first approached you."

"What did your PI say about the Shellys?"

He laughed and shook his head. Seemed perplexed more than anything else. "Looking into the Shellys led my guy in about a hundred different directions, and not one of them was anywhere near definitive. But I can say the couple has ruined a few lives for ratings already."

"What does that mean?"

"My guy said he's only scratched the surface, there's too much there and he was paid to dig up information on Noah. But they're sharks, Amanda. Always on the move, taking a bite out of everything they can sink their teeth into."

"I'm such an idiot."

Mike's anger seemed to dissipate, like a dandelion lost to the wind. He came around from his side of the desk to mine, sat on the edge, then did the last thing I expected by taking my hands and looking into my eyes.

"There was one other thing on the PI's report."

"What was it?"

Mike almost smiled. "He said as far as he could

see, you've been doing everything possible to keep your distance from Noah."

Hope pulled me into a bear hug, squeezing tight enough to take all of my breath. My voice hitched again, and the tears kept spilling, but faith that life might offer me yet another chance was flooding my blood and reanimating my ambition.

"I promise, Mike, it was over before I came back to you last year. And I never want to see him again."

He squeezed my hands and said, "I believe you."

We settled into an exquisite silence, then he gave me a tentative smile. "So, you're serious about selling the restaurant?"

"Yes," I nodded. "It's the right thing to do."

"Do you still want to be my wife?"

*More than anything in the world.*

I nodded, knowing if I did anything else, the dam would shatter again.

He pulled me to my feet, and we stared into one another's eyes. I felt even more grateful for this second chance than I had a year ago, when he took me back the first time, before I truly appreciated what a treasure my husband was. I couldn't then. But now, everything had changed.

Mike shook his head. "There's no way we're letting that asshole kid win."

"It's too late. He's going to tell everyone on live TV, and there's nothing I can do to stop him.

He kissed me on the cheek then whispered into my ear. "Maybe you don't have to."

.

## THIRTY-FOUR

# Noah

I was finishing with my makeup, keeping an eye on both entrances, waiting for Amanda to enter the first day of a much better life for both of us.

Everything about this had been more difficult than I expected. It was never a straightforward proposition, but I'd never seen it as fraught with landmines as it turned out to be.

But now I was dying to see her, to show her how much she'd taught me.

For a month, Amanda had shared her stories with me. She'd taught me what it meant to achieve my dreams, to never settle for anything less than the best, and to do whatever it took to prove I belonged. I was willing to do that when we were baking together, and I believed we'd be peaking in tandem.

But then she left me like I was nothing, and I had to learn to be alone all over again.

Nothing had ever hurt more, and I'd lived a life filled with pain. I thought I was done until the Shellys came into the Milano, then the sun rose on my second chance. And this time, I refused to let anyone steal it.

Any minute now, Amanda would come into the studio and see Clarissa. She was sitting beside me, one chair over, getting her makeup done. The second Amanda saw her former student, she'd know why Clarissa was there. She'd stolen Clarissa's recipe and had told me the story herself. Knowing I was willing to prove as much on air would make Amanda see how serious I was about keeping what should have never been taken away.

"How much longer?" Clarissa asked, a little edgy, her nerves directed toward me rather than Amanda. Getting her to the studio hadn't been as straightforward as I'd hoped.

"I'm surprised she's not here already." I glanced at one entrance, then the other.

"I hope you're right about this."

"Right about what?" asked the woman doing her makeup.

"That being on camera is easier than she's

thinking." I shot her a look through the mirror, ordering her to please not contradict me. "As long as she doesn't overthink it."

I never saw it before, how untouchable Amanda thought she was. I didn't realize it until our confrontation in her dressing room. She actually thought she was better than me. I was good enough to fuck, and better at it than her husband could ever hope to be, but she didn't think I was good enough to be her partner in or out of the kitchen.

Good enough to help her through the hardest month of her life, but not enough to stay with.

And good enough to make all of those promises to, filling my head with beautiful lies, but not good enough for her to deliver on them.

I kept smiling into the mirror. Because anger was a treadmill, and I needed a road.

Clarissa looked over to the eastern entrance, which then drew my attention.

Amanda entered, looking bravely resigned and more beautiful than ever.

This would be so much easier if she wasn't an angel, but seeing her now was yet another reminder of the heaven we could have if we were in it together. I expected her to be tearing at the seams, instead she looked perfectly tailored.

Clarissa smiled, revenge curling up the corners of her lips as she waited for Amanda to notice her.

The makeup artist noticed, and her eyes grew curious. Mine, too.

Amanda slowed her gait when she saw me. Emotional traffic roared in both directions, horns honking and vehicles weaving, a cacophony of deafening silence, less than a second and deeper than an ocean.

Her attention turned from me to Clarissa.

I smiled wide because I had her.

Except I didn't.

Amanda turned deliberately away from makeup and veered hard toward wardrobe. She stopped in front of Zoe and immediately started talking, smiling as she did — a different Amanda, waving happy hands, clearly delighted to be here.

*What the hell?*

Did she not realize what was happening? The danger she was in?

Didn't she recognize—

Clarissa looked at me, her eyes asking the same questions.

I shook my head, muttered, "I'm on it," then I was out of the chair, waving my makeup artist away as I walked toward Amanda.

I waited for her to stop talking, but she was deliberately taking her time.

Amanda finally finished, said goodbye, then slowly turned to face me, still acting as though she held all the power. "What do you want, Noah?"

"Have you reconsidered?"

"Reconsidered what? Doing this show? Having to spend another second around you? Leaving my husband? You've given me an awful lot to think about, so what is it specifically that you're asking?"

"Lower your voice."

"You don't get to tell me what to do."

Her power and cruelty were a slap to my face. For a moment, I could only stare into hard eyes that no longer looked uncertain. I was losing whatever power I'd had the day before, if it wasn't already entirely gone.

A surge of hate flowed forth, fueled by an assault of terrible thoughts.

This? After the month I gave her? It was the best of my life. And hers, too. All of her promises. Knowing how great we were together, pantry to picnic. We could have the best, both in life and the kitchen, but she was going to throw it down the garbage disposal instead. She really was going to abandon me. For that loser, Michael Byrd.

I deserved Amanda. This was my moment. It was promised, and I earned it.

How *dare* she reject me?

"You're going to throw it all away for someone who works so hard to hold you back?" I could barely throttle my fury.

"Did you think you could blackmail me into having a relationship with you?"

"Aren't you forgetting something? Didn't we discuss this yesterday?" I glared at Amanda, suddenly loathing everything about her. "Do you want your dirty laundry going viral? Because it's going to, and we just added more soiled clothes to the pile."

I tipped my head towardAmanda's old victim, watching us with narrowed eyes.

Then I continued, low enough so only Amanda could hear. "After you've lost everything and your husband leaves you for someone more successful, you're going to come crawling back to the best you ever had and the most you could have been. It'll be too late for a partnership then, but maybe I'll pity you enough to toss you a job in my kitchen."

I expected that to end her, but it did nothing of the sort, inspiring a steady smile that left me unseated instead.

Why was she smiling like that? So sad and knowing. It filled my stomach with acid. Then made it slosh around.

"Goodbye, Noah."

Then she turned around and left me, walking with her shoulders straight and her head held high.

My heart should have been too shocked to keep beating, but it found a way to pound harder than ever. My chest was constricting, and I couldn't breathe. Couldn't even bear to look over at Clarissa. She didn't have to hear a word to know the story.

I was so certain this was going to work. I'd felt like a second-class citizen my entire life, but that never stopped me from working hard. I'd had to, because no one was ever going to give me anything. The truth was, even by working my nails into dust, I might never get what came so easily for everyone else.

Too many years of bottom-barrel living congealed into a cold and unforgiving rage.

*Fine.* If Amanda wanted to regard me as though I were garbage, just like everyone else always had, then she was about to find out what it meant to be treated the same way.

I'd been bracing myself for this.

I never wanted it to go down this way. I wanted the two of us to work it out. Preferably as a couple.

But that couldn't happen, because Amanda Byrd was a two-faced lying bitch of a cunt who was making the worst decision of her life. Selfish like always, unable to see how much her false promises tore me to pieces.

Yesterday, if the worst had to happen, I would have regarded it as a necessary evil.

But now? I sneered as I suddenly realized I was going to enjoy destroying Amanda Byrd.

THIRTY-FIVE

## Amanda

As usual, I took my place in the studio kitchen between Harris and Noah.

In the newer, more humiliating version of our show, my old partner introduced the mentor, her apprentice, and that episode's special recipe before he stepped off to the side. And that's where Harris stayed until it was time to insert his commentary before and after each commercial break.

They were both subtly looking over at me, stealing glances for very different reasons.

I was a live wire, and I'm sure the electricity was crackling right off of my skin. This was the hardest thing I had ever done, and while Harris couldn't have any idea what I was going to do, he had to know something was about to go down.

Noah made me want to smile. I'd scared the living shit out of that blackmailing prick. He didn't know what was happening either, but at least he had the inside scoop that it had something to do with him.

I was terrified of what I had to do but resolved to do it. And I was so glad to no longer be afraid of Noah.

The music started, its upbeat tempo still slower than my heart.

I glanced again at Clarissa and offered her my warmest smile. She smiled back, like an involuntary flinch. Noah did me a favor, bringing her here to the studio for me.

He saw our smiles and instantly frowned, shifting on his feet beside me.

I looked past the cameras to where my husband was standing and gave him a loving gaze before meeting my mark as the intro music concluded.

Harris glanced at the teleprompter. "Welcome—"

But that's all he got. Because I looked into the center camera and let it all out.

"I'm Amanda Byrd, and I owe you an apology. I owe a lot of people apologies. If you're watching this, then you probably saw a video of my melt-down a few weeks ago. *Not* my finest moment."

I gave the camera an embarrassed smile. Talking was already aloe on my burn.

Anderson was mouthing things like *No, stop it!* and *What are you doing?*

The floor manager was waving his arms and violently shaking his head.

I could see Harris and Noah in my peripheral vision, both men staring at me like I was nuts. Harris had his mouth open, and the way it was fixed, it looked permanently stuck. His eyes looked like they were bolted to the wreckage of a five-car pileup. Noah's expression was an odd cocktail of raw confusion, brewing rage, awe, and inner destruction.

I ignored them all. There was exactly one person in the studio who mattered, and he was standing behind the cameras.

"Until recently, I always rationalized that kind of behavior. I told myself I was improving the people around me. That they were lucky to have me demanding such perfection, constantly pushing them into a version of themselves they might have never realized otherwise, staying intolerant whenever anyone failed to meet my impossible standards.

I have a lot to be embarrassed about and to atone for."

I gave the camera a little shake of my head, wanting everyone to know that I wasn't making any excuses.

"I know better, so I'll do better. But I should also explain. It was easy for me to justify what I was doing because it was the way I was taught. My teachers, the French chef I was fortunate enough to apprentice under — that's how every one of them pushed me to improve. I was paying it forward and passing it on. I *thought* I was doing my best to mold the people around me, and because I thought they should be more grateful for my experience, I was resentful when they weren't."

Anderson wasn't mouthing anything now. He'd joined the floor manager in maniacally waving his arms, making *Cut!* motions with his hands, doing something that looked almost like a jig — anything to shut me up. This was what Noah had wanted to do, hijack my show and force me to walk the plank in front of a live audience.

That was a recipe that had to be stolen, and now I was cooking his dish while he stared at me dumbstruck.

Everyone was watching, all of them stunned.

Most were trying to stop me, a few were staring in wide-eyed amazement.

All except for Dominic and Melinda. Both were present, by Noah's request I'm sure, from when he wrongly thought that he could control the heat. Neither seemed surprised, but both appeared delighted. Like cats catching their mouse.

And the only person in the room who mattered, still standing behind the cameras, was giving me a thumb's up.

"I'm thankful to the person who filmed my meltdown and shared it with the world." I blinked to keep from crying. I could do that later, for hours if necessary, but right then I had to stay strong. Tell the truth, so I could leave it behind me. "That video helped me to see myself for the first time and understand the kind of person I've become."

I was embarrassed, but I knew this had to be said. "I saw how my behavior looked to my children, and how it might be changing who they were." I shook my head harder. "That's not what I want for them."

I turned to Harris, his mouth still hanging open in astonishment.

"You've tolerated my arrogance and my emotional abuse for too long. I've never acknowledged that you're the reason for our restaurant's success, and I wouldn't have ever had such a stratospheric career without your relentless support behind the scenes. You complained maybe five percent of what you had every right to, and I made you feel awful every time. I don't blame you if you never forgive me, but you deserve to hear me say I'm sorry for the way I treated you."

I waited a beat then repeated it. *"I'm sorry for the way I treated you."*

Harris was struck frozen with nothing to say.

I turned and looked at Clarissa, still standing over by the makeup station.

"Can you come over here?" I called out.

The crew were huddled in discussion, probably trying to decide if they should cut my feed and kill this now before it got any worse. Dominic and Melinda were still sharing a conspiratorial smile. Mike gave me a nod. *Keep going.*

Clarissa nervously skittered across the studio then tentatively stepped onto the set.

"This is Clarissa." I looked at my old apprentice before turning back to the camera. "When I was a student chef, I did something I'm still ashamed of today. I took a recipe that another student created, improved it, then submitted it as my own, claiming credit and winning my way into the most rewarding opportunity of my life."

Clarissa looked into the camera, a doe under high beams.

"I'm sorry, Clarissa. I was supposed to be your mentor, and instead I took advantage of you. You don't have to forgive me, but I want you to know I'm sorry, and I want everyone to know what I did."

Through freshly falling tears, Clarissa said, "We used to call you Bitchface Al Dente behind your back."

I gave her a tiny smile. "I deserved that."

She smiled back. "Yeah, you did."

The floor managers had both given up. So had everyone else. Most of the crowd caught the contagion from Dominic and Melinda and now stood back to enjoy the show. Anderson was shaking his head, but the hint of a smile was finally touching his lips.

Noah had drifted behind me, so I could only imagine the gallery of emotions flickering across his face.

"I want to say I'm sorry to everyone who has ever worked with me. And I have one last apology to make. To my husband." I waved at the cameras. "Hi, Mike!"

Then I turned around, grabbed Noah by his arm, and pulled him closer to me.

He stood there, shocked and gaping like a fish waiting to get gutted.

And then my eyes were back to the camera. "About a year ago, after a similar meltdown, my husband needed a little time away from me. I had some growing up to do. A lot like now." I laughed at myself so that everyone could hear.

"But I didn't take that time to reflect. I used it to escape. Instead of falling deeply into drinking or drugs, I did something equally stupid, and in a fit of spectacularly bad judgment, I had an affair. With my co-host, Noah. Before he was on this show."

I nodded at Noah and gave him a second. But the bastard didn't defend himself.

"Noah, it was wrong of me to start a relationship with you that could never have gone anywhere, and I deeply regret derailing your life with all of my problems."

"That's not—"

"Mike, I don't deserve the second chance that you've given me. You are a wonderful man, too amazing for words."

The camera swiveled around to meet my husband's face.

"You said you didn't need it, but you deserve a public apology. I am so, so sorry that I hurt you. Especially like this. I am constantly humbled by your compassion, your love, and your support. By your almost unreasonable faith in me. And I will do everything in my power to be the wife you deserve for the rest of my life."

The crowd had changed. They no longer hated me.

Most of them were smiling, some were crying, a few were filming the scene on their phones. But everyone had been touched.

"Finally, I have an announcement to make. I'm leaving *Chef Happen*s. You're in the capable hands of Harris and Noah. I'm retiring and giving away every recipe I've ever developed for free — except for the dishes on the Arrivé menu, which now belong to Harris."

The studio was dead silent.

But as I stepped off the set, it exploded into applause and enthusiastic chatter.

I left Noah behind me, knowing the asshole would be alone for a while.

Melinda was already walking toward me, fast as she could without running. When she reached me, she touched my shoulder. Her face was positively beaming. "That. Was. *Gold.* You can write your own ticket now. Tell us what you want, and we'll build it for you."

I smiled at Melinda. "I want to be with my family."

"I'm not sure you understand the opportunity here."

I laughed. "But that's the thing. I actually do."

"You can have it all, Amanda. This is only the—"

"I don't want it all. I want to do better with what I already have."

Mike approached me from behind, put his arm around me, then tried to lead me away.

"Thank you, Melinda. For everything," I said over my shoulder. Then I followed my husband out of the studio.

Outside, he said, "You did great."

"I didn't. But I'm going to. Starting now."

# Epilogue

Bake it Away was opening tomorrow morning, but tonight felt even more important.

Chelsea and I were making cookies in the bakery's brand new, boldly beautiful kitchen. It was open so that patrons could see us baking and hear our harmony, from kneading dough to frosting our finished product.

The menu was small to start because we were running a lean operation. We had everything in this place. Me, Mike, and the children. It was officially a family business.

And since everyone had at least a little say, Chelsea didn't mind telling me our menu was missing something extra special. So, on the eve of our opening, we were making the prototype batch of her Everything Cookies.

I told her we couldn't literally put everything in them, and we had to be consistent so our customers would always know what to expect. Chelsea could choose four ingredients for her delicacy. She decided on plain M&Ms, peanuts, chocolate chips, and rainbow sprinkles, with a basic chocolate chip cookie dough recipe for the base. And yes, that meant double the number chocolate chips. My daughter knew exactly how to frame her argument.

These would probably be the homeliest delights behind the glass tomorrow, but I'd feel prouder of our first batch of Chelsea's Everythings than I would for anything else on display.

We laughed when she tried to manage the jumbo bag of M&Ms and accidentally poured way too many into the bowl.

"Uh-oh," I said. "Do you think there's going to be enough room for the peanuts now?"

Chelsea was a problem solver. She dipped her hand into the bowl and started scooping excess M&Ms into her palm. She looked up at me and said, "Sorry, Mom, but these are mine now."

She had her candy-coated chocolate and I had my wine. I'd make sure neither of us had too much of our vice. But it was fun to share tradition with my daughter, and I was surprised at how fast we found our rhythm in the kitchen. We regularly fell into long silences, shaping the dough, dolloping it onto the cookie sheet, trading the occasional smile.

When Mike and David weren't with us, I often missed them. It was a family business, after all. But there were other times when it was just mother-daughter time, and I relished bonding with my little girl.

Tonight, Mike and David were at the school for the animation contest. It killed me to miss the judging, but I'd been to the premier event when the movies were all aired. Call it parental bias, but our son's entry was the best. And if it wasn't the eve of our bakery opening, I'd have been there for him tonight, too.

Since I couldn't be there, I was determined to enjoy one-on-one time with my daughter.

Chelsea finished snacking on the last of her M&Ms as I put our cookies into the oven.

After I closed the door, I turned back to my daughter. "So, tell me what you learned today."

"We learned about the letter S."

"What about it?"

"We learned it hisses like a snake."

"Snakes are so sneaky."

"And slippery!"

"Suspicious, I think." I wrinkled my nose.

She laughed then said, "Sad."

"Why are the snakes sad?"

"Because *sad* starts with the letter S," Chelsea explained.

"Can you think of a reason why the snake would be sad?"

"Maybe its parents were sad, so the snake was sad, too."

"Makes sense. What if the snake's mommy and daddy were suddenly happy? Would that *surprise* the snake?"

"Yes! She would be *so so surprised*." Chelsea laughed, loving our game because we played it a lot.

"What else would she be?"

Chelsea spread her arms for the next declaration, but went too wide and smacked the bag of flour.

It spilled everywhere, on the table and floor, and into puffs of dust all over the wall.

She was a frightened little cat, hair raised as she looked up at me, fearful of what might happen next. Our harmony gone along with her solace.

But it wasn't like that anymore. Hadn't been for a while.

I gave her a smile. "Why don't you get me a dustpan and brush, then we'll clean it up together, okay?"

"Okay, Mommy!" Chelsea scampered off to the closet.

We cleaned up, then played a few more rounds of Slithering Serpents, the name we eventually landed on for the day's game. The oven dinged as we were finishing up.

I was putting the cookies on the cooling rack when Mike and David came into the kitchen.

David was talking a mile a minute and had started while still out of earshot, so I lost the first part of his monologue.

"—and then it was just mine and eleven other ones, and I didn't know what was going to happen because no one does, that's why they call it a contest and—"

"David, honey."

He paused and looked up at me.

I knelt down and looked into his eyes. "Slow down. I want to hear everything you're saying, okay? I promise. I'm not going anywhere. You don't have to get everything out in one breath."

His shoulders relaxed and he broke into a smile. "Sorry."

"Don't apologize. Tell me your story."

"My three-minute movie won first place in the school's animation contest!"

"Wow! That's terrific!" I scooped him up into a hug and swung him around, enjoying the look on Mike's face all three times I saw it in a carousel passing.

Then I set David down and told him how proud I was.

He barely registered what I said after seeing cookies. "What are those?"

"They're Chelsea's Everything Cookies," I told him.

Chelsea pointed her tongue at David. "You don't have anything on the menu.

"So? You don't have anything in the animation contest." Then to me, he said, "What's in them? Wait … M&Ms … peanuts …sprinkles, obviously … oh, and chocolate chips." He looked up. "Is that it?"

"That's a lot!" Chelsea said. "It's *four ingredients*. Plus double chocolate chips."

Mike was waiting to get me alone. I could see it

in the way he was standing and the longing in his eyes.

I took two small napkins, placed a Chelsea's Everything Cookie on each one, then said, "I'm so proud of you both. Take these into the dining room. Your father and I will meet you there in a few minutes."

The children scampered away, both laughing, and left their parents alone.

Mike took me into his arms, and it felt more like home than home itself. More than my beautiful new bakery, and definitely more than Arrivé ever had.

"How are the new bakers working out?"

Mike was only asking because he loved to hear good news, a slightly different version of the same conversation each day. Keeping tabs as my partner while giving me the podium to say it aloud and hear it for myself.

"They're coming along great, and more importantly, I'm having a terrific time training them. Rochelle is still my favorite. I don't think there's anything that woman can't bake, and I'm pretty sure in another few months she'll be teaching me a few things."

"That's wonderful to hear."

But his face was different. Almost mischievous.

"What?" I asked.

"What, *what*?"

I know when my husband is playing innocent. "Just tell me."

"Tell you what?"

"The thing you're not saying."

His face cracked into a striking smile.

Again, I felt lucky. "Mike …"

"Okay!" He smiled. "Do you think Rochelle will be capable of running the kitchen in a couple of months?"

"That's fast. I don't know. Why?" I felt like I was being tested.

"Because I've just booked us on a two-month foodie tour. Spain, France, Italy, Japan, Thailand, Singapore, and China."

"Oh, my God!" The first tear was already leaving my right eye. "What about the children?"

"My mom will be taking care of things while we're eating our way around the world."

I buried my head against his chest. "Thank you, thank you, thank you."

"I'm sure you'll pick up a new recipe or ten."

"I have the only recipe I need. You and my family, then heat to obsession."

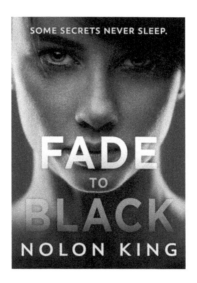

**He stole her childhood.**

Sloan Alexander's life blew up when she accused producer Liam Winston of trying to seduce her at the age of 12. Blacklisted and abandoned, she moved to Europe to start over. Now she's back with a film based on her life and Winston will stop at nothing to silence her.

## A Quick Favor ...

If you enjoyed this book, please take a moment to write a review on your favorite bookselling platform so other readers can enjoy it too. It would mean a lot to me.

Thank you,
*Nolon King*

## About the Author

**Nolon King** writes fast-paced psychological thrillers set in the glitzy world of entertainment's power players with a bold, insightful voice. He's not afraid to explore the darker side of human nature through stories featuring families torn apart by secrets and lies.

Nolon loves to write about big questions and moral quandaries. How far would you go to cover up an honest mistake? Would you destroy your career to protect your family? How much of your soul would you sell to get the life of your dreams? Would you cheat on your husband to keep your children safe? Would you give in to a stalker's demands to save your marriage?

Ingram Content Group UK Ltd.
Milton Keynes UK
UKHW042121120623
423291UK00015B/11